Res
New York r
ELIZABETH PETERS

"No one is better at juggling torches while dancing on a high wire than Elizabeth Peters."
Chicago Tribune

"Peters has few rivals."
Houston Chronicle

"If bestsellerdom were based on merit and displayed ability, Elizabeth Peters would be one of the most popular and famous adventure authors in America. She picks her stories well, tells them nicely, populates them with original characters, adds convincing details both great and small, and has a humorous touch that keeps things as interesting as they are lively."
Baltimore Sun

"No one else can write the kind of mystery Ms. Peters is so adept at producing."
Dallas Morning News

"Peters' trademarks [are] intelligent plotting, engaging characters, and stylish writing, and we can hardly ask for anything more."
Cincinnati Enquirer

"Elizabeth Peters is nothing less than a certified American treasure."
Jackson Clarion-Ledger

"She keeps the reader coming back for more."
San Francisco Chronicle

By Elizabeth Peters

ELIZABETH PETERS

The Camelot Caper

HARPER

An Imprint of HarperCollins*Publishers*

HARPER

An Imprint of HarperCollins*Publishers*
195 Broadway
New York, New York 10007

Copyright © 1969 by Elizabeth Peters
ISBN 978-0-06-211971-1

First Harper premium printing: August 2012
First Avon Books mass market printing: January 2001

HarperCollins ® and Harper ® are registered trademarks of Harper-Collins Publishers.

Printed in the United States of America

Visit Harper paperbacks on the World Wide Web at
www.harpercollins.com

HB 06.02.2024

ONE

The book was small, a paperback edition, with a cover done in shades of blue. In the foreground was the figure of a beautiful young girl, disheveled black hair streaming over her shoulders. She was in genteel dishabille and in considerable distress; her eyes, looking back over her shoulder, were fixed in terror upon the distant outlines of a ruined castle, perched on a cliff, under a darkening sky.

Jessica glanced down at the book, half concealed in her lap by her clenched hands. What ghastly danger from the haunted ruins threatened the poor heroine? A man, of course; it was always a man—either a dark-browed hero, whom the vapid heroine suspected of villainy, or a dark-browed villain whose plot the girl had just discovered. She hadn't read the book yet, but she had read a number of similar volumes, and the plots had a monotonous kinship. She suspected she would never read another such thriller. Fictitious terrors lost their charm when they recalled a real fear.

Jess glanced back over her shoulder, not at a ruined castle or Charles Addams house, but at a prosaic stretch of black-topped road. There was not much traffic, and no car remained for long behind the bus, which was jogging along at a leisurely twenty miles an hour.

Reassured, Jess transferred her attention to the side window, where the view was prettier. For more years than she could remember she had looked forward to that view—the green hills of England, looking newly upholstered in their fresh spring grass, dotted with grazing white sheep, covered over with a sky of china blue. This was the England of which the poets sang—almost. The month was May, not April and, Browning notwithstanding, May was warmer and more pleasant. The first day Jessica had delightedly identified the prickly bushes along the roadside, with their blazing yellow bloom, as gorse. She had found bluebells in the lanes, and smelled the lilac.

That had been yesterday—before the fear began.

Compulsively, her head turned again, her eyes found the road still innocent. The fat lady next to her was looking at her curiously; the plump pink face remained expressionless, but the eyes behind the round, gold-rimmed glasses were shrewd and hostile.

The fat lady's bundles were jabbing her in the hip. Jess slid over another fraction of an inch. She was already squeezed into the farthest corner of the long back seat, and she wondered, irritably, what had prompted the other woman's buying spree. She also wondered how she had found so many worthwhile bargains in the unexciting shops of Salisbury. But "unexciting" was a relative term; judging from the tiny villages this very local bus had passed through, the sleepy cathedral town of Salisbury might look like a metropolis by contrast.

Jess let her aching head rest for a moment against the cool glass of the window. Salisbury . . . the cathedral . . . Sunday morning. A strange time and place for the beginning of the threat which had driven her, in unreasoning flight, onto a bus going she knew not where, arriving she knew not when. She didn't dare ask anyone where she was going; her aim was inconspicuousness, and that question would certainly attract attention. She was conspicuous enough by her very foreignness. Odd, how obviously American she looked; even she could see the difference, and it was not defined by anything so obvious as makeup and short skirts. The English girls she had seen wore skirts which made hers look Victorian, and their false eyelashes outdistanced hers by a good quarter of an inch. The cut of her clothes, perhaps? Her yellow wool suit with its short jacket and straight skirt probably hadn't cost any more than the plaid outfit and purple sweater the girl two seats up was wearing, but it looked . . . well, it looked different. And whatever had possessed her to select yellow? It stood out like a neon sign.

The bus lumbered up a rise and through a copse of trees; Jessica's features, palely limned against the dark background of foliage, made a pallid pattern on the window glass. The blue of her eyes hardly showed; only the fair skin, bleached by a long winter in the office, and the light-brown hair. The effect was spectral; she closed her eyes, too tired to turn for another look behind.

Being afraid was fatiguing. She could understand now why a hunted man might suddenly stop running and surrender himself to his pursuers, even when capture might mean death. In her case, terror was increased by bewilderment. She did not know why she was being threatened, which meant that she had no clue as to how to defend herself.

As she looked back now, a number of incidents fell into place, making a pattern which had not been visible until the one key incident occurred and gave meaning to the whole. A pattern—but only in the sense of consistent behavior. The motive still remained obscure.

But there was no doubt in her mind now that the man who had taken her suitcase at Southampton had not done so by mistake. It had been a close call. She had looked away for only a moment, to hail a taxi. Her two big suitcases had been sent on; they had arranged that for her on the boat, and as soon as she cleared customs she had simply carried her one remaining bag out of the building and had stood by the street looking for transportation. The man who brushed by her was only one of many; there was a crowd near the quay, people embarking and disembarking, seeing friends off, and meeting them. When, having obtained her taxi, she looked down to find her bag gone, her first assumption had been that it had been kicked or pushed away. If she had not happened to look in just the right direction; if her bag had not had that long ragged scratch across one end which made it unmistakably hers; if the policeman had not come strolling by in time to hear her call: "Hey, wait a minute, mister, that's my suitcase. . . ."

The man's reaction had been quite natural. He had glanced back over his shoulder—casually, as was to be expected, a lot of people were yelling at one another, and he wouldn't assume her hail was directed at him if he had made an honest error. But his seemingly casual glance had seen her—and the tall, blue form beside her. He had returned at once and made his apologies. Why should she have realized that the incident had any hidden meaning? She had done equally idiotic things in a fit of momentary abstraction.

She hadn't given the matter a second thought, nor taken any particular notice of the would-be thief. She had observed his mustache only because it was impossible to ignore it—big, brown, and bushy. The mustache had effectively obliterated the features which surrounded it. The man was taller than she was; but then practically everybody was. Medium height, medium frame, medium everything, including the voice. She had heard only a mumbled phrase, in the accent Americans think of as "Oxfordian," and in a tone whose huskiness might have been assumed for the occasion.

Yet perhaps the incident colored her feelings without her being aware of it, for she found Southampton disappointing. The clerk at the hotel was supercilious, the cost of the room was higher than the travel bureau had told her it would be, and the room wasn't ready for her.

It was too late for lunch and too early for tea, so

Jess left her suitcase at the hotel desk and went for a walk. By that time her mood was so bad that she would have sneered at the Emerald City, and Southampton is not the most picturesque of English cities. She got lost, and her feet hurt. When she arrived back at the hotel her room was ready, but the momentary satisfaction of this fact was immediately canceled when she realized that her suitcase had been searched.

The search had been thorough and unsubtle. The contents of her bag looked as if they had been stirred with a spoon, and her tube of toothpaste appeared to be missing. She found it in the bathroom flattened on the floor; its former contents festooned the washbowl like a long white snake.

An older or more determined person might have called the manager and complained. Jessica was not timid; but she was still young enough to dread appearing ridiculous. How could she raise a fuss over a tube of toothpaste? Nothing else had been taken, not even her one piece of decent jewelry, a string of cultured pearls which had belonged to her mother. Two telephone calls later she was on her way to the bus depot and the last evening bus to Salisbury. Really, she kept telling herself, there was nothing interesting to see in Southampton; and now she would be in time for Sunday service at one of England's noblest cathedrals.

The bus was a gleaming modern monster, an express which roared contemptuously past the green local buses. The inn was half-timbered, black on white, straight out of Elizabethan days; the smiling receptionist cheerfully produced a late supper, eggs and thick slabs of bacon, hot muffins, and a huge pot of tea served with cream and lemon and brown sugar. Jess went to bed in a state of deplorable smugness, congratulating herself on her decision.

She woke at dawn next morning, with a renewed sense of the excitement which Southampton had almost destroyed. Her room was a funny little cubicle, all odd angles; the interior walls had the same blackened beams on white-washed plaster as those which adorned the façade of the inn. There was a prosaic washbasin in one corner, and an electric heater beside it. Shivering in the glorious May weather of merry England, Jess flipped the heater on and leaped back into bed until its coils glowed orange-red. She abandoned, with no more than a slight qualm the idea of a brisk morning tub. The corridors would be ten degrees cooler than the room, and she refused even to imagine the probable temperature of the bathroom. After a hasty splash at the basin—the water was blessedly hot—she huddled herself into her clothes, thanking heaven for the experienced friends who had warned her to bring plenty of sweaters. Then she opened the leaded casement window and leaned out.

The fresh morning air felt the way chilled white wine tastes—light, heady, like the concentrated fragrance of spring. She was high up over the old town; across the gabled roofs of Salisbury she saw the spire of the cathedral, as slim and graceful as a girl's lifted arm. The most feminine of all the English cathedrals—she had read that, in some guidebook. Now she understood what it meant.

After a hasty breakfast she was on her way. She

walked fast, because it was that sort of morning, not because she had any sense of being followed. It would have been hard to conjure up a premonition of ugliness in that setting. Down Blue Boar Lane to Castle Street . . . The very names conjured up the past, and there were old houses, converted into shops and inns but lovingly preserved; their curved black timbers looked bowed with the weight of years.

Sunlight streamed down into the narrow streets, floodlighting old façades and sparkling off an occasional gilded crest above a door. The breeze lifted Jessica's curls, and she tied a bandanna over her head. A few minutes later she came out of the populated streets onto what was called simply "the town path," a long graveled foot-and-bicycle way, across the water meadows and over Long Bridge, which crossed—of course, it was the River Avon. Stratford, she reminded herself, was not the only town "upon Avon."

Jess leaned on the rail of the bridge and rejoiced. The scene was straight out of Constable—or, to be more accurate, Constable had captured the scene and the atmosphere. How lucky she was to see it like this, with the vast blue arch overhead spattered with floating clouds. Across the tender green of the meadows her eye passed over the pale, earthbound clouds of flowering fruit trees to fasten on the perfect façade of the cathedral and its soaring tower, set on the meadows like a jewel on a green velvet cushion.

She wandered on, stopping frequently to enjoy a visual gloat, for each few feet brought a change in the picture or in its frame of greenery and flowers, or in the shape of the puffed, gliding clouds. Amazing how satisfying primary colors could be—blue and white and green. . . . But they weren't primary colors, that was the whole thing; the blue was a tone that most artists failed to catch, the green was not one shade but a thousand, shifting endlessly under the sun and shadow and wind—from chartreuse to emerald, through the whole spectrum of greens.

After a certain point the view of the cathedral passed its prime, and she hesitated, wondering whether to turn back or to follow the path to its end. But the decision was not difficult; it was more fun to explore new terrain than to retreat, and the path ended somewhere in town, near the cathedral. Of course, that view from the bridge . . . But it was the sort of thing that should not be experienced too often in a short span of time; like a second piece of chocolate cake, it spoiled the memory of the first taste.

Later, she wondered what would have happened if she had retraced her steps. Had they followed her from the town, and would she have met them out on the empty meadows? Perhaps; and perhaps not. For all she knew, they might have been waiting for her at the cathedral since dawn; it was the one place to which every visitor to Salisbury would come, sooner or later.

By following the path, she reached the close from an unexpected direction and entered the cathedral through one of the transepts instead of through the main doors. She glanced at her watch, and quickened her pace. It was almost ten thirty; if she wanted to see anything of the cathedral before the service began, she would have to hurry.

Jolting along country roads on the elephantine bus, Jess was glad she had had that unclouded half hour. Even now, looking back on it through a fog of doubt and fear, the memory shone bright; the length of the nave, with its soaring arches, the medieval tombs and the spare, stiff effigies of mailed knights, the vaulted cloisters, whose traceried arches framed shifting vistas of green leaves and golden-dusted grass. The last unshadowed sight had been her first view of the Chapter House.

Standing near the center of the high octagonal chamber, she let her eyes follow the line of the single slim pillar up to the roof, where it bloomed into spreading vaults ribbed with stone, which curved back in gracious lines to the tops of the pointed windows. Half mesmerized, she sank down on the stone bench that followed the line of the walls. Here the officials of the cathedral had transacted their business. Each canon had had his own little niche framed by carved stone; she hoped that he had also had a few cushions. The bench was hard, and in winter the chill must have struck at elderly clerical bones even through voluminous woolen robes.

Sitting straight upright, as suited the place, she let her mind wander. How amazing that all this wonder should date from the Middle Ages—the thirteenth century, when men and women still lived like swine in mud-floored huts, and even the lordly gentry in their proud castles endured discomforts which would drive modern workmen into protest marches. Filthy rushes on the icy floor, fleas under the embroidered velvet robes, and the stench from the open pit of the garderobe permeating the Great

Hall . . . And from all the filth and misery came the miracles—stone worked into lines of Euclidean perfection, glass that glowed like jewels, a concept of God and man expressed in structure which surpassed the men who had built and the God whose narrow dictates they had served.

And that was the last romantic thought she had for a long time.

Some sound of the man's approach must have penetrated her reverie, but when she first saw him he was standing still—in the doorway which was the sole exit from the room. Something in his very stance and the fixity of his gaze struck her with foreboding even before she recognized him. Medium height, medium frame, a beautifully tailored dark suit, brown hair . . . A mustache. Good heavens, yes—the bushy brown mustache, and the man in Southampton who had walked off with her suitcase!

Jess had an excellent imagination, nourished frequently on solid doses of detective fiction. Often she had amused herself by noticing such coincidences, and building on them complicated plots of deadly intrigue. Sometimes her plots had been so good that she had half frightened herself.

So she tried to convince herself now, combating a primitive instinct which sometimes is truer than reason; the world is not, actually, a very reasonable place. She rose, stiffly, from the hard stone bench; and the man shifted position, slightly but significantly.

For a long moment they stared at each other across the curiously shaped room. Patterns of dim color from the pale stained glass carpeted portions of the floor and slid eerily across the man's face as he moved slowly toward her.

"I want to talk to you," he said. "Nothing to be afraid of. Just a little talk."

His voice was as she remembered it, artificially husky, but the accent was impossible to hide. The clear, clipped consonants showed through.

"What about?" Jess asked breathlessly.

"Not here. Somewhere . . . more private."

Jess retreated, the edge of the stone bench pressing against the back of her knees. He couldn't corner her here, she thought crazily; there were lots of corners, but they were all wide angles.

"Leave me alone, or I'll call for help. We've nothing to talk about."

"The ring. Where is it? You did bring it with you, didn't you?"

"The ring . . ." Jess repeated stupidly.

"That's all I want. If you'll just—"

He was still moving toward her, his arms lifted like those of a man trying to catch a playful dog. She didn't like the way he moved his arms. Or his face. Or, in fact, anything about him.

The lofty room was so empty, and so silent. From the cloister outside Jess could hear birds chirping, and a murmur which might have been distant voices. What had happened to the hordes of tourists? Just one little tourist, that was all she needed—one sweet old lady from Moorhead, Minnesota, one French student, one Dane. . . .

"If I give you the ring, will you leave me alone?"

"Certainly." This time, in his eagerness, he forgot to disguise his voice; it rang clear and mellow, a pleasant baritone. Something else was clear, even in the single word. Jess knew, with a sureness that defied analysis, that he was lying.

What would happen if she screamed? Would anyone hear her? The cathedral was too far away, cut off by massive doors, but there must be people in the cloisters. Yet she hesitated, not because she was not convinced of her danger, but because of the damning pressure of conformity. A well brought up young lady does not shriek in a church.

She started, convulsively, as a vast clamor of sound burst through the door—the bells, high up in the spire, but sounding as if they were just outside. The bells of Salisbury Cathedral, ringing for the service.

Later, Jess remembered that the man had also started at the sound, and realized that he must have been almost as nervous as she was. Even if she had been calm enough to note this at the time, it would not have consoled her; according to the authorities on murder whom she had read, nervous criminals were the most dangerous.

One reassuring point kept her from complete panic. What could the man do to her here? He seemed to have no weapon; surely he would have produced a gun or knife by this time. He couldn't risk killing her in such a public spot, with the constant danger of interruption. Kidnaping was even more difficult; she would struggle and kick and . . .

And . . . what? All he had to do was to get close

enough to hit her, once. Then he could carry his swooning fiancée, or sister, through sympathetic crowds to a waiting car.

He took a step forward and, with a gasp, Jess backed away. She had overcome her scruples about screaming now; but now it was too late. The clamor of the bells went on without stopping, urging late-comers to hurry.

He was close upon her now, his outstretched arms a bar to flight, reaching out . . .

All at once the room was filled with people: short people, tall people, fat ones and thin ones, but all middle-aged or older, all carrying the insignia of their class: cameras. American tourists, God bless them, in the wrong place at the wrong time, as they so often were; a black-robed verger hurried in after them, wringing his hands.

"Ladies and gentlemen, please! The service is about to begin. Please—ladies! Those of you who wish to attend the service—"

A portly gentleman removed a chewed but un-lighted cigar from his mouth, contemplated the end of it, and looked at the guide.

"How long does this service last?"

"Approximately forty-five minutes, sir. Now, la-dies and—"

The portly gentleman put the cigar back in his mouth.

"I'll meetcha later, Martha," he said. "Out in front."

There was a hearty murmur of agreement from the other men in the group. The guide looked sadly at the leader of the rebellion, and then glanced back over his shoulder in the direction of the invisible spire, from which the bells had ceased to ring.

"Very well, gentlemen. If you . . . Ladies. Please. This way."

Four ladies had come in; five went out. Jess was as close as she could get to the chubbiest of the five. The verger was behind her, making shooing motions; as she scuttled through the doorway, Jess saw the man with the mustache come forward from the bench and follow after.

She had hoped to make a dash for freedom when she got into the cloisters, but she didn't know her way well enough, and there was such a feeling of safety in the comfortable contours of the lady tourist. Jess had the usual contempt for the "average tourist"—which means all tourists except oneself—but now she was ready to overlook all their other sins for the sake of their amiable curiosity, and their naïve assumption that anybody from the States was practically a member of the family.

"You on a tour?" her new-found friend asked cheerfully. "Sure is hard on the feet, isn't it? We're on our way home now. Harry says if he has to look at one more church he's going to turn Mohammedan, but his bunions are bothering him. Harry says . . ."

Jess couldn't have spoken if she had wanted to. She nodded and smiled; the monologue did not end until they entered the cathedral and were shushed by the indignant verger. He indicated a row of seats, and Jess slid in, behind her compatriot.

The music had already begun. All the cathedrals had fine choir schools, and the singing bore little resemblance to the volunteer choir of the white

Methodist church back home. The high boys' voices lifted over the deeper tones of the men, and for a moment the sheer beauty of the soaring song, filling the lofty vault, made Jess forget her panic. Then she turned her head, to accept the little book the verger was offering; and she saw the man with the mustache heading purposefully for her. His face was set in a scowl and his right hand was in his pocket. A gun? A hypodermic needle? A knife? Suppose he stood next to her and stuck the needle . . .

Her wide eyes and frightened mouth caught the verger's attention, and he turned to follow her gaze. Jess saw his black-clad shoulders stiffen with indignation. Visitors were not permitted to wander about the cathedral during the services, and this visitor was clearly in pursuit of the pious young lady, whose expression had displayed her disapproval. The verger gave Jess an austere, ecclesiastical smile, and pounced.

Jess watched, with relief and sudden amusement, as her follower was intercepted, cut off, and ruthlessly shoved into a distant seat. The verger took up his position in the aisle, next to the pursuer's chair, and fixed him with a cold stare. Jess had a feeling that if the man had moved he would have been smothered under a wave of outraged black officials, and the body quietly removed. The ultimate sin here was creating a disturbance.

For the first time she felt safe, and she drew a long, quivering breath. The music stopped, the echoes died in the vast arches; the white-gowned celebrant approached the altar, and amid the rustle of the crowd, kneeling, the words rolled out:

"Almighty God, unto whom all hearts be open, all desires known, and from whom no secrets are hid; cleanse the thoughts of our hearts by the inspiration of thy Holy Spirit . . ."

Jessica wished her pursuer would heed that beautiful thought. She also wished that this particular secret was not hidden from her. What was the man after? The ring? Impossible. Absurd.

"Glory be to God on high, and on earth peace, goodwill toward men . . ."

Goodwill? Jess felt very little, at that moment. The ring, the ring, the ring . . . It ran through her head as an insane counterpoint to the glorious old Litany, and her view of the ritual movements of the celebrant and his assistants was blurred by an inner vision, of the d—no, no, not here—the cursed ring, nestled in a corner of her purse.

The letter had asked her to bring it, so she had; she carried it in her purse because that seemed safer than a suitcase, and because the old man had laid such stress on it. But surely he only wanted it for sentimental reasons. Her mother had once taken it to a jeweler, who had reported that it had no intrinsic value. The stone was an agate of some sort, clumsily cut; the setting was gold, but of poor quality. Certainly the ring was not very pretty. It was big—made, obviously, for a man's hand—and heavy enough to bend a finger. Some old family trinket, perhaps, but not worth stealing.

"Let us pray for the whole Church of God in Christ Jesus, and for all men according to their needs . . ."

Jessica woke up, startled to find herself the only

one still standing. She dropped down, banging her knees painfully on the floor; the cushion had disappeared, and she had to fumble under the seat for it. By that time, the celebrant was immersed in prayer for the Queen, the Royal Family, and the good estate of the Catholic Church—a statement which startled Jess temporarily out of her grimmer thoughts until she remembered that this was how the Church of England referred to itself.

The prayer then referred to all those who were in any way afflicted or distressed, in mind, body or estate. Jess heartily endorsed the sentiment. She did not need to look over her shoulder to know that an angry gaze was aimed at her bowed head. What was she going to do? Prayer was good for the soul, but God seldom interferes personally to lift up the fallen sparrow. The verger might help to delay her pursuer while she dashed out, but after that, even in the street . . .

Again she was late in following the response, as the rest of the congregation surged to its feet. Half turning, she saw the man with the mustache, and she saw another thing that froze her in position, while the sound of the service faded to a dull drone in her ears.

The enemy had also turned; his hand moved in what appeared to be a signal. It was not difficult for Jess to pick out the man at whom the signal was directed. People were not allowed to stand at the back of the church during the service, like spectators at a play. But one man was standing, ignoring the verger's attempts to make him sit down, or leave. She could not make out his features, but she saw the lift of his hand as he answered his confederate. He was tall and rather thin, dark-haired, wearing one of the aged raincoats that were so popular in England.

This time when Jess fell to her knees she meant it. A second man at the door; how many others, inside and out? She had to do something. She had to think of something. Frantically her mind took up, and discarded, possibilities, while the murmur of voices rose around her.

"Trusting not in our own righteousness, but in Thy manifold and great mercies. We are not worthy so much as to gather up the crumbs under Thy table . . ."

As the congregation rose, and the beautiful, modulated voice proceeded, somewhat incongruously, with banns and notices of monthly meetings, one thing became plain to her, one thing that she must do. But how to do it? She had not made up her mind when the angelic voices rose again, and two church officials came slowly down the aisle. She paid little attention until the American lady's elbow nudged her.

"It's the collection, dearie. If you need any English money . . ."

"Thanks, I've got some."

Jess fumbled in her purse. She couldn't find her change purse. The maroon velvet collection bag, on its little pole, was bobbing along the row in front of her. What a genteel little bag it was, compared to the collection plate at home. . . . Her fingers found the change purse, with its unusual contents, and a great blinding light seemed to burst in her brain.

The verger who extended the bag to her could not see what she dropped into it—she was careful not to open her fist until it was inside the opening—but he heard the solid, musical jingle of several heavy objects falling among the coins already inside the bag. Nothing smaller than half crowns could make such a noise, and he gave the young lady a polite smile before he went on. Foreigners; it wasn't their church, after all; rather nice of them to be so generous, even though Alf would have it that they were being patronizing, especially the Americans. . . . The man in the next row dropped in a pound note, and he forgot the young American lady. Ostentatious, that one was; made sure everyone had a good look.

Jess relaxed, feeling pleased with herself. Now, at least, she had something with which to bargain, if bargaining became necessary. Again her neighbor's elbow caught her in the ribs and a sibilant whisper came to her ears.

"They're all going up there. What should we do?"

"If you want to take communion . . ." Jessica began doubtfully.

"I'm a Baptist," said her companion, as if she had suggested a small Black Mass.

"Well, then, let's just stay here."

The other woman nodded, watching the proceedings with a disapproving eye. Jess joined in the Lord's Prayer, trying to drown out the odd noises her stomach was making; she was nervous, not hungry, and the qualms in her interior increased as the stream of communicants began to thin out. Soon the service would be over. She had disposed of the ring; but what was she going to do with her own palpitating person?

All too soon the celebrant turned to the congregation.

"The Lord be with you."

Jess missed the response; she was busy tensing her leg muscles.

"Go forth in peace," the celebrant intoned.

Jess thought it was a splendid idea. She acted upon it while the congregation was muttering the final "Thanks be to God." Before anyone else had moved, she was out of her chair and through the doorway into the cloisters, leaving behind several disapproving ecclesiastics and—she hoped—two frustrated villains.

It wasn't far to her hotel, and ordinarily she would have walked. Under the circumstances, she hailed the first taxi she met. As it chugged off through the calm streets she knew she had found only a temporary haven. Salisbury boasted no more than a dozen hostelries; she had looked at the list the previous night, when deciding where to stay. They—the Enemy—could call each hotel in turn, and simply ask if she were registered. If they knew about the ring, they must know her name. In fact—her breath caught as the realization dawned—they might already have located her hotel. Pursuit could be hot on her heels, seconds away instead of minutes.

In her haste she gave the driver a ten-shilling note and waved away his shocked remonstrance: "Here, now, miss, the fare's only two and six! You don't—"

The hotel desk was unoccupied. After a second Jess pounded on the bell, and a man appeared, carrying a napkin and looking annoyed. Breath-lessly Jess plunged into her story; and her heart sank as she saw the change in the man's expression.

"But, my dear young lady—"

"Don't you believe me?"

"Why—certainly I believe you. Only—isn't it possible that you are exaggerating an incident which—er—"

"It wasn't like that at all," Jessica said, with as much dignity as she could command. It wasn't much; her five feet, two inches, and 105 pounds were not impressive.

"Well! Naturally, if you insist upon the police . . . However, the sort of thing you have described simply doesn't happen here. Not unless . . ."

His voice trailed away, meaningfully, and Jess stared at him, feeling cold and more than a little sick. He didn't believe her. No one would believe her. Why should they? The man was right, the things she had described didn't happen to people—unless . . . Unless they were criminals, trying to double-cross other criminals, or under-age females trying to es-cape guardian or parent, or sick people suffering from delusions of persecution. Unless, in short, they were undesirables who were not entitled to the protection of the law.

Jess gripped the edge of the desk with cold fin-gers as the full helplessness of her position struck her. A stranger in a strange land, she knew no one who could vouch for her character or mental stabil-ity. Her tale of pursuit and persecution was ren-dered unbelievable by the very fact that she could give no logical reason for her predicament. The men who were after her, one of them, at least, was English and a member of a respectable class of society, to judge by his speech. Presumably he knew what this was all about; certainly he would have provided himself with identification and with a story plausible enough to deceive casual strangers who would not, in any case, want to get involved. If she went to the police they would pat her on the head and call a doctor. She had no witnesses. The man had not actually threatened her; in fact, it would be her word against his that he had said anything at all.

All this passed through her mind in a flicker of thought; she saw her conclusions mirrored in the desk clerk's inimical stare. She turned away, and stumbled up the stairs.

As she had hoped, he had returned to his interrupted lunch when she came back downstairs, on the tips of her toes. The bell at the outer door jingled when she opened it, but she darted out and was gone before anyone could appear.

The street outside held no sinister strangers; apparently they had not located her hotel. She ran at first, but the suitcase was too heavy to permit such a pace for long. She had no map of the town and remembered only vaguely the location of the bus station. She had to stop a pedestrian and ask directions. It was unlikely, she reassured herself, that the pursuers would find a person met so casually.

The bus station was crowded, not only with tourists but with local people on Sunday excursions and visits. Standing on the platform, Jess looked uncertainly from the glass window of the buffet to the shabby waiting room. Where was she going?

There were about a dozen numbered loading platforms; buses stood waiting in four of them, the others were empty. Where *was* she going? Instinct provided the answer: London. The anonymity of a huge city, where, in hiding, she could catch her breath and try to find a clue to this insanity. The American Embassy. It was silly to assume that they would be any more inclined to believe her, but at least they were Americans. For what that was worth . . .

Yes, London. She searched the station for a bus schedule, found it incomprehensible, and then caught sight of an elderly man in some sort of uniform who seemed to be answering questions put to him by travelers. She went up to him.

The next bus for London did not leave for an hour.

Jess was unable to hold back an exclamation of distress. The man looked at her benevolently.

"From the States, are you? Americans are always in a hurry. You'd find the train quicker, miss, I expect; but the express doesn't go until six."

"Thank you."

He would have pursued the subject, out of sheer benevolence, if Jess hadn't retreated into the waiting room. She stood inside the door biting her lip in agitation. This would never do. They would soon be on her trail. Locating her hotel would take next to no time, and if the clerk, alerted by her odd behavior, inspected her room, he would realize that she had gone for good. The money she had left on the table would prevent any legal action on the part of the hotel, but the pursuers would immediately head for the railroad and bus stations. Good old reliable instinct had led her to the latter rather than the former; there was only one railroad line, but buses went out in all directions.

But, if this fact was to be of use to her, she would have to give up the London bus and take one almost at random. London was a logical destination, and the bus official would remember her question. The thought of an hour's delay, huddled in the waiting room or the ladies' wash-room, with mounting suspense weighing at her nerves, made up her mind. She walked straight out of the waiting room to Platform Six, where the driver had just gotten into the bus, and climbed on after him.

"Just in time," he informed her, with a cheerful grin. "Here, let's put your case under the steps; no room for it in the aisle."

As the ponderous vehicle backed skillfully out of its niche Jess had a panoramic view of the bus station and found it free of suspicious men with bushy mustaches. There was only one problem. She hadn't the faintest notion where the bus was going.

TWO

Now, as the afternoon sunlight deepened from gold to copper, Jess still didn't know where the bus was going. It had picked up other passengers on its way out of Salisbury; when they left the town behind, a pimply youth came to collect the fares. Unluckily for Jessica, she was unable to overhear the name of a single town on the route. The other passengers knew, not only where they were going, but the price of the ticket, and handed over the money without comment. When the young man reached Jess, in the farthest seat of all, she was speechless. She simply proffered a ten-shilling note and a feeble smile.

"All the way?" the boy inquired, and gave her back four shillings.

Jess could have kissed him, pimples and all. However, she still had no idea of her destination. She could tell from the sun that their general direction was northeast. That was good; London lay northeast of Salisbury. But this was obviously a local bus, and the fare to London would certainly be more than six shillings.

The bus ambled along; its meditative pace should have been calming to the nerves. When it stopped, in villages whose names, when she caught them, meant absolutely nothing to Jess, it sat chugging asthmatically for long minutes, while the driver helped an old lady off and walked her down the street to her house, or delivered parcels to shops. Once he ducked into a doorway under a sign bearing the legend, The Cross and Anchor, and came out five minutes later wiping his mouth with the back of his hand, amid a chorus of good-natured jeers from the passengers. They all seemed to know him by name.

Jessica's stomach made sympathetic noises. She hadn't eaten since breakfast, and panic, she had found, dried one's throat. A nice cup of hot tea would have been more to her taste than the beverages on tap at The Cross and Anchor, but at that point she would have settled for a glass of water.

In her capacious handbag, bought especially for the trip and almost as big as her suitcase, she had a general guide to England and a map. She had already examined the map and found it useless; the villages on their route were too small to be mentioned.

They passed a church and a scattering of small thatch-roofed houses, then the bus jerked to a stop in a village somewhat larger than any she had yet seen. It possessed a marketplace, with an ancient stone cross, and a particularly appetizing tea shop. Jess's mouth would have watered if she had had any extra saliva. For a moment she considered getting off the bus, but she knew such a move would be folly. Eventually her pursuers would pick up her trail. Someone might have seen her board this bus, and even if she had not been seen, there could not be more than half a dozen buses that would have left the station before the trackers reached it. All they had to do was to follow these buses, and if the pace of this one was typical, that process wouldn't take forever.

Three of the passengers got off in the market-place; there were now only seven people left in the bus, including herself. No, she couldn't leave the bus in this sleepy hamlet without being observed. She would have to stay on the bus, "all the way"—wherever that might be.

The driver finished his philosophical discussion with an elderly native who was sitting by the market cross, looking as if he had grown there, and the bus started off again. The little boy on the other side of the fat lady said something in a soft, plaintive voice, and the woman—his mother?—said robustly,

"Well, you can hold it in a bit longer. We'll be home soon."

Jess was sorry that subject had come up. Almost too tired and uncomfortable to worry, she leaned her head against the windowpane and idly contemplated the lurid cover of the thriller in her lap. She had pretended to read it, not only to occupy her mind—it hadn't worked—but to put off the lady beside her, who looked as if she might enjoy a chat. From her sole bus trip before the debacle, Jess had learned that the standoffishness of the English was a myth; they were the friendliest souls in the world, especially when traveling, and loved to talk to foreigners. On the Southampton-Salisbury trip this trait had given her much pleasure, but she wasn't in the mood for idle chitchat now.

She opened the book again, noting that she seemed to be on page forty-six; at least that was where her thumb had been inserted as a bookmark. Not surprisingly, she couldn't remember anything of the first forty-five pages. "Althea crouched against the wall, her heart pounding. How long had she been entombed in this dark, dank hole? Four hours? Five? It seemed like an eternity."

Jess wondered who Althea was. The heroine, clearly; only heroines crouched in dark dank holes for that length of time. She didn't remember how Althea had gotten into the hole, or why, and she didn't care. Silly wench, Althea. She swallowed, through a dryness that felt like a patch of the Sahara, and tried to ignore her other distressing discomforts, and wondered how on earth the heroines of these stories managed to get around the simpler, more basic necessities of life. Four or five hours was a pretty long stretch, and when you were as nervous as all that . . .

It was useless, she couldn't keep her mind on Althea's troubles. Silly woman, she thought again, and wondered if her predicament would sound as absurd to an outsider as the dangers of Althea and her fictional sisters usually sounded to her. It was difficult to describe peril unless it consisted of something as concrete as a bullet or a bloody knife. But she had learned that danger could be implicit in a look, and that the movement of an arm could convey a threat.

She sighed, and closed the book on poor Althea

and her pounding heart. Once again she half turned, to scan the road behind. But this time the road was not innocuous. How long had the car been there? It was an open car, a convertible, and it was close—dangerously close—to the bus. She could make out the features of the two men quite clearly. The brown mustache was unmistakable.

For several seconds Jess was too paralyzed to move. Pounding hearts indeed, she thought; hers was banging around like a loose pebble in a box. Could they see her? She thought not. Thanks to the fat lady's bundles she was jammed into the corner, where a stretch of blank wall separated the back window from the one on the side. This was not one of the new all-glass sight-seeing buses, and she had to look sideways as well as back to see out the window. It was pure reflex that made her shrink back, with a little gasp of terror.

The fat lady leaned over and put a firm hand to her arm.

"Now then, love, what's the matter?"

"The matter?" Jess squeaked.

"Why, child, you're as pale as a ghost. Don't be afraid. This isn't the States, where the gangsters and hippies are shooting people down in cold blood all over the streets; no doubt they'll have followed you from home, those two back there, but you're in England now, don't you fear; we don't let such things happen here."

"How did you know?"

"Haven't I watched you, nervous as a cat, peering out that window the whole time and not being able to read your little book? I'll tell you what we'll do;

you'll just get off the bus with me and we'll fetch Thomas Babbitt. I knew you were an American, of course. My niece married one, naturally he was a man, but I know what it's like over there."

Out of this morass of inconsequentiality and shrewd analysis, Jessica's reeling brain focused on one point.

"Who," she asked feebly, "is Thomas Babbitt?"

"The constable, of course. He'll get rid of those two. He's my sister's boy. Mrs. Hodge, that's my name, Mrs. Edward Hodge."

"How do you do. But, Mrs. Hodge—you're very kind, but . . . Those two back there. I'm afraid one constable wouldn't be—"

"Armed, are they?" Mrs. Hodge had pale-blue eyes, just the color of the glass eyes of a doll Jess had once owned. They widened with delighted horror. "With guns? Pistols?"

Jess got a grip on herself.

"I don't know. They may be. But I can't risk your getting hurt, you or anyone else. They may not even wait till I get off. They may stop the bus. They can't be sure I'm on this one, you see."

Mrs. Hodge pressed her lips tightly together and nodded till the blue flowers on what was surely her "Sunday hat"—as opposed to her "other hat"—wobbled insanely.

"There, I knew it, a nice girl like you wouldn't be involved in anything criminal. That Bonnie and Clyde, now, I thought of that at first: gangsters rubbing out the one that double-crosses them, eh? But it's not that. No, you don't need to tell me; it'll be—" She glanced at the little boy, who was staring in fascination, and lowered her voice. "It'll be the white slave trade. Well!" She nodded again, and the flowers danced. "They can't do that sort of thing, not in England."

Kindness and sympathy, however muddleheaded, had the wrong effect on Jess, who suddenly felt she might burst into tears.

"But you can't stop them," she faltered. "I can't get out without being seen, they'll follow us, and if they—"

"Not in England," Mrs. Hodge repeated. She raised her voice in a ladylike bellow.

"Miss Aiken—Mr. Woodle—Sam—"

Jessica jumped several inches; the other passengers, now four in number, turned casual faces toward the back seat. Evidently they were familiar with Mrs. Hodge's voice and her habits.

Light-headed with hunger and nerves, Jess began to feel as if she had slipped out of the real world into some sideways dimension, as Mrs. Hodge, in a cheerful shout, outlined her version of her problem. It was quite in keeping with the mad logic of this unreal world that all the other passengers accepted the improbable story with perfect equanimity. The red-faced man in baggy tweeds—Mr. Woodle—expressed the general sentiment.

"Americans," he snorted. "Gangsters. Can't have that sort of thing here. Let 'em come." He brandished his stick, a heavy gold-headed affair, and narrowly missed hitting himself in the nose as the stick bounded off the low luggage rack above his head.

"We can't fight 'em," yelled Mrs. Hodge, "They've got tommy guns. Maybe bombs."

A disembodied voice floated back from the driver's seat. Sam never took his eyes off the road, but he hadn't missed a word.

"Trick 'em," he shrieked. "Not very bright, these gangsters."

"Quite right," shouted the genteel maiden lady midway down the bus. "Do I understand that the young woman believes that these villains do not know with absolute certainty that she is presently within this vehicle?"

"I don't think so," Jess muttered dazedly. The information was passed on to the audience by Mrs. Hodge, and an animated discussion followed, at the top of everyone's lungs.

"We none of us seed her," bawled the fourth passenger, a wizened little old man who might have been a farm laborer. "She never was here."

"But I am here," yelled Jessica, entering into the spirit of the thing. "How can I hide, on this—"

"Better to say, I think, that she got off the bus earlier," howled the maiden lady.

"Wow," said the shrillest voice of them all. "Mum, look there."

Master Hodge, probably the most sensible member of the crowd, had been keeping an eye out the back window. He drew Jess's attention to the road just in time for her to see the car pull out and pass. Moments later came the driver's warning yell:

"Watch ouuuuuuut!"

The words blended harmoniously with the squeal of the brakes as the bus shuddered to a halt, twisted half across the road in a wrenching movement. Jess knew what had happened even before the maiden lady screeched, "They've stopped ... blocking the road ... They are getting out of the automobile. They are coming—"

Then Mrs. Hodge—five feet tall, 160 pounds, bespectacled and on the wrong side of forty—achieved her finest hour.

"She got out at Woodhole," she called; simultaneously her large pink hand clamped on Jessica's shoulder and forced her down onto the floor of the bus.

There was very little floor available, not more than a foot and a half between the last seat and the back of the one ahead; but Jess was amazed to find how much of her own small person could be crammed, with Mrs. Hodge's vigorous assistance, into that space. Moving with the skillfulness of a housewife shaping a loaf of bread, Mrs. Hodge's hands tucked a good deal of Jessica under the seat. The part of her that protruded was, at least, down below seat level.

Speechless and snorting in the dust, Jess's distorted view of the outside world was obliterated by a rain of parcels, all of which landed on top of her—Mrs. Hodge's parcels, topped off by Mrs. Hodge's large coat. She felt the seat above her sag, heard a surprised squeak, and deduced, correctly, that Master Hodge had just been added to the agglomeration on top of her. Though she could see nothing, except a dimly lit collection of cigarette butts, candy wrappers and one banana peel (fresh), she heard every word. Sam had stopped the engine.

"Good evening, ladies and gentlemen," said one of the most cultivated voices she had ever heard off the screen. "My abject apologies for stopping you so abruptly—"

"Watdidja do it for then?" Sam asked unpleasantly. "Stealing buses, now. Think you can get to Cuba on this here?"

He cackled; the passengers joined in loyally, the maiden lady's shrill chuckle and Mr. Woodle's bass guffaw rising over the rest.

"Jolly good," said the voice, unconvincingly. "Yes indeed."

"But I'm late now," said the maiden lady indignantly. "For the bowling league. The rest of them will never forgive me."

"Illegal," said Mr. Woodle. "Against some sort of law. Several, possibly."

Mrs. Hodge decided to enliven the proceedings.

"Don't you come near me," she howled. "Take my poor little savings, if you must, but don't lay a hand on me or me child!"

"Don't worry, madam," said Mr. Woodle stoutly. "If he takes another step toward you, I'll—"

" 'Ave the law on 'im, I will," remarked the elderly laborer vindictively. "Just you wait till we gets to town. I'll 'ave—"

Jess, shaking with a horrible combination of laughter and fright, realized, too late, that she was on the verge of a mighty sneeze. The floor of the bus had collected the dust of ages. Fortunately her muffled explosion was drowned by the laments of Mrs. Hodge, now on the brink of convincing hysterics, and by the general uproar. The voice of the intruder rose over the cacophony; it sounded slightly hysterical itself.

"Please, please, ladies and gentlemen! Madam, calm yourself! I wouldn't dream," the voice added sincerely, "of coming any closer. Look here, just let me say something, can't you?"

"Speak up, then," Sam growled. "Wasting our times like this. I'm behind schedule as it is, and the company—"

"Please! Sir—madam—friends—er, that is—I'm a medical man, looking for a young lady, run away from my nursing home, placed there by distraught family; thought she was recovering nicely, not dangerous, we don't think, but—"

"You don't think?" Mrs. Hodge repeated. "What's this, now? You've let some loony escape, that'll maybe murder the lot of us? Call yourself a doctor!"

Jess could almost feel sorry for her pursuer; she imagined him perspiring gently, mopping his forehead with a large white handkerchief. But her sense of humor, ordinarily good, was soon subdued by a new fear. The tale was lame enough and, thanks to the man's confusion, poorly told. But what if her allies believed it? The man's accent was certainly not that of an American movie hoodlum. Would Mrs. Hodge—could Mrs. Hodge—believe that a respectable Englishman might be involved in the white slave trade?

She need not have feared her friends' loyalty. It was their enthusiasm that almost finished her; the discussion went on so long that she felt sure she would be asphyxiated before the intruders left. The passengers were having the time of their collective lives; by the time they got through, Jess almost believed that she had left the bus twenty miles back, "at Woodhole, right at the Burning Babe—rolling her eyes something frightful, gentlemen. I thought at the time, I thought . . ."

The rolling eyes were Mrs. Hodge's contribution; it was Sam who added, "Talking to herself she were. Made me come over queer, it did."

Jess was of the opinion that this was overdoing it. But the general effect was convincing. The pursuers had little choice; they could not search the bus without exposing themselves, and they had no reason to doubt the story. She heard the spokesman begin his apologies; then the airless space and her stretched nerves got the better of her. She was dimly aware of the bus jolting on, but she lay in a daze until a firm hand plucked off several layers of camouflage and dragged her up into the open air.

"Fainting away, poor child," said Mrs. Hodge. "Mr. Woodle, let's have your flask back here."

Jess tried to object, but her position, on her knees on the floor, was not conducive to rebellion; she took a swallow of brandy, gasped, gagged, and was finally allowed to droop forward, her head and arms on the seat.

"It's all right now; they've got out of sight," said Mister Hodge, nose flattened against the rear window.

"She'd best stay down, all the same."

Jess agreed; the effect of brandy on an empty stomach made her quite sure that a disaster of some sort would occur if she tried to stand. When she found herself sliding helplessly across the seat, she thought at first it must be the brandy. Then she realized that the bus had made an acute-angle turn at its top speed.

"Sam, where are you going?" asked the maiden lady.

"Thought we'd better get off our route, just to play safe," Sam shouted; now that the bus was moving, conversation had returned to its former intensity. "Sorry about the bowling, Miss Aiken."

"The bowling is tomorrow night," yelled Miss Aiken. "An excellent idea, Sam."

"I think it's safe for her to get up now," said Mrs. Hodge, and assisted Jessica onto the seat. "You're a sight, child—covered with smuts. Sam never sweeps this bus, that's clear. Get your handkerchief, my dear, and your bits of makeup, while we discuss what's to be done. Where were you going? Have you friends who'll look after you?"

Jess thought of the old house in Cornwall, and rejected it, violently and at once, with an instinct which she was not to understand for another twenty-four hours.

"London," she said, groping obediently for her lipstick. "I thought . . . London."

The suggestion had to be submitted for committee approval, and everyone agreed.

"Scotland Yard," Mr. Woodle said. "That's the place. They'll know how to deal with these international crime rings."

By now they were careening wildly along narrow lanes flanked by thick-grown banks so high that the bus moved through a false twilight. Jess wondered, as branches snapped past the windows, what they would do if they met another car. She decided not to think about it.

The brandy had gone to her head, and she felt giddy and relaxed. Most helpful of all to her shattered nerves was the atmosphere. The unquestioning, positive goodwill of these strangers created a small, warm world around her—a world as insane, in its own way, as the unexplained persecution to which she had been subjected, but one which restored her shaken faith in humanity.

"Where are we?" she asked. "If I can get to a train station . . ."

"I've a better idea," said Mrs. Hodge. "Sam—we're not far from St. Mary's Underhill, unless I'm mistaken."

"Right," Sam bellowed back.

"Then that's the place we want. Drive around a bit more, Sam, till it starts to get dark. Now, child, here's what you'd best do. Harry Marks in St. Mary's has a brand-new automobile, the young fool, that he can't afford, and he's always behind on the hire-purchase payments. He'll drive you straight to London and be glad of the money. Tell him you're a friend of mine and he'll not dare to overcharge you. D'you need money?"

She had her pocketbook open before Jess could reply, and the girl felt her eyes fill with tears as she caught the plump hand.

"You're being so kind," she muttered. "And I'm a stranger . . ."

"Nonsense," said Mrs. Hodge calmly. "There are

only two sorts of people in the world, right ones and wrong ones. I can tell the right from the wrong, at my age. Now. Do you need money?"

"I don't have much English money," Jess admitted. "I had planned to cash a traveler's check at the hotel."

"Traveler's check?" Mr. Woodle came reeling down the aisle and took the seat in front. "I can cash one for you if you like. Give you a good rate of exchange."

"Shame on you," Mrs. Hodge began indignantly.

"No, please—I'd be very grateful. I have plenty of money, really, but perhaps—what's his name? Harry?—would rather have cash than a check, and on Sunday—"

"Quite right," said Mr. Woodle briskly. "Ten or twelve pounds should see you through. Now the exchange rate as of yesterday morning . . ."

According to plan, it was dusk when the bus wheezed to a stop in the village of St. Mary's Underhill. It was the smallest village Jess had yet seen, which was saying a good deal, and she regarded its tiny huddle of buildings with dismay. Half a dozen cottages, hugging the ground. . . . Neurotic houses, lonely and dark in the twilight. Only one of the buildings had any lights, the building in front of which they had stopped; but the light filtered, meager and unwelcoming, through closely curtained windows. A sign swung above the door, but it was too dark for Jess to read it.

"The Blue Boar," Sam announced, swinging Jess's bag down with a gesture which, in a southern European, might have been a flourish. "Let me give you a hand, love."

Her suitcase beside her, Jess turned to survey her friends and fellow conspirators, all of whom were now at the windows on her side, grinning and waving encouragement. Mrs. Hodge stood in the doorway of the bus. Her mouth was grave, though her eyes still twinkled with reminiscent enjoyment.

"Send us a postal card, child, will you? Mrs. Hodge, Westbury, that's all the address you'll need."

"I'll telephone," Jess promised; no extravagance seemed quite good enough. "Thank you—all of you . . ."

"You'll be all right now," Mrs. Hodge said firmly.

"Come along now, Mrs. Hodge." Sam pushed her back up the stairs and mounted them himself. "We don't want to linger here, in case they should pick up our trail."

As the bus lumbered off, Jess saw Mrs. Hodge's round face at the back window. One of her hands was raised in a sign Jess knew only from books and movies; with a queer contraction of the heart, she realized that Mrs. Hodge had lived with that victory sign and the years of disaster it had valiantly denied. Then Sam turned off the interior lights and the bus became a dark shadow which might have been some smelly prehistoric beast retreating into the night.

Jess turned to contemplate the doorway of the Blue Boar, and took an instant dislike to the place. It was probably snug and sheltered inside; from the outside it gave precisely the opposite impression. Lifting her eyes for a last look at the village, she saw a huge square darkness outlined against the luminous sky. St. Mary's itself, no doubt; the tower of the church from which the village took its name. But what a tower for a cluster of six cottages and a pub! It should have been a symbol of comfort, but the towering bulk loomed like a curtain designed to cut off the friendly stars. With a shiver Jess picked up her suitcase, squared her shoulders, and reached for the doorknob.

THREE

The door opened onto a corridor, poorly lit and prosaic. The whitewashed walls were dirty, the floor was worn, and the single piece of furniture, a table on the right, held a used beer glass, one grimy gardening glove with the thumb out, and a collection of rusty nails.

There were three inner doors, one on either side and one at the end of the hallway. They were all uncompromisingly closed, but from behind the door on the right Jess thought she heard a clinking sound. She turned the knob and pushed the door open.

She had guessed correctly; this was the bar. Knowing English pubs only from guide-book descriptions, Jess found this one a crushing disappointment. There were no blackened oak beams, no quaint old prints, no fireplace. Correction, she thought; there was a fireplace, but it was no robust, stone-manteled Tudor survival. Small enough to look grudging, it had been refaced in a kind of fake brick, and contained, instead of a fire, a portable electric heater, which was not turned on.

The furniture consisted of a slot machine, a calendar with a picture of a drooling Scottie and four tables placed up against a bench built around two of the walls. Someone had made a desperate attempt to brighten the room up by painting the walls bright coral and upholstering the bench in red. The attempt had failed, and clearly the decorator had given up when he got to the carpet; it was gray, figured with blue and rust. The bar proper was at the back of the room, to her left; a wooden counter with three stools in front of it and shelves of bottles and glassware behind.

Also behind the bar was a man. The publican, Jess wondered? Mine host? The jolly innkeeper? He was no Chaucerian Harry Bailey; Jess had never seen a glummer face, and the sight of her did nothing to increase the fellow's happiness.

Jessica would have left if there had been anyplace else to go. Suitcase in hand, she closed the door behind her and advanced, with as much dignity as the brandy circulating through her bloodstream allowed, toward one of the tables. She sat down gingerly on the bright-red bench. The eyes of the man behind the bar never left her, and his mouth never opened.

Jess cleared her throat.

"I'm looking for a man named Harry Marks."

The pause was long, but not pregnant; it was dead, without even a hint of potential life. Finally the affable bartender grunted, "Not here."

He took a glass off the shelf and began to polish it.

"I see he's not," Jess said coldly. "But I was told

that you would know where to find him. I want to hire his car."

Another unpromising pause ensued.

"Can't."

"What do you mean, 'can't'? You can't find him?"

"I mean, you can't hire him nor his car." The bartender leaned forward, both elbows on the bar, and eyed her with sour pleasure. "He's gone and he won't be back. Not before morning. And in no fit condition to drive then."

Jessica's mental state is better imagined than described. She felt as if she had been hit over the head with a large blunt mallet. After the first shock she lost her temper.

"Of all the nasty men! I wouldn't have believed anyone as nasty as you could live in the same country as those wonderful people on the bus! You love giving people bad news, don't you? What's your problem—your stomach, or your wife, or—Don't you dare glare at me! Just keep a civil tongue in your head and tell me how I can get out of this horrible place tonight."

"With me," said a voice from the far, window end of the room. "Anyone who can talk to Alf like that deserves a lift."

Jessica's new bravado, and her breath, went out of her in a gasp. It was not only the shock of finding that there was another person in the room; it was the familiarity of the voice.

Then the speaker extracted himself from his shadowy corner behind the curtains and came out into the light; and she realized that the voice had seemed familiar only because of its accent. The man was someone she had never seen before. He was tall, and painfully thin, with a long narrow face. His hair was black and untidy, his eyebrows were lifted; but the rest of his features were overshadowed by a nose of such lordly proportions that she forgot all else in the wonder of it.

The man saw her stare and, with the readiness of experience, interpreted it correctly.

" '*C'est un roc!*' " he exclaimed, striking an attitude. " '*C'est une péninsule!* When it blows, the typhoon howls! When it bleeds—the Red Sea!' "

"You shouldn't be so morbidly self-conscious about it," Jess said. "It's not that bad. Certainly not as bad as Cyrano's."

The newcomer sank ungracefully into the chair opposite.

"An American. The accent, plus the off-the-cuff psychological analysis of people you've just met . . . But—a pretty American. That does compensate."

"Thanks a lot."

"Come now, you're capable of better repartee than that." His long mouth curved up in an unexpectedly attractive grin. "Why so pale and wan, ladee? Hungry? I could do with a bite myself. Alf, with your usual gourmet skill, conjure us up a couple of plates of bacon and eggs. The same again for me, and a large sherry for the lady."

"I don't want—"

"But you should. Food, first and always; then we'll make plans. What's your name? Mine's Randall. David Randall. Do not call me Dave."

"Jessica Tregarth."

"Ah, the Cornish Tregarths. Good God, don't start so. I never heard of you or your family. Don't you know that old rhyme about the Cornishmen—Tre, Pol and Pen? Jessica. It doesn't suit you. I shall call you Jess."

"I wish you wouldn't."

"But if you're going to be intimately occupying the front seat of my automobile all the way to London, we must be friends. The intimacy is inevitable; I don't drive a Rolls. Look here—don't be put off by my feeble attempts at light conversation. If you want to leave this metropolis tonight, it will have to be with me."

From the open doorway behind the bar floated a smell which made Jess realize that she was really very hungry. In her preoccupation with her stomach she lost track of the conversation—if it could be dignified by that name. Randall leaned back in his chair and studied her with an odious smile. He said no more until Alf reappeared with two thick white plates and deposited them on the counter with an aggressive thump. Randall unwound his long legs from the chair and carried the food to the table. Jess was embarrassed at the speed with which she emptied her plate.

"That's better," Randall said. "Ready to leave now? You'd better powder your nose, or whatever. Actually, your nose is in need of some attention. What did you do, fall off a horse? A bicycle? I've been trying to puzzle out how you could have reached this oasis. But of course I'm too well bred to ask."

"I came by bus," Jess said.

Alf's snort and Randall's delicately raised eyebrows conveyed the same reaction. Alf put it into words.

"Nearest bus goes to Castlebridge. Three miles from here."

"It was a bus from Salisbury." For the first time in hours Jess felt like a human being—warm, fed, and safe. Her sense of well-being went to her head and joined forces with the brandy lingering there. She took a deep swig of sherry and said recklessly, "Two men are chasing me. I don't know who they are or what they want, but they're chasing me. I got on the bus to get away from them, but they followed the bus and stopped it back there—somewhere— and got on, and told everybody that I was an escaped lunatic, but the other passengers were awfully nice, they hid me under a seat and told the—the—"

"Bad guys?" said Randall helpfully.

Jessica glowered at him.

"Pursuers," she said, articulating clearly. "That I wasn't there. Then the bus driver brought me here. She said to find Harry and hire him to take me to London."

She finished her sherry.

"Female bus drivers," Randall muttered.

"He was not."

"Never mind. Look here, my girl. I hope my sense of humor is as good as the next man's, and I do not take my profession at all seriously. But couldn't you have invented a better story?"

"I don't know what you're talking about." An involuntary hiccup escaped Jess. She looked disapprovingly at Randall. "I don't even know who you are," she said sadly. "And you want me to go off to London with you."

"I'm not sure I do," Randall admitted. "But there's no help for it. You can't stay here. Alf doesn't have any rooms; and there's not a hotel or inn for miles. The locals have gone off to the fair, tra-la, tra-la, and will not, as Alf said, come reeling home until morning."

"Closing time in a quarter of an hour," said Alf inexorably.

"Yes, there's that. You're sure I haven't met you somewhere? That you don't know who I am?"

"Who are you?"

Randall sighed.

"Never mind. The sooner we start, the sooner we'll arrive."

"But I don't even know who—"

"I know, you said that. If you're afraid of being murdered in a ditch somewhere, let me remind you that Alf is a witness to your departure with me, and that there's nothing good old Alf would like better than to put someone in the dock. Especially me. I wouldn't risk it, however great the provocation, and I am beginning to suspect that the provocation will be extreme. Come along—here we go . . ."

Later, Jess had a vague memory of pouring quarts of cold water on her face before she joined her unwilling chauffeur at the front door. The cold water helped, and so did the night air pouring in the open car window. Randall drove at a speed which, as she sobered up, made her wish she was still drunk. But for the first part of the journey there was little traffic, and Randall was an excellent driver. Jess curled up in the bucket seat and began to enjoy the ride. It had been too dark to see much of the car, except that it was low-slung and expensive-looking, and it certainly rode like a dream. She felt as if she were sitting motionless with a dark landscape flowing smoothly past the window. Then they turned onto a main road. The lights of oncoming cars began to appear, and Jess finally spoke.

"Where are we?"

"Near Reading, if that means anything to you. Feeling better?"

"Much. I owe you an apology."

"But it was a lovely yarn," he said easily. "Who put you up to it?"

"Yarn? Oh, I'm not apologizing for that, that was true. But I'm sorry I was so rude when you were kind enough to offer me a ride."

"Oh, we're going to carry it out to the bitter end, are we? All right. Let it not be said that I couldn't take a joke. Where are you going, specifically? London is a good-sized village, you know. Quite a burg, as you Americans say."

"Americans don't say that, and you know it. You've spent some time in the United States, haven't you? It didn't affect your accent, but you seem to have acquired a few colloquialisms. And I don't mean 'burg.'"

"Accent be damned," said Randall, stung. "I fancied I had a rather neat New York twang."

"Pure Oxford."

"Cambridge, as a matter of fact. Where you Americans get the mistaken impression that—"

"It's a beautiful accent. I love just listening to you talk."

As she had expected, this kept Randall quiet for a few minutes.

"Not to be repetitive," he said at last. "But where *are* you going?"

"Some hotel, I guess."

"The Hilton?"

"Heavens, no. I haven't got that kind of money. I do have a hotel reservation, come to think of it. But I had my luggage sent on there from Southampton, and if they manage to trace it . . ."

"They? Oh, yes, the bad guys. Do forgive me; they had momentarily slipped my mind. Yes, well, that's quite right; it wouldn't be difficult for them to trace your luggage, and if you don't materialize at that hotel, they'll try others. The sort of places where an American would stay. I rather imagine you'd like me to recommend a nice, obscure hostelry?"

"Never mind," Jess said wearily. "I don't blame you for thinking I'm kidding you. I guess I should be grateful you don't think I'm crazy. Yes, please, I would appreciate a recommendation."

"Good. I know just the place."

They proceeded in strained silence for another mile or so. Then Randall said,

"If you don't mind, I'd like to hear that saga again. You rather overdid the incoherence the first time round."

Jess was tempted to employ a rude American colloquialism, but she reminded herself that, after all, it was his car.

"Not bad at all," he said, when she finished. "Better than I thought. Offhand I can't think of a plausible pattern. Is there one?"

"A what?"

Randall beeped his horn—it sounded like a small chamber orchestra—flicked his lights, and went roaring out and around the car ahead. Jessica flinched. She wasn't used to passing on the right.

"A pattern. That's how these things are written, of course. Like a what d'yecall'em—piece of woven cloth, warp and woof and all that. The writer knows the entire pattern, but the only part he displays to the reader is the warp, or perhaps it's the woof— half of the whole, in other words. Naturally it appears to be incoherent and unconnected; that's the mystification. In the last chapter he weaves in the missing threads, and then the innocent reader sees what it's all been about."

"Oh, skip it. If you don't believe me, why do you keep harping on the subject?"

"As I said, it's not a bad plot. I particularly like the part about dropping the ring in the collection bag. Though antique family jewelry is a bit passé. Microfilm dots, or sealed containers of new mutated germs—that's more in vogue."

"Nuts," said Jess.

"But your main plot problem at this juncture," Randall went on blithely, "is that you've lost the enemy. How the Hades do you expect them to find you in a hive like London? You'd better go to the Hilton, or to that hotel where you've booked a reservation."

Jess growled under her breath.

"It's a nice little problem," Randall said, squinting at the excessively bright lights of an approaching car. "I mean, how do we get the villains back on your trail without making you sound a complete idiot? That's one of the difficulties of this form of fiction; the heroine has to be an idiot or she wouldn't get into such idiotic predicaments. A sensible female would go straight to the police."

"Who would, of course, believe me without question."

"Yes, I know, that's the conventional excuse. Wait a sec—no, that won't work. Even if they tracked you to the Blue Boar, Alf couldn't tell them where you'd gone. Not that he wouldn't tell them if he knew. He adores causing trouble. But he couldn't. Hmmmm."

They drove the rest of the way in silence except for Randall's muttering, and Jess amused herself by studying his profile in the lightning flashes from oncoming headlights. Vindictively concentrating at first on the size of his outstanding facial adornment, she found herself growing to admire it. It was a well-shaped nose, for all its size, and only slightly curved: Roman in its narrowness and beaky arrogance. She tried to picture him in a helmet, with a row of bristles on top like a shoebrush, barking out orders in Latin to a troop of legionnaires. She failed. The rest of his face didn't fit. His chin was firm, but hardly belligerent, and his mouth was shaped with a precision that verged on delicacy. If it had not been overshadowed by The Nose, it would have been a sensitive mouth.

Then the fatigue that had been accumulating all day hit her like a hammer, and she did not awaken until the recurrent flash of street lights vexed her eyes.

"Almost there," said her companion equably, as she hastily withdrew her head from his shoulder.

If they had passed any of the famous landmarks of London, she had slept through them; when they turned into a quiet, almost empty street she had no idea where she was. Randall pulled over to the curb. Without waiting for her, he mounted a flight of stone steps and rang a doorbell.

To Jess, blinking groggily out of the car window, the place did not look like a hotel. It was one of a long row of similar houses, tall and thin, separated from one another only by narrow passageways, and fronting directly on the sidewalk. This house was distinguished from its neighbors by a black-painted door and a big brass knocker, but it had the same air of smug, Dickensian respectability and in fact dated, as she was to learn, from that very era.

Before long the door was opened by a stooped, elderly man who greeted David with a cordial handshake. They exchanged a few sentences, and then the other man came out to the car and reached for Jessica's suitcase.

"Good evening, Miss Tregarth. We've only one single left, and it's on the fourth floor. No lift, I'm afraid . . ."

"That will be fine."

He went on into the house with her bag, and David opened the car door. Jess was sodden with fatigue; as she clumsily maneuvered herself out of the car, she dropped her purse. Half the contents slid out onto the sidewalk—wallet, pen, lipstick, and the pocket thriller she had been trying to read.

Randall bent to pick them up. When he straightened he was smiling, but not pleasantly.

"Jolly good joke, Miss Tregarth. For a while I

almost . . . We'll have a laugh over it next time we meet."

He didn't even wait for her to answer, but roared off with an indignant swish of his exhaust. Jess was left staring bemusedly at the purse and the book which he had thrust into her hands.

The knock on her door sounded like thunder. Jess sat up in bed, brushing tangled curls out of her eyes. She was startled, but not alarmed; at first she couldn't even remember where she was, let alone what had happened the day before.

"Your tea, Miss Tregarth," called a voice from outside the door. "May I come in?"

The knob turned before she had a chance to say anything, and she dived under the sheet. The elderly man who had met her the previous night entered, carrying a tray. He gave her a pleasant smile, and Jess smiled back, a little uncertainly; she felt like a hick from the backwoods. She hadn't ordered tea. Was this a normal service of English hotels? A gracious gesture, certainly, but it struck her as somewhat arbitrary that the manager of the hotel should decide when his guests ought to get up.

"I do hope you slept well," said the manager, bellboy, and waiter calmly. "You looked frightfully tired last night."

"I did, and I was," said Jessica over the top of the sheet. "And I'd forgotten that what you call the fourth floor is what we call the fifth."

"That's so, isn't it?" The man put the tray on a chair and drew it up to the side of the bed. "Ordinarily, of course, I wouldn't have dreamed of disturbing you. But Mr. Randall rang up, and said to make sure you were awake before I put him through to you. He has such a sense of humor."

"Doesn't he, though," Jess said coldly. "Thank you for the tea."

"Mr. Randall said to give you five minutes, then he'll ring back."

When he had withdrawn, Jess contemplated her pot of tea with mixed emotions. Amusement finally won out. Whatever David Randall was up to now—and she suspected it would not be to her taste—she owed him something for finding this gem of a hotel. Her funny little room, up under the roof, must have been part of the servants' quarters of the original house. It was the oddest blend of old and new; there was a telephone, but no bedside table, a washbasin in the corner and a ceiling that sloped so abruptly over her bed that she had nearly brained herself when she sat up. And the manager—was he the manager? Or Lord High Every-thing Else? Had he made the tea, besides carrying it up five flights of steps? It was excellent tea; by the time the telephone rang she was ready to face even David Randall.

"Awake?" said the familiar voice.

"I'm awake, but I don't know why."

"You've been sleeping for hours. It's almost mid-day."

The dulcet tones sounded different. Jess peered suspiciously into the mouthpiece.

"Are you drunk?"

"No, but I soon shall be. Meet me. I might even give you lunch."

"You can just keep your lunches. I don't think I want to meet you."

"I think you'd better."

"That sounds like a threat," Jessica said slowly. All at once she was struck by a bombardment of doubts. His fortuitous appearance—his odd behavior—and he knew where she was. The flaw in the plot, he had called it. But it was no flaw, if he was one of the enemy.

"It is a threat. But not from me. They came, I saw, they conquered."

"They—oh, no! You don't mean—"

"Yes, I do mean," said the peculiar, blurred voice, with a theatrical gasp. "We must have a chat. Have them call you a taxi; I presume you don't know London well enough to get around. Tell the driver you want number thirteen, Lincoln's Inn Fields. Got it? The house is a museum—Sir John Soane's Museum."

"But I'm not even—"

"Then get dressed. In something less conspicuous than that glaring yellow costume you wore yesterday. Drab brown, that's the thing. Ask the guard to direct you to the Monk's Parlour. If I'm not there, wait for me."

It was half past twelve when Jess paid off the taxi and climbed the steps to the entrance of Sir John's museum. It was not precisely the most popular tourist haunt in London; there were more guards than visitors. When she asked for the Monk's Parlour, the guard directed her downstairs. She had been too preoccupied to do more than glance at the other rooms of the house, which was a handsome building in its own right, but the Monk's Parlour brought her up short. It would have attracted the attention of a dope addict in the grip of the drug.

The room was gloomy and low-ceilinged. It looked smaller than it was because it was crammed with the most grotesque collection of miscellany Jess had ever seen. The walls were covered with fragments—bits of sculpture, and isolated gargoyles, and staring antique faces, looking like blind decapitated heads in the thick dusk. Though the house stood on a London street, the window of the room looked out on a vista of ruins—columns and arches and melancholy fallen stones.

Jess staggered back against the stair rail. The place reminded her of something, and as the first shock wore off, she began to remember. Something in a college course, about a Gothic craze that had swept England in the late eighteenth and early nineteenth centuries. In literature it had produced such gems as Walpole's *Castle of Otranto*, and Mrs. Radcliffe's *Mysteries of Udolpho*. The genre had been delicately and devastatingly spoofed by the rapier-witted Miss Austen in her book *Northanger Abbey*.

The craze had extended to architecture as well, with Walpole's beloved Strawberry Hill as the classic example. Towers and battlements and crenellations sprang up; the grounds were adorned with fake ruins hung with fake moss, and riddled with grottoes filled with fake antique statues. Patently Sir John had been a convert.

The atmosphere of the Parlour was not soothing

to shaken nerves; she couldn't imagine a more likely spot in which to be strangled, after having her virtue threatened, as Mrs. Radcliffe might have expressed it. Whatever David Randall's motives, he must be crazy to suggest meeting in this Gothic nightmare.

It was not long before she heard footsteps and saw on the stairs a pair of legs which, from their length, could only be David's. Then the rest of him came into view; and she knew why the aristocratic voice had sounded blurred.

Jessica was rendered speechless, which was not a common state with her; she had never thought of this possibility, although she realized that she should have done so after hearing what David had told her on the telephone. David cleared his throat nervously. He appeared to be embarrassed, though she couldn't imagine why; she would have expected, and understood, rage, indignation, or reproach. Before either of them could gather enough wits to open a conversation, more footsteps were pounding down the stairs. David moved aside to allow a young couple, very mod and long-haired, to enter the room. They giggled, jointly, and did not stay long; but David said, "This place is too popular. Let's go into the sarcophagus room."

"Sarcophagus! Not even Sir John would—"

"Oh, yes, he would. Haven't you seen enough of his taste to know that he adored sarcophagi?" David took her arm and steered her through the appropriate doorway. The object was unquestionably a sarcophagus, even to an eye unaccustomed to such decorative items: an extremely large, grubby, white stone sarcophagus, an ancient Egyptian sarcophagus, covered with neat rows of hieroglyphic signs which had once been filled in with blue paste. Most of the paste had gone, and the little that remained had turned a dirty gray. The horribleness of the object was completed by the smeary, dusty glass case which covered it.

The two stood side by side in the narrow aisle along the far side of the huge stone coffin.

"Look like an enthusiastic student," David advised. "Friends assure me that this specimen is a perfectly stunning sarcophagus, as sarcophagi go."

"It needs a good scrubbing. David—I'm so sorry—"

"Here, none of that! Unreasonable as I am, I can't think of any reason why you should be sorry. You told me the literal truth, and I sneered at you. But I shan't apologize, because I don't want to welter in bathos with you."

"Bathos, indeed. I am reminded, I must admit, of one of your minor poets."

"Which one?"

"Blake."

She thought that would baffle him; she was impressed and obscurely pleased when, after a moment of frowning thought, he burst into a peal of laughter. The sound rang hollowly in the high, glass-roofed chamber, and bounced back off the sarcophagus. David winced, cursed, and dabbed at his lower lip with a handkerchief which was already bloodstained.

"Damn, the cut keeps opening up again. I've got

to learn not to guffaw. But that's not bad—as you Americans—"

"Oh, stop it."

"Fearful symmetry, eh? What a way to describe my classic features."

"They look pretty fearful now," Jess said grimly. "Couldn't you put something over those bruises? It makes me uncomfortable just to look at them."

"Not half so uncomfortable as it makes me to feel them. I thought seriously of starting a beard."

"It's not funny."

"Not very, no."

"What happened?"

"Let's discuss it over lunch. I don't think I can stand the sight of this sarcophagus much longer. It seems safe to assume that I wasn't followed; the gentlemen would have made an appearance by now, in this nice quiet cul-de-sac, if I hadn't lost them."

"Is that why you suggested meeting here? Good heavens, you are crazy. Let's get out of this horrid place."

Jess was given a demonstration of solid British phlegm when the waiter in David's favorite restaurant greeted him and his altered face without so much as a raised eyebrow. When the preliminaries of ordering were over, David finally gave in to her repeated demands for an explanation.

"They found the Blue Boar," he began. "How, I don't know, but I can think of several ways in which it might have been done. Alfie had gone to bed by the time they arrived, and his natural ferocity was not soothed by being rousted out in the middle of the night. He talked. He knows me by name, you

see; my rich old maiden aunt lives in the neighbor-
hood, and I generally stop at the Boar for a quick
one before I head homewards, Auntie being a bit of
a teetotaler. I could kick myself. An obvious clue
like that one, and I overlooked it! That sort of thing
is supposed to be my specialty."

"What do you mean, your specialty? What do
you do for a living?"

"Haven't you guessed?" He gave her an off-center
grin. "Where's the book that fell out of your bag
last night?"

It was still in the bag. Wordlessly Jess produced it,
and David laid it flat on the table and transfixed the
blue cover with a long forefinger which jabbed the
heroine in the middle of her stomach.

"*The Spectre of the Château*," he read, in rolling
tones. "By Desmond Dubois. That's me. I'm Desmond."

"You write—you write this—this—"

"Trash? Yes, and I do very well, thank you. Do
you see, now, why I suspected you of ribbing me? I
thought one of my dear old pals had set you up as a
gag."

"Yes, I do see. Oh, dear!"

"Serves me right. That's why our mutual friends
caught me off guard; I never believed in them. Some
of my artistic acquaintances keep unorthodox hours;
when the doorbell rang, I staggered to the door and
flung it wide, with only natural curses hovering on
my lips. Even when the pair persuaded me back into
the flat, I thought they were kindly burglars."

"When did you realize who they were?"

"When they asked about you, of course. The odd

thing was, they made no attempt to disguise themselves, not even a kerchief around their stalwart jaws. One was slight, medium height, brown hair, fair complexion, and the most hideous mustache these eyes have yet beheld. The other was a bit taller, dark, olive skin, and a nasty sneering look about the eyes. Rather like an American hoodlum."

"The same ones," Jess agreed.

"Well, naturally, I asked them what they wanted of you. Equally naturally, they refused to answer. They had somehow got it into their little heads that we were more than casual acquaintances."

"But—they must have known I met you by accident."

"We might have met accidentally, and still parted friends—very good friends. I gather jolly old Alf gave them an unexpurgated version of what he assumes my character to be."

"Even so." Jessica leaned forward and looked at her companion with unreasonable exasperation. "You could have lied to them, couldn't you? Told them you dropped me at the darned old Hilton. Or at a subway station. Or something. Did you have to be so—so s-stupid and noble, and let them hit you, and—"

"Good God, don't do that!" David glanced uneasily over his shoulder. "If you cry, I'll never dare come back here. Naturally I lied. Told them I'd dropped you at some obscure hotel in Bloomsbury, I'd forgotten the name, but it was just off Russell Square."

"Then why did they hit you?"

"Well." David looked uncomfortable. "I couldn't blurt that information out the first time they asked, could I?"

"I see. It was necessary to retain the image. The perfect English gentleman. Chivalry. The old school tie. Playing the game."

"It was necessary," said David, in a restrained shout, "to be convincing!"

A waiter hurried up, hands fluttering in agitation. David gave him a sickly smile and lowered his voice.

"Now look what you've done. See here, you bird-brained American, this isn't Chicago; we are not accustomed to crooks invading our homes and, when they do, we bluster and fume. As it was, I created one hell of a disgusting image. A true gent would have let them beat him to a pulp. I objected just long enough to sound sincere. Even so, I assume they had sense enough to watch my flat. That's why I was late meeting you today."

"I think you overdid the sincerity," Jess said, studying his bruises. "Next time, try for more cowardice."

David blushed.

"Flattery will get you—What? Oh, yes, waiter, I would like a sweet. Trifle? Fine. Cream. Jess?"

"Nothing, I'm stuffed. How can you eat so much?"

"I'm frightfully nervous. Let's not exchange any further compliments. The question is: What do we do now?"

Jess took her time about answering. For some unexplained reason she found herself unable to meet his eyes, so she concentrated on his hands. They were competent-looking hands, as thin and wiry as the rest of his body, with long spatulate fingers.

"That's obvious, isn't it?" she said at last. "We go

to the police. That is, if you don't mind backing me up. At least I now have an independent, reliable witness to support my story."

"It won't do."

"Why not?"

He did not answer; the waiter had arrived with a tray, and Jess watched admiringly as he poured cream lavishly over a dessert clearly stuffed with calories. She stirred her coffee delicately, waited till the waiter had left, and repeated.

"Why not?"

"Use your imagination. 'You say these men took nothing from your flat, Mr.—er—hmm? And you opened the door to them? Well, sir, I'm afraid . . . Of course, sir, we'll try. Would you like to look at some photographs, sir? Oh—you don't believe that they were professional criminals? Then, sir, what do you think they wanted? Ah . . . I . . . see, sir. And what, sir, did you say your profession was, sir? Ah. Yes. Sir.'"

He spooned the rest of his dessert down his throat and sat back in his chair.

"You must be exaggerating."

"I didn't believe you. Why should they believe me? I'm not even beautiful. It would be different if we had the slightest clue as to the motive for all this trouble. Jess, are you sure you—"

"I'm sure. Nothing makes any sense."

"There's got to be a reason." David put both elbows on the table and buried all ten fingers in his hair. It was, as she soon learned, the position he favored when thinking. "Tell me the story of your life."

"But . . ."

"Wait just a moment. I forgot. We have a clue after all, if what you told me last night is accurate. The ring. What sort of ring, where did it come from—full data, if you please."

"It's ugly," Jess said. "And worthless. The metal is gold, but it's impure, and poorly shaped. The size? Oh, big—a man's ring, it's miles too big for me, and the setting must be an inch in diameter. The stone is a hideous dark thing, opaque—agate, probably. It isn't even cut, just sort of rounded off. The whole thing is terribly crude. Oh, I forgot—on the stone there's a roughly scratched sign. A sword, according to my father, though it doesn't look like a sword. But that was the family crest, so—"

"It belonged to the Tregarths? Your father's side of the family?"

"Yes. Oh, I suppose I'd better tell you about that, too, but it sounds so medieval. Or do I mean Victorian? Anyhow. My grandfather is still living, down in Cornwall. Father had a terrible fight with him years ago, and walked out—clear across the Atlantic. I never knew what the fight was about; my father died when I was small, and Mother never talked about his family except to say they were a bunch of rats. Of course she never knew them, only what he said about them; he met her in the States and married her there.

"Then, a few months ago, I got a letter from my grandfather. He's awfully old and I guess he's mellowed; he wants to see me before he dies."

"How did he find you?"

"Mother wrote to him when Father died. Not a

nice letter. She's moved since then, of course, but she's still in New York; it wouldn't be hard to find her. The letter was sent in care of her."

"You're living with your mother?"

"No, I moved out two years ago when I got my job. I see Mother now and then; we get along reasonably well. She's been working since Father died, and has a good job as a buyer for a big department store."

"All right for that. It must have occurred to you, surely, that your problems are somehow connected with your grandfather. I take it the ring was his?"

"Yes; he asked me to bring it with me. He didn't exactly say that Father had stolen it, but he managed to convey that idea. Goodness knows I don't want the darned thing."

"Oh, I don't know; it sounds just the sort of thing they're selling these days in the pop-art establishments. But I don't see the meaning of the cursed trinket. Is it the designation of the rightful heir? Did your father try to rob his elder brother of a million pounds by stealing the ring?"

"My father was the only son. He had one sister; she's still in Cornwall, taking care of Grandfather. She's a widow; I guess her son would be the heir. 'Your cousin John,' my grandfather called him. But, goodness, David, there isn't anything to inherit! There never was a title, nor a great estate, and since the last war what property there was has lost its value along with so many other things. Mother was bitter about that."

"Your mother sounds like a woman after my own heart. Practical. Well, that's a pity; I shan't be able to marry you for your money." David signaled the waiter. "Have some more coffee, we still have matters to discuss. Okay, as they say in—Sorry. Our course of action seems clear. Obviously we must converse with Grandpapa. Stopping off on the way to Cornwall to recover his ring from the cathedral treasury at Salisbury."

"David . . ." But the speech she had started to make stuck in her throat. She felt like a child, trying to force itself to return a much desired but inappropriate gift.

"What?"

"I can't—you mustn't—"

"Get involved?" He put his coffee cup back in its saucer with a neat, precise movement, and grinned at her. The distortion of his mouth made his smile a caricature, but above the preposterous nose his eyes were warm with amusement. "My dear innocent, I am involved. Don't you see that I am their only link with you? When they fail to find you skulking in Russell Square (and just the place for it, too), they'll apply to me again. With thumbscrews, mayhap, or a portable Iron Maiden . . ."

"How can you joke about it?"

He put his hand over her clenched fist. With a slight shock she realized that this was the first time he had ever touched her, except for the conventional gestures of courtesy. Perhaps that was why his fingers felt unusually warm and strong.

"Darling Jess, it is a joke. The whole thing is farcical. Very little has been done to either of us, really. When you consider how violent they might have been, you ought to be reassured. In a way they were rather laughable villains. That damned mustache—"

"What do you mean?"

"Why, it was a fraud, of course. False. Didn't you see that?"

"I didn't have time to think about it," Jess admitted.

"I did. No one would deliberately grow a thing like that. Oh, it's a nice touch; it definitely does distract the viewer from more important features. But don't you see, it's such a juvenile attempt at disguise, almost a . . . What's the matter now?"

Jess closed her mouth with a snap.

"So that's it," she muttered.

"What? What, what, what?"

"I wondered why he looked familiar," Jess said slowly. "The mustache put me off. But without it—he's the image of . . . of my father."

David, in the act of lighting a cigarette, inhaled involuntarily and burst into a fit of coughing. When he had gotten his breath under control, he said indignantly, "For a minute there I thought you were losing track of the plot. This is a suspense story, not a tale of black magic. Ghosts are out. You think, then, that the Second Murderer—sorry, the Second Villain—might be . . ."

"Oh, I'm sure! The resemblance is too strong for coincidence. It must be Cousin John."

FOUR

*"Are you sleeping, are you sleeping,
Cousin John, Cousin John . . ."*

"I wish I were," Jessica interrupted. She stared gloomily out the car window. The suburbs of London were just as depressing and unpicturesque as their American counterparts. Row on row of drab little houses, rendered even more dismal by the cloudy skies. The weather had returned to normal; a gentle drizzle was falling.

*"Morning bells are ringing,
The hero's boldly singing. . . ."*

"That's a terrible line. And what makes you think you're the hero?"

"Nuts-to-you, Cou-sin John. I must be the hero. I'm the only one around except Cousin John, and he is obviously the villain."

"It's still a terrible line."

"Dear me, you are crotchety in the morning, aren't you? I'm glad I found out about that. Cheer up, we'll be out of London before long, and then you can enjoy the spectacle of the English country-side in a thick fog."

"Hmmmph." Jess leaned back and put her cold hands in her pockets. She was wearing her brand-new pink raincoat and cap, which she had bought especially for the trip. It was bright on a dull day, no doubt about that, but it was too thin for an English spring. The cold was damp and penetrating, and she was too proud to ask David to turn on the heater. So she tried to concentrate on the view out the front window, obscured by streaks of rain and by the mo-notonous movements of the windshield wiper.

She knew she ought to be rising above such mi-nor troubles as rain. She was lucky to be where she was. Their departure from London had been a mir-acle of complex planning, most of it done by David; she suspected that about half the complications had been David's enthusiasm for a good plot. Some day she really must read one of his books.

Still, his basic idea had been sound: it was likely that the villains were watching his apartment. His departure from it had involved two old pals, a back entrance, and a suitcase lowered, by rope, from an upper window. The last, surely, was pure *joie de vivre*, as was David's refusal to leave the hotel—now their hotel—for dinner. Grudgingly, she revised the last judgment; when David gave up eating, he had to have a good reason. He had consumed six tomato-and-egg sandwiches, and three bottles of beer, but this had obviously only taken the edge off his appetite.

Carp as she would, the plan had justified itself by its results. She had not seen hide nor hair—including the hair of the mustache—of the man who might be Cousin John. Or again he might not be. . . .

She was awakened by David's announcing a stop for coffee.

"You do sleep a lot," he commented.

"But not at night."

Over their elevenses which, in David's case, amounted to a substantial meal, he studied her so critically that she brushed nervously at a recalcitrant curl on her cheek.

"Smudges?"

"No, I was just wondering whether you owned any garment that was halfway unobtrusive. Is that one of those strange American garments that glow in the dark?"

"Certainly not. It's a nice cheery pink for gloomy days. Heaven knows this climate demands something cheerful."

"Oh, it's becoming to you," David admitted reluctantly. "The way that silly cap sits on top of your hair . . . But a rain hat is supposed to keep the rain off, isn't it?"

"I have naturally curly hair," Jessica said.

"Beauty does not compensate for stupidity. When we reach Salisbury we shall buy for you a nice nondescript raincoat."

"David, do you think they can possibly catch up with us?"

"Frankly, I can't imagine how. But I believe in taking all possible precautions. We've only seen two men; for all we know, they may have a regiment on tap."

"That's a cheerful thought. . . . Are you going to eat all those muffins?"

"I *have* eaten all of them," said David, popping the last one neatly into his mouth. "Ready?"

It was appreciably warmer when they returned to the car, and as they drove on a few bold rays of sunlight tried to peer through the clouds. The countryside, dripping as it was, had a beauty that grew on Jessica. The sheep were furry bundles against the rich green grass; they seemed to be quite undisturbed by the damp, and Jess cooed over the romping lambs. In the gray atmosphere the bright yellow blooms of gorse looked luminous, like little lamps along the road.

"I've got a new version," David said suddenly. "Are you plotting, are you scheming, Cousin John . . ."

"That's the worst one yet." Jess couldn't help smiling. "You know, the more I think about it, the more preposterous it seems. How could that—that awful man be my cousin?"

"Well, we've got to call him something," David pointed out reasonably. " 'Cousin John' has an air of distinction, a personal touch, which appeals to me. What about the other lad? Any other relatives? Hey, now, I've got it—he's Aunt What's-er-name in disguise."

"Aunt Guinevere, of course! I should have recognized her immediately."

The car swerved dangerously before David returned his eyes to the road and his hands to the wheel.

"As my most recent hero, an American private eye, is fond of remarking—you've got to be kidding."

"I was, you must have known. . . . Oh, you mean her name? Guinevere? I never told you my father's full name, did I?"

"Lancelot? Agrivaine?"

"Not quite that bad, but bad enough. Gawain."

"Poor devil," David said feelingly. "Who was the Arthurian fanatic? Grandpa or Grandma?"

"Grandpa." Jess turned her head to study David's profile. His hair needed combing. "In fact—I hesitate to mention it for fear of making you nervous in my presence—but I am, by right, Queen of England."

"How nice," David said enthusiastically, and once again Jess was obscurely pleased at the quickness with which he followed her. "Through dear old Mordred? Not a very nice ancestor."

"No one so disreputable. An affair between Arthur and a local Cornish lady."

"Odd, how bastardy becomes merely quaint after a certain length of time. Yes, that's charming; has a certain weird logic, as well. Arthur was born, or conceived, or something, in Cornwall; and isn't the Duchy one of the claimants of the site of Camelot?"

"Heavens, I don't know. I never was interested in—oh! Oh, look—how lovely!"

One ray of sunlight cut like a sword through the hanging clouds to illumine the lifting spire. They had come upon Salisbury unaware.

"Nice if you like that sort of thing." The spire disappeared behind closer buildings; David swung around a corner and came to a stop at a traffic light. "It's not my favorite cathedral."

"Which is?"

"Depends on what one is looking for. Over all—Wells, I think, though quite a few people howl in horror at the upper arches. Ely is great in its way, the fan vaulting in the cloisters at Gloucester—you aren't listening."

Jess, gawking out the window at a black-and-white timbered house, said dreamily, "I love this town. Even after what happened."

"Like to do a little sight-seeing?"

"You're mad."

"After luncheon, naturally." David tried to make a right turn, caught the warning sign, muttered, and turned left. "Damn, they've one-wayed all the streets. Sweet Jess—now that has an almost Elizabethan ring to it, doesn't it?"

"What are you talking about?"

"I was ponderously working up to a suggestion." David made a noise of satisfaction and swung the car into a public parking lot. "At this hour the reverend gentlemen will all be feeding. Where I too would be. Afterwards they probably take naps. It would be the height of rudeness to disturb their innocent slumbers."

"You're making that up," Jess said.

"All but the part about luncheon. After all, what's your hurry? You've seen the cathedral, but have you seen the fifteenth-century house that's now a cinema? Or St. Thomas's, with the medieval doom painting on the arch? If we wait till midafternoon to call on the vicar, he may offer us tea. That will make a nice entry for your diary. Tea with the vicar! What could be more truly English?"

He wasn't a vicar," Jess said, some hours later. It was raining again. She stopped under the shelter of the big stone gateway and glowered at the wet street.

"I don't know what he was," David admitted. "Not the Bishop . . . These blokes have such idiotic titles. All pre-something or other, and all different. And it wasn't even a very good tea."

Bareheaded and bland, he turned to look back at her. The shoulders of his raincoat were already dark with water.

"What are you stopping for?"

"It's raining."

"Nonsense. Just a little mist."

"Talk about sense enough to come in out of the rain," Jess jeered. "You people make an absolute fetish of it."

The gateway was one of those which gave entrance to the cathedral close. It was a gorgeous crenellated stone gate with little leaded windows in the upper part, and the Royal Arms, painted in crimson and gilt, above the arch. It led into the High Street, which was, at the moment, almost hidden by a swaying curtain of rain.

"Now you've done it," Jess said, viewing her companion with disgust; he had stepped back under the arch's questionable shelter with the air of a man humoring female whims. "You're soaked. We can't go on till you've dried off. You'll catch cold."

"Nonsense." David sneezed. Cyrano had not exaggerated by very much; the effect did suggest a typhoon. "This can't last long. It'll be clear by dark."

"Then let's wait a little longer. As you said, what's our hurry?"

"All right." David brightened. "We might have a spot of tea."

They found a tea shop just down the street, and David used an unexpected streak of masculine charm to persuade the waitress to turn on the electric heater near their table. Jess had had two cups of tea at the canon's home, and really yearned for something stronger. But she was learning David's whims, and thought it best to humor him. His interest in tea was not in the beverage but in the food that went with it.

Three sandwiches seemed to stimulate David's brain.

"I just thought of something," he said.

"What's that?"

"Grandpapa. We agreed he might know something. Why don't we ring him up?"

"No telephone," Jess said smugly. "I thought of that yesterday while you were out."

"Mmm." David consoled himself with a muffin. His tousled black hair had stopped dripping and was now steaming alarmingly; he looked like something materializing in a cloud of ectoplasm. "Well, let's have a look at our prize, then. I didn't have a chance to examine it there."

Jess burrowed in her purse. As usual, the object she wanted had worked its way to the bottom and was buried under a clutter of debris.

"Do you think that sweet old man believed the story I told him?"

"My story. I thought it up."

"It was pretty thin. Not the ring slipping off my finger when I dropped in the money, but the very idea that I'd try to wear such a monstrosity."

"That wouldn't surprise him," David said comfortably. "You represent two categories which are as alien as Martians to the innocent ecclesiastical mind."

"Americans. And . . . ?"

"Women. Good Lord, don't tell me you've lost it again."

"No, wait. Here it is."

David extended his hand and she placed the ring on his palm. He turned it over, and then slipped it on his finger.

"It is heavy," he said, holding it up for inspection.

Jess was not so much aware of the ring, which she knew well, as of its appearance on a man's hand. It was crude and archaic, but for the first time it looked—well—right.

"Too big for me," David said, unaware of her relapse. "The original owner must have had hands like hams. Or—wait a minute. Didn't they wear rings on their thumbs?"

He made the transfer and considered the effect.

"Fits better. Well. I don't see that this object suggests anything meaningful. It's just as you described it."

"I know."

"Well, then, on to Grandfather Tregarth. You will observe that I was right; it has stopped raining."

"David."

Jess dropped another lump of sugar into her

empty cup and mashed it with the tip of her tea-spoon.

"Getting all noble and courageous again?" he asked.

"It's not fair—"

"Or could it be that you don't want me around?"

She reacted so briskly that the teaspoon clattered into the saucer.

"You know it's not that! Without you I'd be out of my mind. But I don't see why you—"

"Why?" He grinned at her. "Don't you know about that famed British chivalry? Jess, you couldn't rid yourself of me now if you tried. I'd put on a beard and follow you. I'm curious to know what is behind this. One never knows; I might be able to use the plot. The old font of inspiration has been running dry of late. . . ."

"You're just saying that."

"Jess, you think too much. I'm of age, and as much in my right mind as anyone—which may not be saying a great deal. If I choose to pursue this little caper, it's my responsibility and my neck. Be-sides, we've lost Cousin John and his friend; nothing else can happen."

This blithe comment should have caused a trickle of premonitory terror to slide down Jessica's spine. Something trickled, and she did shiver; but the trickle was cold water, from the back of her collar, as she stood up. She had no premonition; only a cow-ardly sense of relief.

They walked under leaden skies and dripping wa-ter from the eaves of the shops, but, as David men-tioned four times, the rain had stopped. Toward the

west, a livid bar of red light indicated, the weather
prophet announced, that the next day would be fine.

It was almost dark when they reached the parking
lot, and Jess, barking her shins on a fender, cursed
the economy-minded Salisbury City Council, or
whatever body guided the affairs of the town. Why
couldn't they put more lights in their parking lots?
Then she saw that there were lamps, but that two of
them had gone out. The lot was only half full by
now. The weather, and the hour, had driven many
shoppers and sightseers indoors.

Without thinking, Jess went to the wrong side of
the car, and there was a brief altercation while
David pointed out her error. Another car had parked
in the space next to his, and the gap between the
two was narrow; slim as she was, she had to squeeze
sideways to reach her door. Always the perfect gentleman, David followed her and bent over the lock,
trying, with some difficulty in the dark, to insert
his key.

Both doors of the adjoining car opened at the
same time. Jess had only time enough to realize
what a neat, tight little box was formed by the sides
of the two cars and the door of the one when the
dark shape beside her brought an arm down and the
wet pavement beneath her feet dissolved into mist
through which she fell into blackness.

She woke up to find David's feet in her face. There
was no mistaking the clammy feel and smell of
wet leather.

Her first reaction was relief that he was there, in
any position or condition . . .

Which thought led her, after a hazy moment, to violent attempts at movement. David's feet were ominously still. Supposing he was . . . Her mind, still fogged by a splitting headache, recoiled from the word with a surge of terror.

The first attempt to move was as futile as the second, third, and fourth attempts. She subsided, gasping for breath behind the gag that muffled the lower part of her face. Her wrists and ankles were tied. She was lying on a surface which she thought must be the floor of a car, to judge from the vibration and sense of movement. Most of David seemed to be on top of her; his weight, as well as her bonds, made movement impossible.

Dead weight. Now the word fought its way past her defenses, and she began to wiggle again.

This time her contortions produced results, though not the ones she had hoped for. A voice from the front seat of the car said, "One of them is awake."

There was a squeak of springs and, after a moment, a second voice reported, "He's not."

"What about her?"

"Can't tell."

No wonder you can't, Jess thought furiously. Burying me down under here like a turnip . . . Then she froze, as the first voice said, with an indifference that chilled her more than the actual words, "Give her another tap on the head, why don't you?"

The second man made deprecatory noises.

Jess recognized this voice, though it lacked the artificial huskiness which had once disguised it. The dulcet tones were those of the man with the mustache, the one they had christened "Cousin John."

His companion must be the thin dark man. They had never decided on a name for him. David had maintained that "X" or "the second villain" was too anonymous; he had suggested Algernon. Tears began to slide down Jessica's cheeks.

She wept in strangled silence for a time. The gag was wet anyhow; nasty, sloppy things, gags. Her headache had become an almost tangible weight on her head, and she lost track of time for a bit. Then the car jerked, banging her head painfully against a metal object on the floor. It jerked again, and jerked to a stop.

At first she assumed that this was the end of the road, and her other, more unselfish emotions were swamped under a wash of sheer terror. Then the voices took up a furious dialogue.

". . . damned heap of rubbish! I told you the motor needed—"

"And just when, may I ask, have I had the time to take it to a garage?"

"Could be out of petrol."

"Not bloody likely."

The car door slammed, and Jess perked up, as much as she could perk under one hundred and eighty pounds of David. This was the sort of maddening accident that could only happen to very amateur crooks; and it was something the good guys ought to be able to take advantage of. But how could she, with her bodyguard not only unconscious, but weighing her down like a tombstone?

Footsteps crunched on gravel, moving from the side to the front of the car. By straining her neck to the breaking point, Jess made out the wavering light of a flashlight. She also found two stars. They were, then, out in the country; there would be other lights visible in a town, and other sounds. That ended any hope of rescue by a policeman or inquisitive passerby.

The footsteps crunched again.

"Petrol. Tank absolutely dry. Of all the dam' fool, negligent—"

"Well, I am sorry."

"That's a help. You'd best start hiking."

"Oh—hell. I suppose I must. It must be all of four miles!"

"Would you rather I went?"

"Much rather," said Cousin John candidly.

"Very well. If some fool of a do-gooder stops, and gets a look at those two, in the back . . ."

"Damn and blast! Do you think that's likely?"

"It's a possibility we must consider; and, frankly, old boy, I would rather not leave you to handle it. You haven't the sense of a cat or the courage of a rabbit. Now hop to it, and don't dawdle."

"It's difficult for me to resist such effusive compliments."

"You can beg a lift back, but it will take all of an hour to get there, unless you're fortunate enough to pick up a ride."

"I daren't let anyone bring me back. Not with those two—"

"Precisely. That is why I shall, during your absence, shift the evidence temporarily. Another job which, I fancy, you'd rather not handle."

The only answer was an eloquent sniff, followed by footsteps rapidly retreating out of earshot.

"Bloody fool," the man in the front seat muttered. Jess heard a match scrape, and smelled cigarette smoke.

Jess was feeling sick enough without the addition of another unperfumed smell. The brief dialogue had told her a good deal about the characters of their abductors; of the two, she thought she preferred Cousin John. He was a rat, but at least he had human foibles and the rudiments of a sense of humor. The second man seemed to think of them as two unwieldy parcels; the very tones of his voice were as bloodless and inhuman as the click of a calculating machine.

When the car seat in front squeaked, she went rigid, expecting murder. The front door opened, but the back door did not. The man's footsteps sounded gratingly on gravel, and then, abruptly, stopped. Was he standing by the car? She couldn't hear him breathe, or smell the cigarette any longer. Probably he had gone off into the fields. He would have to scout around a bit in order to find a hiding place for their bodies, in case Cousin John returned with a potential witness.

But he would soon be back. Nothing very complex in the way of a hole to hide in would be necessary at this hour, and in this place. If she had had Cousin John to deal with, Jess would have decided to wait until she had been dumped in a handy ditch before making any attempts at escape. Mr. X was another cup of tea. He seemed quite capable of silencing them, perhaps permanently, before he left them in the field.

She began to wrestle, ineffectually, with her bonds, and then went stiff as a board when a voice addressed her by name.

It was David's voice, breathless and soft, but unmistakably David's. He heard her gurgled response, and said quickly,

"Don't yell, for the love of God. Oh. Forgot. You can't yell. Turn your face this way, can you, and excuse me if I hurt you, I've got to work fast."

His bound hands banged her painfully on the nose before his fingers found the edge of the gag. He jerked it down with scant regard for the skin on her lips.

"Now turn over, get your hands up here. Can't you kneel?"

"Not with your feet on my stomach."

"Always complaining. Is that better? All right, I've found your arm. There. Now, hold still. . . ."

The process seemed to take forever, and at every second Jess expected to hear the man returning. She could see out the car window now, and the view she saw was that of a peaceful pastoral landscape, wooded and gently rolling, under a high, bright moon. It was deserted. Not a human form was visible, not a light showed, except for the round silver penny of the moon and the dreaming stars.

Then at last her hands fell free and she turned, rubbing them, and fumbled for David's wrists.

"Don't bother with that, get my back pocket. There's a knife. No, the left pocket."

When she had sawed through the ropes on his hands he snatched the knife from her and swung his feet up on the seat. He was still hacking at the ropes on his ankles when, in the bright moonlight, she saw the man coming back.

Her gasp alerted David. He muttered something blasphemous and slid down onto the seat in an approximation of his former position.

"Take the knife," he hissed.

Four hands fumbled clumsily, and Jess found herself holding the knife. She had better sense than to try to free her feet then. Instead she subsided onto the floor, face down to hide the absence of a gag, her hands behind her. She had no idea what David was planning to do. Something clever, of course; a writer of thrillers ought to be overflowing with escape plans. Certainly his performance so far had been admirable. She couldn't blame him for not being on the alert in Salisbury; she hadn't expected any trouble either.

The rear door of the car was pulled open, and David propelled himself out onto the kidnaper.

Winded by the foot he had planted in her ribs, Jess lay still for a moment. The metal implement—jack, or wrench, or whatever it was—was jammed up against her hipbone, and she picked it up and tossed it onto the seat. She had just begun to saw at the ropes on her ankles—David's pocketknife felt like a relic from his school days, untouched since then—when the car rocked wildly. One of the combatants had been tossed against it. Jess sawed harder. Her head emerged from the doorway just in time to see David aim a vicious judo chop at the other man's neck. It landed on a shoulder instead, as the man ducked; from David's pained expression Jess deduced that the shoulder was heavily muscled, or padded, or both. The other man hit David in the stomach and added a crack on the jaw that echoed through the windless night like a shot.

Jess reached back into the car and picked up the wrench. David had slumped to his knees and was embracing his opponent's legs. In the eerie light of the moon the two looked like priest and suppliant, or a king being begged for mercy, or a judge. . . . The tableau held just long enough for Jess to reach out and bring the wrench down, with annoyed precision, on the victor's head. She suspected it was the same wrench that had knocked her cold earlier, and appreciated fully, for the first time, the meaning of the phrase "poetic justice."

David stood up, taking his time about it. Jess made no move to assist him; she just stood and shook, while her weapon slid out of her hand.

"Are you all right?" she squeaked.

David wiped his mouth meticulously with the back of his hand and studied the result.

"I think," he said, wheezing, "I broke my hand, when I hit him."

"Hit him, indeed. I suppose you've been reading your own fiction. You have to practice that judo stuff. Or whatever that was supposed to be. Otherwise you just—"

"If you say one word—just one," David said, taking her by the shoulders, "I am going to shake— you—till your teeth—rattle."

"You haven't got the strength. Oh, David, please don't faint or anything; if you do I'll start screaming."

David straightened and eyed her with a cool

dignity which was only slightly marred by the blood on his chin and the extreme pallor of his face.

"Faint, nonsense; I'm trying not to be sick all over the road. The last time anybody hit me in that precise spot I was nine years old, and I . . . For the love of God, what are we standing here for? Let's run."

"You can't walk, let alone run! You're leaning on me, hadn't you noticed? Can't we flag down a car?"

"If our other pal meets a kindly driver along the way, in or out, he could be back at any moment. And it would be just our luck if he happened to be in the car we flagged down."

He was right. They had hardly cleared the fence on the other side of the road when a truck pulled up by the car and the moonlight shone fair and free on the curling mustache of Cousin John.

Absentminded he might be, but he was not slow; from where she crouched behind the fence Jess saw his face tighten as he glanced at the suspiciously silent scene. The body of his fallen ally was not visible from where he stood, but he must have suspected that something was amiss. He turned and said something to the invisible driver of the truck, which promptly made a U-turn and roared back in the direction from which it had come. As soon as it was out of sight, Cousin John put down the gasoline can he was holding, and trotted around the car.

Jess understood why David had not rushed out to demand assistance from the driver of that truck. If cornered, both villains might turn violent; she could not be sure they were not armed. But when he

pulled at her sleeve and gestured meaningfully toward the fields which stretched out behind them,
she resisted.

"They'll see us," she whispered. "And hear us."

"If we squat here much longer, they will also feel
us," was the critical reply. "With a club. Come along,
while they're getting reorganized."

She saw his point; still, it was an effort to raise
herself up out of the comforting dip in the ground
where she had at least had the illusion of shelter, and
dash off, in full view, amid a crashing of dried leaves,
sticks and loose stones. She heard a wordless bellow
from the road, but never knew whether it was
prompted by Cousin John's discovery of his fallen
cohort, or his sight of them. But when she looked
back, she saw the now familiar silhouette tumble
over the fence, pick itself up, and dart after them.

The moonlight, which made them so visible, had
one advantage. It let them avoid the more obvious
pitfalls. However, it cast queer, tricky shadows. As
often as Jess swerved to avoid an imaginary hole she
fell into one which she had not seen. The field, which
had looked so smooth and flat at a distance, was covered with pitfalls—concave and convex, sharp, wet or
muddy. There were fences. There were hedges—
thorny hedges. There were streams, and mud puddles, and broad stretches of boggy land through
which they dragged their feet with the horrid slow
motion of nightmare. Before they had crossed the
second field, Jessica's vivid pink raincoat was no longer a landmark; a tumble into a particularly large
puddle had coated it with the drab brown David had

mentioned as desirable. David had lost his jacket wriggling through a prickly hedge and his face was zebra-striped with scratches from the same source.

If either had thought of returning to the road, that idea was discouraged by the sight of a pair of headlights traveling with specific slowness parallel to their own panting, crashing route. As she caught her ankle wrenchingly in a rabbit hole, Jess wished she had tapped Villain Number Two much harder.

The only comforting segment of a generally hellish situation was the knowledge that it was Cousin John who was chasing them across the fields. Jess had heard enough from him to know that he would particularly loathe this activity; she guessed, as well, that their best hope of eventual escape lay in the fact that Cousin John was just as inept as she at broken field running. Twice she had looked back to see the pursuing shape flounder and fall; the joy of that sight, plus the echo of curses carried on the gentle breeze, had given her a new burst of strength.

At last even David's long legs tired, and he drew up with a snort like that of a winded horse and pulled her close to him—not so much, she suspected, to support her frail frame as to lean on her. Despite the cool night air, his shirt was plastered to his back and chest. He had also acquired his share of mud.

"I can't—go much—farther," she gasped, when she had collected enough breath to speak.

"He stopped . . . too," David said. "Lazy clod . . ."

"What are we . . . going to do?"

"Find . . . something—eventually. . . . House, town . . ."

"Where are we?"

David groaned.

"No idea."

"Can't you spot . . . star or something?"

Sheer indignation made David forget his heaving lungs.

"God save us, woman, do you expect me to scan the heavens for the North Star while I'm running an obstacle course? And what the hell good—Look out, here he comes again."

"Cousin John" might not care for exercise, but he was, if nothing else, persevering. He came on. And on. And on. As the moon climbed and shrank, the pursuit degenerated into a trot, and then into a walk. Jess stumped along beside her tall companion without even bothering to look back. She knew Cousin John was back there somewhere; she also knew that he probably wouldn't catch up with them. She didn't care. She wished she were back home. She wished she were in London, in bed. She wished she were dead.

The moon threw their shadows along the grass ahead of them, strange elongated caricatures knobbly with the unevenness of the ground. Jess had long since abandoned the view. She imagined that it was quite lovely by moonlight. The peaceful fields of Somerset. Or was she in Wilts?

"Hell with it," she said indistinctly. David, stumping along with his hands in his pockets and his shoulders hunched, nodded.

"Beautiful, succinct description of the situation."

Jess stumbled and caught at David's arm for support. He promptly collapsed, and both ended up on their knees in a patch of bog.

"You're just as tired as I am," Jess said.

"Tired." His arms draped loosely around her, his chin digging painfully into the top of her head, David sighed. "The degree of my fatigue may be measured by my lack of enthusiasm for what might otherwise be a position fraught with—"

"Why can't we go back to the road? Someone must come along it eventually."

"Someone is on it right now. Of the two, he's the one I'd prefer not to meet."

"We've been walking for hours," Jess groaned.

"But we haven't covered much distance. Still, I'd have thought we'd have reached some signs of habitation by now. This part of the country isn't . . . Wait a minute. I think . . . Look over that way."

He dragged her to her feet and pointed. Jess squinted in the direction his outstretched arm indicated. On the horizon, she made out a regularly shaped silhouette which did not look like trees or hills.

The sight seemed to restore David's energy, though Jess was more skeptical; there were no lights visible in the oddly shaped structure, which could not, surely, be a house. . . . As she stumbled along, she found the silhouetted outline more baffling the nearer they got. A modern factory? Surely not here. A ruined castle? A ruin . . . Yes. Her footsteps faltered. David tugged at her, and she went stumbling along behind him, staring and staring . . .

Clear against the darkened sky, silver-pale and ghostly, crowned by stars and a high white moon, was a cluster of immense monoliths, some single stones, some paired and topped by lintels to make huge hollow doorways. Once those empty doors had let into a space which, if never roofed, was nonetheless filled with something more than vacant air, when the faith that had—literally—moved small mountains was a living force, not a memory for students.

She had read about the place, of course; it had been on her list of "Things to see in Salisbury," for it was less than ten miles north of the town. That had been a long time ago; at least it seemed like a long time, before the insanity that had brought her to this muddy field in the dead of night, wet to the hips, tired to screaming point, being towed along by an equally muddy vagabond in his shirt sleeves. . . . But as the incredible stones lifted up above the horizon, she knew that the sight was almost worth the effort: Stonehenge by moonlight.

The size of the place made its appearance deceptive: it was still a long way off, though it seemed to loom. David's new energy petered out before they got close, and he stopped for another rest.

"One thing about you," Jess said. "You do show me all the sights."

David glanced down at her. He lacked the strength to scowl, and she thought that she had never seen anyone look quite so disreputable. Dried blood and wet mud masked his face, his upstanding hair was filled with burrs and leaves and twigs, like the coiffure of a primitive maiden, and his shirt was torn in at least six places. Inevitably that thought made her hands move to her own hair. David, watching, produced a wan but malicious smile.

"Believe me, darling, I couldn't care less what you

look like. I'd much rather admire a telephone. I don't know whether there's a caretaker in charge of that rock heap, but there's sure to be a souvenir stall or shelter of some kind. If it's locked, I shall break it open."

Now that they were nearing a goal which had seemed, for a long, mad period, to be nonexistent, Jessica's sense of caution reawakened. There was no sign of Cousin John, but when she looked back she saw a flash of light where there should be none. David squeezed her arm.

"Torch," he said. "They've been signaling, haven't you noticed?"

"The other one is still on the road?"

"Algernon? (I've decided we will call him Algernon.) Yes, he's there. I know this whole performance has seemed unnecessarily boggy, but, you see, one of our problems is that we must reach Salisbury well ahead of them. Otherwise they can simply meet us by my car. And we can't leave the car."

"I know, I realized that . . . oh, David, I hate to admit it, but that place really is gorgeous by full moonlight. Look at it."

"I am looking at it. And I wish it were—"

And then, appallingly, the arm under her fingers stiffened till it felt like stone. She heard his breath catch, with a sharp note of terror it had never held even during the worst moments of their capture. In a voice she would not have recognized, a voice muted by horror, he whispered, "Oh, God. Oh, God—look. Look."

Then she saw it too, and the shock made her physically dizzy. Passionate disbelief and equally firm faith in the reliability of her own senses met and clashed. For across the leveled grass that surrounded the temple of the sun worshipers a wavering snake of dim light was slowly moving. It was moving toward the temple, and from it, carried faintly through the still night air, came a ragged chorus of chanting.

FIVE

David started to laugh.

It began slowly, a throaty chuckle that shook his arms and chest, and then mounted in intensity until he was roaring, vibrating from head to foot, slapping his knees. Tears poured from his eyes. He said something, but the words were unintelligible, drowned in the terrible sound of laughter. Then he staggered off across the field, toward the moving procession of light.

Jess reached out for him—too late, but she would not have been able to stop him in any case. Hysteria, she thought; I don't blame him, it's too much. I can't let him go. What did the Druids do to their victims? Bury them alive? Cut out their hearts? No, that was the Aztecs, or somebody. . . .

She took one step after him, fighting the most insidiously terrible of all fears, and then a horrid qualm stopped her in her tracks. It was the upsurge of a doubt that had haunted her for some time, and it could be summed up most aptly in the phrase: "Whose side is he on?"

With her last remaining shred of common sense,

she argued with herself. Make up your mind, Jess—
ghosts or crooks, you can't have both. If David is in
league with Cousin John, he can hardly be on familiar terms with the spirits of long-dead Druid
priests too.

Having made up her mind, or what was left of it,
she began trudging across the field. It was not long
before she made out the true nature of the shifting
train of lights, but the sight did nothing to reassure
her. The lights came from torches, borne high by
shrouded white figures. Hooded and robed, they
stretched in a short procession from the road, beyond the monument, almost to the entrance. They
were standing quietly now; the singing had stopped.
David was in earnest conversation with one of the
pale shapes. He turned, and his face cleared as he
saw her coming.

"There you are. What took you so long? Jess, this
is Sam Jones of the Mystical Order of Sunworshipers."

The bus seemed to careen down the road but
maybe, Jess thought vaguely, that was because she
was rolling from side to side. In the back seat of the
bus—always in a back seat, she thought resentfully—
wedged in between Sam—good ol' Sam!—and
David. They both had their arms around her, and
she had her arms around them, and they were all
singing.

"Jolly good fello-o-ow," sang Jess, but her small
voice was drowned out by the roaring chorus from
the other passengers. It had something to do with a
girl named Mabel.

Some time later, as the lights of Salisbury appeared, they all seemed to be singing a verse of a classic folk song.

"This is number four, and his hand is on the floor . . ."

"That's not right," Jess objected.

"No?" Sam stared at her in distress. The hood had fallen back from his head, displaying a shining bald pate. His face was almost as round and pink and featureless, his snub nose and pursed rosebud mouth swallowed up in rolls of affable fat. "But you taught it us—taught us it—taught it. Jessie. Nice girl, Jessie."

The bus stopped. The song died.

"All out," called the driver, the only sober person on the bus.

Sam shook himself like a duck coming out of the water. The rolls of fat under his chin wobbled. With the almost miraculous capacity some people have for overcoming the weakness of the flesh, he spoke in a voice which was relatively coherent.

"Back. High time, I expect. Well. Jolly good fun, wasn't it?"

"Great, great, great fun. Great, great . . ."

"Jess." Someone shook her. David? She beamed at him.

"Great fun, David? Jolly good show."

"Jess, my love, you're drunk as a skunk. How am I going to get you to the car?"

"Carry me," said Jess, and flung herself into his arms. He fell back against the seat.

"Can't. I'm a bit under the weather myself."

"She can't be drunk," Sam said firmly. "Not on our mead. It'sh—excuse me—non-intocshicating.

Here, I'll help you. Where's the car, old boy? We'll have a parade. 'Nother parade."

The farewells took some time. Sam was in command of himself, and kept giving Jess firm, stiff handclasps, but one young man insisted he must kiss her good night. Jess, full of generalized love for humanity, was willing to oblige, but David objected, and the young man had to be restrained. Then David drove slowly out between rows of Sunworshipers waving torches. Jess was too giddy to wonder why he had arranged this, or why he gave a vulgar grunt of satisfaction after glancing into his rear-view mirror, or why they left the town at such breakneck speed. But about an hour later she did begin to wonder where they were going, and whether they were going by road or cross-country. The effect of the mead was wearing off.

"Ow," she said, as they hit a massive bump, and she rebounded from the ceiling. "Where the hell are you going?"

David did not answer at once. Jess saw his mouth set and the muscles of his forearms writhe as he manipulated the car over a particularly vile stretch of road. Again he shot a glance at the rear-view mirror, and nodded. Almost at once the tires sang sweetly on concrete. The car swerved, first right, then left, and stopped. David switched off his lights. He sagged forward, arms embracing the steering wheel, head against it.

"Are you going to faint?" Jess asked.

David heaved himself erect.

"No, I am not. I have never fainted in my life. I have no intention of fainting, now or any other time. What the hell do you take me for, one of my own imbecilic heroines?"

"It's neater," Jess said ominously, "than being sick."

"I'm not going to be sick either. If you plan to be, please get out of the car first."

"I guess I won't, then. What on earth *was* that stuff?"

"Mead. Honey and something extremely alcoholic. Supposed to be the brew of the ancient what's-their-names."

"Men of iron."

They sat in silence. It was a profound country silence—noisy, in other words, reverberating with the mating calls of nocturnal animals and insects, the rustle of foliage as small things came and went, the gurgle of water, the hoot of an owl, the flapping of bats. The night air was cold and sweet, laden with various smells which city-bred Jessica could not identify, but which she connected, sentimentally, with such English items as hawthorne blooming in the hedges and lilac blowing in the breeze. David's teeth began to chatter.

"Haven't you got another coat?" she asked. "You're shivering."

"Oh, that's fear. Sheer, cold, terror."

"Where's your suitcase?"

"Never mind. You can keep me warm." He gathered her in, and lifted his voice in song. "And all night long I held her in my arms," he caroled, "just to keep her from the foggy, fo-oggy . . ."

"Be quiet, you fool."

"I can't help it," said David, shaking. "That wonderful bunch of damned fools. If they hadn't come along when they did . . ."

"I almost died when you went running toward them," Jess chuckled. "And when you introduced Sam—with his little round pink face peeking out of that hood—"

"Don't speak so disrespectfully of good ol' Sam," David warned; both of them went off into a paroxysm of mirth.

"That's all very well," David said, sobering. "But they saved our necks, just the same."

"What were they doing at Stonehenge in the middle of the night?"

"Holding their annual rites. They're quite sober citizens most of the time, but one night a year they run amok and pretend to be ancient Britons. God bless 'em. Our other pals were waiting for us at the car, you know."

"I didn't see them."

"You didn't see *anything*. But they were there. The crowd held them up just long enough for me to get out of sight. I made sure we kept out of sight by taking every damned side road I could find. The result is, I don't know where we are. And the reason why we are sitting here now, behind this handy hedge is not, as you might suppose . . ."

His lips left her hair and slid down, inquiringly, across her cheek.

"To make sure they aren't following us," Jess said, stifling a yawn.

"Hmmm. I guess you're right; that must be the reason." David removed his arm and deposited Jess in the far corner. "I suppose it's just as well. Never

start anything you can't finish, and at this moment . . . All right, where were we?"

"Waiting to see if somebody is going to chase us
some more," Jess said drowsily. "Oh, dear, I'm so
sleepy. . . ."

"Yes, right; we've got to find a hole into which to
crawl, or we'll both collapse. But I doubt if any decent hotel would accept us. You aren't in such bad
condition, your coat absorbed most of the mud; but
I seem to be attired mainly in a collar and one shirt
sleeve."

"That blond got at least one sleeve," Jess said in a
voice which was suddenly no longer sleepy.

"Let's not exaggerate. She was only—"

"Orgies," Jess muttered.

"If it comes to that, why was little Oscar so sure
he had the right to kiss you good-bye?"

"Oh, that." Jess yawned and relapsed into her
semi-coma.

"Yes, and while we're on the subject I seem to
recall seeing you and Sam . . ." A gentle snore interrupted him. He swore, and put the car into gear.

Sunlight pounded on Jessica's closed eyes with
little warm fists. She became, not so much conscious, as aware of her body. It was a vile body. It
ached, and somewhere in its cavernous interior there
was a vast discomfort.

"Here," said David's voice, somewhere off in the
distance. "Drink this." A cold glass touched her fingers.

"No," Jess said. A hand heaved her up, and the
glass moved to her lips.

The next few seconds were exciting; but virtue, and a healthy life, triumphed. Jess found herself sitting up, her eyes open, and her stomach under control.

The room was cold, and unfamiliar. There were goose bumps all over her arms and chest . . . She grabbed at the sheet.

"Who undressed me?" she croaked.

David's face swam into her vision. It was smiling, but that was the only thing that could be said for it; he had collected several more bruises, and the circles under his eyes were a delicate shade of lavender.

"Much more original than 'Where am I?'" he said. "To answer your question—it had to be, I, myself, or Bill—and I know you wouldn't like a stranger taking such liberties. Come now, my own, you know I couldn't put you to bed wearing that muddy coat. You are still extremely grubby; being a true gent, I did not feel that I could proceed beyond a certain point, so therefore I suggest that you take advantage of the amenities across the hall, which may also restore the rest of your faculties, such as they—"

He vanished precipitately when Jess raised her fists. She crawled out of bed and found the bathroom.

Washed and dressed, she found the kitchen by following the smell of coffee. The house was a tiny sliver of a place, all dark-paneled, with floors so uneven that she almost rolled down the stairs. The kitchen looked like a picture out of a book on pioneer architecture; no cabinets, no tile, no porcelain, no stainless steel sinks. A thin layer of dust covered everything, including the windows, which were uncurtained; but sunlight poured in through the panes and there was a huge red geranium on the window sill.

"Coffee coming up," David said. "I'm making it; learned the proper style in New York. Meet your host, by the way. Frederick George William McAllister the Fourth. Known as Bill."

Jess turned and let her hand be swallowed up by the hand of an enormous young man with a face like that of a white rabbit, eyelashless and eyebrow-less, and the most beautiful head of long blond hair she had seen in or out of *Vogue*. When he spoke, her aching head vibrated; his voice was a deep bass.

"How do you do," said Frederick George, known as Bill. "Shake hands in the morning, don't they? In the States. Odd idea."

"No, they don't," said David rudely. "Sit down, you fool."

"Can't, till she does."

Jess sat down. The beautiful blond rabbit sat down at the table opposite her and fixed her with an intent stare. She saw that he did have both lashes and brows, but they were so blond that they didn't show six inches away. However, Jess did not find his stare unnerving; it was clearly an approving stare.

"Where am I?" she asked. It might be an un-original question, but it seemed to her a pertinent one.

"Bill's house," David answered. He carried coffee and toast to the table and sat down. "Specifically. Wells, generally. I finally located a signpost last night, after you'd gone to sleep, and remembered that this was where Bill lived."

"It was kind of you to take us in," Jess said.

Bill smiled. His pale eyes moved down from her hair, across the emerald-green sweater, over her bare arms, and back again. His smile broadened.

"The amenities having been dealt with," David interrupted, "let's get down to business. I've been telling Bill about our situation."

"My situation."

"No longer yours alone." David rubbed his bruises with a thoughtful forefinger. "Anyhow, he has several cogent points. He conceals his intelligence—and very well, I might add—under that custardy exterior of his."

Bill blushed happily at this two-sided compliment.

"Bill points out," David continued, "that the behavior of our pursuers is, to say the least, peculiar. It had already occurred to me that they are very amateurish crooks. Running out of petrol in the middle of a snatch, for God's sake! So we may safely assume that this is a private vendetta. I mean, you're not being chased by the C.I.A. or N.K.V.D., or some other set of ominous initials."

"Well, for goodness' sake, I never thought I was."

"I know, I know, but let's be pitilessly logical. It was a possibility, if not a very strong one."

"Not with Cousin John."

"Ah." David swallowed half a piece of toast and pointed a long hypnotic forefinger at her. "As Bill brilliantly reminds me, our identification of the gentleman as Cousin John is so very tenuous as to be valueless. We do not, in fact, know who he is."

"But this affair has to involve family matters,"

Jess argued. "It can't be anything else. I've never had any government job, or worked for any mysterious scientists, or anything. I mean, I don't have any deadly secrets."

"Bill is willing to concede that," David said magnanimously. "Bill asked whether there could be any question of an inheritance."

Jess looked at the silent Bill in some confusion. He smiled amiably.

"No," she said, returning his smile; he had such a pleasant face. "There's no money, from what I hear."

"Just for the sake of argument," David said, "if there were, who would inherit?"

"Cousin John, I guess. Grandfather cut my father out of his will years ago; his lawyers told Mother that when she wrote after Dad died. But there isn't anything—"

"So you have been told. But, as Bill ably suggests, the old boy may have been hoarding diamonds or securities all these years. Suppose he repents his harsh treatment of his only son. People don't repent much, in real life," he added parenthetically, "but in fiction they do it all the time. Supposing poor old Grandpapa wants to give you your rightful share. Cousin J. would have to take steps."

"Why?" Jess demanded in exasperation. "I mean, does a normal person go rushing out to eliminate all the other prospective heirs? Even assuming there was anything to inherit, which there isn't! I never heard such nonsense. And you're forgetting the ring."

"Proof of identify," David said airily.

"Nuts," Jess said rudely.

Bill beamed more broadly, and David nodded,

rendered momentarily speechless by the last of the toast.

"Bill's precise comment," he said thickly. "We do not, he says, have enough information to form any theory. Any at all. Our course of action is clear."

"Maybe it is to Bill," Jess said; like David, she was beginning to talk about him as if he were not present. "But not to me."

"Simple. We must capture one of the enemy and interrogate him."

"And how do you propose to do that?" Jess extended one finger and scraped up the crumbs from the toast plate. No one had offered her anything to eat, and she was getting hungry.

"Well, we must remember that these blokes, while capable of astonishing lapses, are not stupid. It was rather bright of them to lay in wait for us at Salisbury, after losing us in London. One of them must have seen your futile gesture with the offering bag."

"He could have," Jess admitted.

Bill cleared his throat. It sounded like an elephant bull calling his mate. David glanced at him.

"Yes, right. Bill raises the question of why the enemy didn't steal the ring back once they had us in their clutches. Now we'll agree that they didn't have time to search us in the car park; they had to tumble us into their car and get away as quickly as possible. No doubt they planned on searching us at their leisure once they got us to their lair—wherever that may be."

"But they left my purse," Jess protested. "Right by the car where I dropped it. They ought to have known I'd put the ring in my purse."

"Not necessarily; you might equally well have tucked it into your fair bosom, or handed it to me to keep. Still; it's one of those lapses Bill mentioned. Can we deduce from that particular lapse that both are bachelors—not only bachelors, but men who don't know much about the peculiar habits of women? All right, maybe we can't. Of course, they could easily have gone back to collect our luggage once they found we didn't have the ring on either of our persons."

"I suppose so."

"Bill is convinced of it. Now, then. We might make a dash for Cornwall. But that course of action has several serious flaws. Either your grandfather is unaware of what has been happening—he'd surely have warned you if he expected trouble—or he's one of the crooks. If he is, we'll be leaping straight into the proverbial fire by looking him up. If he is innocent, and potentially helpful, we're still in trouble; the villains will surely have the family homestead surrounded, since they expect you to go there eventually. We've got to have more information before we make a move of any sort. That's what Bill thinks."

"Bill is right on the ball," Jess said. She licked her fingers.

"Bill is what you Americans call a brain," David said. "Jess, I don't like to criticize your table manners, but must you lick your fingers in that vulgar fashion?"

"I'm starved," Jess said simply. "You ate all the toast."

Bill the brain opened his ponderous jaws and spoke.

"There are eggs. In the fridge."

Jess looked from one expectant face to the other.

"Oh, all right," she said bitterly. "I might have known. Show me how to work that atrocity of a stove."

David rose with alacrity.

"While you're cooking, I'll outline Bill's subtle scheme for trapping the nefarious wight we have christened 'Cousin John.'"

You're sure this was Bill's idea?" Jess asked. They had just left an inn in a town improbably named Brompton on Avon, and were speeding down a country lane. Branches waved in the breeze and birds sang furiously.

"I helped," David said. He jerked the wheel to avoid a ruminating cyclist wobbling down the center of the road, and Jess fell heavily against him. She righted herself.

"We're doing it backwards," she complained.

"We must; it's a very delicate maneuver. They haven't scouted this route yet, both the landlord and that other bloke said no one had been inquiring after us. Now, when someone does inquire, he'll learn that we were at the inn during the small hours demanding petrol and the road to Wells. The landlord promised to be quite annoyed about being knocked up at an ungodly hour. If our pals miss this place, they'll locate one of the others."

"This isn't going to work," Jess said dazedly. "I don't even understand it myself."

"Certainly it will work, you're simply being difficult. Put yourself in Cousin John's place. What would he do after he lost our trail? First, surely, he'd investigate the hotels in Salisbury, in case we doubled back; he knows we weren't in such splendid condition last night. The process would take part of this morning, since most hotels close early here in the provinces and wouldn't have been open for inquiries last night. Then, when he draws a blank in Salisbury, he'll start on the roads leading out of town. That will be a tedious process; it was late when we left the Sun-worshipers, and we might have passed unobserved. As, in fact, we did. Now we've simply made sure someone did observe us."

"Yes, but . . ."

David looked sullen.

In the end, the plan succeeded only too well. They were parked on a side street in Salisbury, arguing, when David suddenly collapsed on the seat, flattening Jess under urgent hands.

"What—"

"Sssh. That was them!"

"They . . . No! Was it?"

"Indubitably." David shook hands with himself. "Jeer at Bill, will you? They're on the right road."

He switched on the ignition and made an illegal turn.

"David, you fool—you're not going to follow them!"

"If they are stupider than I expect, we'll let them spot us," David said blithely.

This drastic measure proved to be unnecessary. The villains were shrewd enough to find one of the clues which David had so laboriously planted. However, David insisted on driving perilously close behind them and once, when they stopped unexpectedly, he had to take evasive action which landed him in a ditch, from which he had to be extracted by two sarcastic farmers. They reached Wells more or less simultaneously, before Jess quite had a nervous breakdown, and David cackled fiendishly when the enemy located the hotel at which they had registered that morning. By midafternoon everyone was in his proper position, near the cathedral.

Wells Cathedral sat placidly on its foundations, looking almost exactly like the colored photograph on the cover of the little guide Jess had bought. Even the sky had made a noble effort for the tourists; its blue was artistically spread with fleecy white clouds.

"This is just about my favorite cathedral," David said. He added in a sotto-voce growl, "Look at it, you goat. You're supposed to be acting like a tourist."

"I want to know where *he* is."

"Back there by the gate. Muffler wound round his mustache, poor fool. Didn't you see him back at the hotel, lurking till we emerged?"

"Yes, but . . . I keep wondering who's chasing whom."

"Bill is following *him*. Come along and stop fretting. You're spoiling the effect."

They strolled across the bright green grass, accompanied by a number of other sightseers. Jess was delighted to see them. If there was no safety in numbers, there was, at least, company.

Once inside, though, she paid Wells Cathedral the supreme tribute. For a full two minutes she forgot all about Cousin John.

"I thought you'd like it," David said complacently.

"It looks almost modern in parts. Those funny upside-down arches. What are they for?"

David plucked the guidebook out of her hand.

"Ermmph. Inverted arches. They were added in the fourteenth century, to support the additional weight of the tower."

"Thanks. May I have my book back now?"

David turned and let his eye wander over the vaulted interior of the Cathedral.

"He's not in sight. I hope we haven't lost him. Jess, don't you have a mirror or some such gadget you can peer into? I can't keep turning around all the time."

Jess fumbled in her purse and located her compact.

"I can't keep powdering my nose all the time either. I don't even know what we're doing here. What are you going to do with him if you catch him? *If*, I said."

David paused beside a chest-high monument which supported a life-sized effigy. The hands were laid on the breast and the features were worn down in a manner which added nothing to the beauty of the face.

"A Saxon Bishop of Wells," Jess read. "I'd hate to have had him for a spiritual comforter."

"Never mind him. Look."

Jess looked. Behind the shelter of the tomb, he flipped his coat aside. Protruding rakishly from his belt was a dull-gray object which was unmistakably the butt of a gun.

"You can't. You wouldn't!"

"I couldn't even if I would." David fought his impulses, but not very hard; whisking the gun out of his belt, he pointed it at her and pulled the trigger. "Bang," he said.

"A toy. That's why you went to that toy shop yesterday." Jess was torn between laughter and exasperation. "What possible good—"

"We have to urge him out to the car, haven't we? Once in the Jaguar, and the villain is ours. Off we fly, into the open fields somewhere, and then—"

"There he is," Jess exclaimed, squinting into her mirror. "He just ducked behind that pillar."

"Hmm. It is a trifle crowded here. Let's gently wend our way toward some more private spot."

He ambled along the north aisle. Jess trotted behind.

"David, do stop and think. You can't make him walk all the way back to the car with that silly little gun. He'll just run away."

"Really? Well, perhaps not. How's this? I stick him up with the gun and then you hit him on the head."

"No."

"Why not? We can say he had a fit, or something, and we can carry him—"

"No."

"Spoilsport. All right. Then I stick him up with the gun—"

Jess started to protest and thought better of it; this was one part of the program which David intended to carry out, with or without her cooperation.

"And then Bill rushes in and bonks him on the head. Rest of the plot according to plan. Where is he now?"

"It's practically impossible to see anything in this," Jess grumbled, shifting the mirror. "Yes, he's still coming. More to the point: Where is Bill?"

"He'll be here when we need him. Let's duck in here. Read the guidebook, dammit, and give him a chance to see where we've gone."

"Where are we going?"

"The Chapter House stairs, up to the gallery over Chain Gate. Here, you duffer . . ."

He flipped the pages of the guidebook and read, in a self-conscious falsetto, "The ethereal beauty of this stair, as one comes upon it through the north transept, has caused many a visitor to call it 'the heavenly stair.' Indeed its clustered columns, sharp vaulting and—"

"Oh," Jess said.

For the second time that morning she was given a moment of sheer unadulterated pleasure, and she agreed wholeheartedly with the pompous description in the guidebook. At first glance it was hard to see why the stairs should be so beautiful. They were wide, shallow, simple stone stairs, worn down in the middle with the mutely impressive evidence of sheer age. About midway up the flight, a second, smaller flight went off to the right toward the Chapter House, the main stair proceeding onto a gallery which crossed the street; this, as David read, was for the convenience of the sleepy clergy on their way to sing the Night Office in the Cathedral.

The light fell through high windows down upon the stairs, and the worn, oblique sections of stone caught it and sent it back, faintly golden. It looks like ripples, Jess thought; ripples of light rising instead of falling; a stairway of filtered sunlight, flowing up toward Heaven. The shape of the curved small flight that led to the Chapter House lifted like some material lighter than stone, in a curve so gracious that it looked natural rather than planned.

With David tugging at her, they went up the stairs into the Chapter House, and Jess was conscious of an odd sensation in her insides.

Her first encounter with Cousin John had been in the Chapter House at Salisbury, and this Chapter House strongly resembled the other. An octagonal room, its lofty ceiling seemingly supported only by the single ribbed column in the center, which soared like a waterspout that broke on the ceiling in a stone spray, its walls were ivory in the light from the high windows.

David's eyes scanned the room and found it good.

"Stand there by the column," he whispered. "Where he can see you. I'll—you're not frightened, are you?"

"Yes."

"Why? I'll be just over there. Not a good hiding place, but at least he can't see me until he gets inside."

He tiptoed across the floor and climbed up onto the stone bench where he hovered like Dracula about to pounce.

Jess made discouraging gestures.

David scowled and remained where he was.

Footsteps scuffled up the stairs. They stopped. Then they came on—the steps of a single person. David reached under his coat. The footsteps came closer. They hesitated; came on; and through the wide doorway trotted a very old lady with white hair and a purple velvet hat.

She looked up at David.

"That is not courteous, young man," she said in a quavering voice. "Someone might like to sit on that bench."

"I beg your pardon, madam," said David, climbing down. His face was beet-red. He took his handkerchief from his pocket and dusted the bench. "Would you care to sit down?"

"No, thank you, I am not at all tired. Four miles of brisk walking each day keeps me fit. I merely voiced a general statement."

Jess, who had been a delighted spectator, stayed where she was. The elderly lady walked slowly around the room, inspecting it; Jess momentarily expected that she would run a gloved finger over the molding to test for dust. Then she nodded to David and went out.

David, whose ruddy complexion was due not so much to embarrassment as to amusement, made strangling noises.

"God, what a fool I looked," he said calmly. "Let's try it once more, shall we?"

He returned to his pose on the bench, and Jess leaned against the pillar. The episode had removed most of her nervousness; it was hard to be afraid and hysterically amused at the same time. It was David who had turned her little drama into comedy. He was having the time of his life. Being beaten up, kidnaped, and run like a fox across brambly fields— none of these discomforts disturbed him in the least. She wondered if he met all of life's misadventures in the same spirit and decided that, if he could be amused by what had happened so far, few things would seriously distress him. And the nicest part was that his *joie de vivre* was communicable. For long moments she was able to forget the potential dangers, and enjoy the fun.

Footsteps again—soft, but heavier. She knew them; all at once she was back in the Chapter House at Salisbury, and he was coming, and it was beginning again, the fear and the flight. She stiffened, and her mouth went dry.

Then she saw David. His face radiated delight; he made silent gestures of pleasure, concluding by placing a finger across his lips. She grinned at him. He scowled and shook his head violently. He clasped his hands and pressed them against his chest. He opened his eyes till the whites showed, pantomiming terror. Jess obediently struck a pose; and just in time.

Under the arched doorway tiptoed Cousin John.

He saw Jess at once. His mustache twitched, and a line appeared between his brows.

"Now, see here, young woman," he began, and took a step into the room.

This move brought David into his line of sight, and David was a vision to strike terror into the boldest heart. He was in the act of jumping, arms extended and fingers clawed, lips drawn back in an anticipatory grin. He looked like an immigrant from Transylvania, and Cousin John, understandably, was taken aback. He retreated, with a yell of consternation. David missed the grip he had intended and landed heavily on his knees, clutching the other man around the legs. They both fell over. David was on top, at least partially; his arms clutched the other man's thighs and his chin dug into Cousin John's stomach.

There was a moment of mutual hesitation, while David tried to improve his position and Cousin John shook off the dizziness which had followed the abrupt contact of his head with the stone floor. Then David tried to get his arms free, and Cousin John began pounding him on the back with his clenched fists.

How long this ineffectual combat would have continued Jess never knew; the inevitable interruption occurred. The sound of feet on the stairs was neither slow nor quiet; it sounded like the advent of a troop of infantry.

The combatants heard the footsteps and were galvanized into action. Jess saw nothing but a flurry of movement somewhere under her hero's prone form, but it produced amazing results; David jerked up as if he had received a stiff jolt of electricity. His eyes narrowed with pain and indignation, and he grasped Cousin John by the collar and banged his head against the floor. The sound made Jess slightly sick. Cousin John went limp and David staggered to his feet, his face green.

The newcomers stopped on the threshold. There were four of them: a weary-looking mother with two little boys, and Bill.

Of the four Bill appeared to be the most distressed. He stood still, gaping, while the two grubby children rushed forward, shouting joyously.

"Look, Mum, a corpse."

"Is he dead, mister, is he dead?"

"He's—er—fainted," David wheezed. "Bill, give us a hand."

"What? Oh," said Bill. He advanced delicately, like a cat investigating a brand-new smell.

"See here, you can't move him," the woman exclaimed.

Bill, who had lifted the fallen man's shoulders, obediently let him go, and again Jess winced at the sound of a head banging against stone.

"Pick him up," David snarled. "Madam, will you please not interfere?"

"But, really, you mustn't move him." The woman advanced. "That's one of the things they teach the kiddies in school. Not to move an injured man."

She knelt beside Cousin John. Above her bowed head David lifted both fists and his face to heaven; and one of the staring urchins bellowed, "Mum, he's going to hit you! Help! The man's trying to hit my mum!"

David was clearly torn between a desire to carry out this suggestion and an equally strong urge to throttle the shrieking child. At this inauspicious moment "Cousin John" opened his beautiful blue eyes.

After the first dazed stare, his eyes made a rapid circuit of the ring of staring faces, registered recognition, and then began to flutter weakly.

"Oh," he moaned, clutching at his jacket pocket. "The pain . . ."

"There now," said the unwelcome Florence Nightingale. "It's probably a heart attack. Just lie still, young man, and we'll fetch a doctor."

"I'll take him to a doctor," David said desperately. "Come along, er—Mordred, old boy."

"Mordred?" the woman repeated doubtfully.

"We call him Mord," David said hysterically.

"Bless you, old chap," Cousin John said in faint tones. "You have such a good heart. . . . And speaking of hearts, I think I'd prefer to stay here."

"Certainly you must," the woman said. "Ah, I hear people coming."

"Probably to investigate the massacre," David said, through his teeth. "Madam, could you possibly quiet that abominable child?"

"Perhaps one of them is a doctor," the woman went on.

David hesitated, and broke.

"I'll fetch a doctor," he said, and fled.

Jess was right behind him.

SIX

The trio traversed the clipped greensward outside the Cathedral at undignified speed. Bill had been the first to leave; he had quietly faded away before the denouement.

"What rotten bad luck," David panted.

"You could have thought of something," Jess said.

"What, for instance?"

"You could have said you *were* a doctor." They came out of the gate around the cathedral close into the town square, and all three slowed to a more sedate pace. "You could have said he was subject to seizures, or was crazy, or something."

"Hmm." David gave her a look of grudging respect. "Do you want to collaborate on my next? Well, I'm sorry; but that woman rattled me, and that ghastly, screaming imp . . . Bill, you weren't much help, I must say."

Bill said nothing. He simply widened his eyes alarmingly and shook his head.

"Something odd, though," David said thoughtfully. "The other chap—Algernon. Where was he while all the fun was going on?"

They found out when they got back to the hotel. Both rooms, Jessica's and David's, had been thoroughly ransacked. Jess recognized the true Algernon touch; there was a kind of contempt in his failure to conceal his activities.

"The ring?" Bill inquired.

Jess jumped. He spoke so seldom that it was like hearing a desk ask the time of day.

"Jess carries it with her," David said. "They didn't . . . Jess, why the ghastly countenance? Don't tell me you left it here?"

"Not the ring, no, I've got that." Jess was white with anger. "The son of a gun stole my passport!"

Mutual recriminations were flying thick as hail several hours later, as the conspirators sat over spiritous liquors in the bar of the King's Arms. David had discovered that the enemy were registered there by the simple expedient of spotting their blue convertible in the inn yard.

"It was a stupid thing to do," Jess raged, for the fifth or sixth time. "But how could I imagine—"

"Don't they warn you at the State Department, or whatever, not to leave the blasted thing lying about?"

"You said that!"

Bill cleared his throat, and the pair subsided.

"And I don't understand why we came here," Jess muttered. "They'll catch us red-handed."

"That hardly matters now. Everybody knows that everybody's chasing everybody. I thought we'd wait till they go out, to feed, or look for us, and then try a spot of room-searching ourselves."

Jess sighed and drank beer. She had chosen to

drink beer rather than anything stronger because it looked as if they might have a long wait. She knew better than to object to David's ingenious plan; when he got an idea, he stuck to it.

They had gotten a table by the window. Even so, they almost missed the exodus, being involved in another argument, this time over why the enemy had stolen Jessica's passport. Two of them were arguing; silent Bill drank his beer. He had an enormous appetite for it, but it did not distract him from the matter at hand. Silently he glanced out the window; silently he nudged David.

David took one look and bounded to his feet.

"They're escaping—the cowardly swine!"

"Where? Where?" Jess tried to see out the window. David shoved her.

"Hurry, can't you? My car's a block away, we'll never catch up with them."

Bill coughed.

"Splendid thought," David said approvingly. "Very well, troops. On your mark—get set—"

They erupted out of the door of the hotel in time to see the blue car drive off. David snatched Jess's hand and dragged her down the street to the spot where they had left the Jaguar. She didn't notice, until he shoved her into the front seat, that somewhere along the way they had lost Bill. Before she could inquire about him she saw him—a block and a half away. He was conspicuous, not only because of his height and his golden locks, but because he was running down the middle of the street, arms up and knees bending, in approved professional style. He left a trail of staring pedestrians behind him.

David pulled out from the curb in front of a truck, which responded with a squeal of brakes and a spate of curses. David paid no attention. They passed Bill, still chugging along, turned left at the next corner in response to his signal, and caught sight of the pale-blue convertible two blocks away. The hunt was up.

Jess's suggestion that they force the other car off the road was not well received. David claimed that there was too much traffic, but Jess suspected that his real reason was fear—not for himself, but for the gleaming smooth finish of his car. She did not press the point. They had left Salisbury well behind when David said suddenly, "Unless I miss my guess, they are heading for Glastonbury. What do they think this is, a sight-seeing tour?"

There was no sensible answer to this question, so Jess didn't try to answer it. Instead she asked, "What about Bill?"

"Oh, Bill never leaves Wells. He likes it there."

"He does?"

"I mean to say, he's something of a recluse."

"He is? Oh. But isn't he going to be hurt at our rushing off this way, without so much as a fare-well?"

"Who, Bill? Why should he be hurt about that?"

"'If I forgot your silly birthday, would you fuss?'"

David grinned.

"'By and large we are a marvelous sex,'" he agreed. "But we may not have seen the last of Bill."

"Why? We've got our suitcases. It was smart of you to put them in the car, I must say."

"Thank you for noticing the only intelligent

thing I've done today. No, I meant that we might have to go back to Bill's to sleep."

"But it's late now. Why can't we sleep in Glastonbury, if that's where they're going?"

"Because, my sweet, you do not have a passport."

"Oh, they never ask for it."

"Don't they?"

Their destination was Glastonbury. They were soon traversing its sedate streets, and in the near distance Jess saw the tall symmetrical shape of a tower-crowned hill which she knew must be Glastonbury Tor. She had done her homework with guidebooks from the ship's library, and now she hung out the window to get a better view. The high hill where, according to legend, Joseph of Arimathea had concealed the Holy Grail, looked green and beautiful in the evening light. David had to repeat his last question.

"What? Not usually. They just give you a form and if you already know your passport number, and where it was issued, and that stuff, you don't even have to produce it."

"Oh."

"You sound disappointed."

"A dastardly alternative had shaped itself in my mind," David admitted.

"Oh, look at that tower! Is it the Abbey?"

"No, you unromantic wench. Don't you ever think of anything but sight-seeing? It's the parish church of some saint or other. I haven't been here in . . . Look out! This is it."

He came to a screeching halt somewhere near the curb. When Jess had withdrawn from the windshield, she said irritably, "It's a miracle you haven't collected a ticket."

"A ticket to what?"

"How long were you in New York?"

"Oh, that sort of a ticket. Why? I'm an excellent driver."

Jess rubbed her forehead.

"You're illegally parked," she said gently.

"I want to be sure they're settling down for a while."

The blue car had stopped in front of a hotel. Cousin John got out, entered the hotel, and reappeared with one of the employees, who began to unload suitcases. David then consented to move on.

Thus far Jess had not been captivated by Glastonbury. Its little shops and dull houses might have been those of any provincial town. But she fell in love with the hotel David selected. Its façade, of creamy stone, had three floors of tall narrow windows framed by carvings, and a gilded set of coats of arms above the entrance.

"What is it?" she asked. "Not a replica of something, I hope."

"Replica?" David was outraged. "The George is an old pilgrim inn, built to hold the overflow of guests who came to visit the Abbey. No later than the fifteenth century, if that impresses you, and I suppose it does, Americans always . . . Oh, come along."

He perspired gently while Jess filled out her registration form, inking in a set of numbers in the appropriate spot with perfect aplomb.

"Bright of you to have memorized the number," he said out of the corner of his mouth.

"I didn't."

"Oh."

After they had inspected their rooms they met in the bar, over Jessica's protests. She was getting tired of beer, she wanted to go see the Abbey, and anyhow she failed to see the point of sitting around in bars all the time.

"This happens to be the bar of the George," said David patiently, "and its windows happen to look out upon the High Street and the market square. This is the center of Glastonbury. Sooner or later those blokes will have to pass this point."

"Unless they decide to leave town the way they came in."

David banged his empty glass down on the table. An assiduous waiter, mistaking the cause of his temper, hastened up with a refill.

"Thank you. Why should they do that?"

"I beg your pardon, sir?"

"I was speaking to the lady."

Jess waited till the waiter had left.

"I don't know why they should leave town. I don't even know why they came to town."

They could carry on this sort of aimless bickering for hours, and they did, while the shadows of evening fell and a mellow light painted the market square of Glastonbury. Then David stiffened.

"I won't say I told you so," he remarked.

The villains had just appeared, strolling down the street like any visitors. Both wore what might be called casual attire, but the effect was as different as day and night. Algernon was dressed completely in black—slacks and a turtle-necked knit shirt; the color did not improve his sallow complexion or his generally villainous air. Cousin John, by contrast, was a vision of what the well-bred gentleman wears while week-ending in the country—tailored tweeds, a spotless white shirt, and a beautiful fawn sweater. Only the mustache spoiled the picture, and Jess was now certain that it was false.

Over his arm Cousin J. carried a dark garment, presumably his coat. His right hand held a little book; and as Jess stared he stopped dead in front of the inn, book in hand. He looked at the inn's façade; he glanced at the book, and nodded. He spoke to his companion, and read from the book.

"Overdoing it," David muttered.

"Do you think he knows we're here?"

"How could he? No, he's playing tourist. Look, there they go. And here we go."

They followed at a careful distance, but their precautions were needless. The pair ahead never looked back. They ambled off down the street and vanished under a wide gateway; and David caught Jess by the arm.

"They're visiting the ruins," he said incredulously.

"Oh, good!"

"Probably bad. Wait, we'll have to let them get ahead."

"Why?"

She saw why when David finally consented to pass through the gate. It led into a narrow street, closed in by high walls, with no place for concealment. At the far end was a small building with a ticket window and turnstile.

Their quarry had vanished when they ventured into the alley but, as David pointed out, they could only have vanished into one place: through the turnstile into the enclosure which contained the ruins of the once rich and famous Abbey.

The woman who took their money warned them that the place would be closing in half an hour. Nevertheless, Jess insisted on buying a small illustrated guide.

As they went through the turnstile they saw straight ahead the best preserved part of the old church: the Lady Chapel, whose creamy walls seemed, at first glance, almost intact. But the roof was gone, and the windows, framed with carved foliage, gaped empty; lichen and ivy had rooted in the cracks of the walls, and a fine crop of green grass sprouted on their tops.

The modern precinct was several blocks long—Jessica's ability to estimate size was no more precise than that—and almost as wide. At the far end, away from the entrance, lay the stately remnants of the church to which the Lady Chapel had been an adjunct. Like monolithic stone sentinels, two tall piers towered in isolated majesty. The top of the vast arch of which they had formed the sides had fallen; but somehow the eye was led up, to complete its form in imagination. The westering sun cast a theatrical glow, gilding the stone and brightening the green of trees and close-clipped grass. Except for the octagonally shaped Abbot's Kitchen, most of the other buildings of the monastery were represented only by foundations, carefully preserved and marked. Preservation, not restoration, had been the aim of the scholars who brought Glastonbury back to life. It cast a spell, a unique kind of magic from which few visitors escape, unscathed. Jess, being particularly susceptible, succumbed at one glance.

"The Great Church," she muttered, flipping the pages of the guidebook. "Piers of the crossing . . . What's a crossing, David?"

"This place is too big. Where the hell are they?"

"Who? What's a crossing?"

"Where the transepts, crossarms, of a church meet the nave," David said absently. "Where did they go?"

"I want to go down there."

"Where? Oh. Might as well." David shrugged. "Look sharp for wandering villains."

Jess had no attention to spare for villains; it was hard enough trying to read the guidebook and look at the sights simultaneously.

"Look at this," she exclaimed, stopping before a marker.

"Huh?" David glanced at it disinterestedly. "Oh, yes, your ancestor."

" 'Site of King Arthur's tomb,' " Jess read. " 'In the year 1191 the bodies of King Arthur and his queen were said to have been found on the south side of the Lady Chapel. On nineteenth April 1278 their remains were removed in the presence of King Edward I and Queen Eleanor to a black marble tomb on this site. This tomb survived till the dissolution of the Abbey in 1519.' Isn't that exciting?"

"No."

"Oh, you're about as romantic as—as an oyster." Jess sighed. "Imagine—King Arthur! I remember now, this is the Isle of Avalon that the books talk about. It doesn't look much like an island now," she admitted doubtfully. "Was it ever?"

"Dunno."

Jess made exasperated sounds and flipped the pages of her book.

"Yes, it was. Not in water, but in marshland. 'Linked to the main uplands by a narrow tongue of land running southeast—'"

"Will you stop that!" David snatched at the book and she ducked, clutching it.

"Aren't you interested in King Arthur?"

"No, I'm much more interested in Cousin John." He scowled at her, and then said maliciously, "It probably wasn't Arthur they found anyhow. When was it—twelfth century? Those credulous boobs probably dug up some old abbot and decided he ought to be Arthur. Even the bones are gone now, there's no way of knowing what they found, if they found anything, and didn't invent the whole story."

"You're the kind of guy who would tell little kids there isn't any Santa Claus. The bones survived till the Dissolution. What's the Dissolution?"

"Henry the Eighth, you ignorant colonist. Don't they teach any civilized history in your country?"

"I know all about Henry the Eighth," Jess said coldly. "He declared himself head of the church and stole all the monasteries. He had six wives, and I can name them all. Which I'll bet is more than you can do."

"Ann Boleyn," David said. "Let's meander over this way. I thought I saw a familiar form by the

Abbot's Kitchen. Katharine of Aragon. Anne of
Cleves. Uh . . ."

"Catherine Howard, Catherine Parr, Jane Sey-
mour. What's this part?"

"Kitchen, cloister, refectory," David said with resigned patience. "Or rather the foundations of same,
the upper parts are gone. I don't think I am very
happy. Have you noticed how dark it's getting?"

He was right. The shadows on the grass had faded
as the light dimmed. One bright star hung low in a
darkening sky. Just then an unharmonious but peremptory noise from the direction of the entrance
made David glance at his watch.

"Closing time. Jess, look here—I know you
haven't been watching, but I have. Neither of those
blokes has left."

"So, they're staying till the last minute."

"Possibly. But I am beginning to have a strange
premonition. This way, please. Let's go back to the
entrance, and lurk."

It was not difficult to lurk; the ruins provided
splendid cover, with strategically placed gaps for
spying. From behind a wall of the Lady Chapel they
could see the part of the path directly in front of the
turnstile, and it was not long before their vigilance
was rewarded by the sight of Villain Number Two.
He strolled by them, his hands in the pockets of
his baggy trousers, his lips pursed in a whistle, and
went out the exit without so much as a backward
glance.

Jess caught David's eye, and saw, reflected, her
own question. Algernon was the last man to seek out
the holy ruins of Glastonbury for their own sake.

Why had the precious pair come here? And where, now, was Cousin John?

Wherever he was, he meant to stay there. The last tourists straggled out, the caretakers closed the gift shop and ticket window. The last footsteps died away; and a profound stillness gathered, with the dusk, over the towering ruins of King Arthur's Isle of Avalon.

By this time the adventurers were in the crypt, behind an altar. David had insisted on the retreat, not only to avoid any vigilant custodians checking on absentminded visitors, but to give himself, as he expressed it, time to think. Jess didn't feel that the crypt was conducive to thought, except thoughts of murder, ghosts, and decay. It was not totally black-dark, being open at one end where the Galilee joined onto the Lady Chapel; but the high remaining walls of the latter structure cast shadows, thick shadows which left the lower portion in darkness. The place felt damp and smelled damp. But, she had to admit, it had one advantage. No one could approach their hiding place without being seen and heard.

"I'll bet he sneaked out when you weren't looking," Jess whispered. "David, how are we going to get out? We can't stay here all night."

"Oh, we can get out. Hop over the turnstile and bang on the gate till someone comes."

"And how do we explain our failure to hear the all-out signal?"

"I can think of one explanation," David said, and chuckled evilly.

"You have a low mind. Let's go look for him, since we're here."

"We'll have to wait for moonrise. I didn't bring a torch."

The wait seemed interminable, but it could not have been more than an hour in objective time; and when the moon did rise Jess forgot her cramped limbs.

The far wall of the Lady Chapel had three arched windows, the one in the center higher than the two on either side. They showed, at first, only as star-sprinkled shapes of black against the deeper black of the wall. Gradually they paled, and Jess caught her breath as the moonlight spilled through the silvered tracery and lay like water on the inner floor. When David moved, she followed him in a kind of trance.

Stonehenge by moonlight had evoked history, restoring a simulacrum of something which had existed three thousand years before. Glastonbury, under a full spring moon, was sheer romance, a shining ghost of what had never been, a truth that was eternal because it had lived, never in time, but in the hearts of men. The colors were gone; only black and gray and glaring white defined arches, carvings, foliage; Jess would not have been surprised to see the bark Malory described come gliding across the shimmering grass, with the three mourning queens and the still figure of the hero at their feet.

A rude noise from David broke her poetic reverie.

"Hssst! Look there!"

The dark figure, featureless in silhouette, was no vision out of Malory, but it was almost as incredible.

Motionless against the silvery space between the mutilated piers of the crossing, it seemed to be swathed from neck to heels in something that resembled a monkish robe. Jess clutched at David. The silhouette moved, flapping its long sleeves like wings; then it glided behind the farther pier and vanished in the shadows.

"What on earth?"

"It's Cousin John, all right," David said grimly. "Doesn't he have fun, though? Let's see what he's doing."

David flung himself down on his stomach and began to crawl. Jess followed, muttering curses; she wore a new pale-blue summer suit which had a semifitted jacket and a skirt which fitted only too well, being extremely tight and short. The dew had settled on the grass; she was immediately soaked from her chest to the hem of her skirt.

The low stone wall which sheltered them was followed by the higher shelter of the only remaining section of the nave walls. They now had to cross the same open section, between the piers, which the figure had already crossed, and David stopped, presumably to consider this problem. Jess was more preoccupied with her skirt, which she had pulled up to facilitate crawling. As she tried to adjust it, David looked back. His eyes popped.

"Haven't you ever seen a girl's legs before?" she demanded, in a hoarse, aggravated whisper.

"Never under such provocative conditions . . . sssh. We'll have to make a dash for it. Take my hand."

They darted across the open space; when they

reached the sheltering shadow of the far pier, David caught her and swung her into his arms.

"None of that now," she muttered, poking him.

"I just want to talk to you."

"It seems to me I've heard that—oh! What's that?"

A rustling, like the frisson of dried leaves, or the leathery wings of a giant bat . . . David dropped Jess and whirled around, in time to see the cloaked figure flit mysteriously across the far end of the nave and duck behind a pile of stone. He started out after it. Halfway to the stone pile he stumbled, floundered grotesquely, and fell.

Jess's heart stopped. There had been no shot, but . . . An arrow? A poison dart?

"You are a fool," she told herself; but she was relieved to see David beckoning her to join him. He had simply tripped. The grounds were well kept, but protruding stones and bits of foundation, carefully preserved, were hazards to runners.

"Did you hurt yourself?" she asked, dropping down on the grass beside him.

"No. I was just thinking—"

"Oh, Lord! Sorry, I didn't mean to startle you—there he goes again."

He was on the southern side of the ruins now, among the buried foundations of the domestic offices.

"All right," David said, sighing. "What I was thinking was that there may be some point to this fatiguing sport; and the point may be to separate us. Keep with me, can you?"

"Oh. Oh! Do you think Algernon could have sneaked—snuck—uh—"

"Try 'crept.' I think too much, that's the trouble, and I know too little. But I prefer to take no chances. Come along, let's play games with Cousin John. How I'd love to get my hands on that capering comedian!"

The game was "hide-and-seek," and there had never been a better place for it; a pack of children would have run wild. Shadows, trees, rocks and ruins; open doors and gaping windows and grassy banks—there were a hundred places in which to hide, and a dozen ways out of each one. The black-cloaked figure seemed supernatural. It vanished into shadows from which no escape seemed possible, and materialized yards away. It did not run, it floated; and the folds of its black garment billowed in the breeze, giving it impossible shapes, as fluid and amorphous as an amoeba. Jess could have sworn that sometimes it stood still and flapped its arms at them.

After a merry romp clear across the grounds, around the octagonal angles of the Abbot's Kitchen, and over the spot which had been the cemetery, they cornered it, finally, in the Lady Chapel, which was one of the few places that had corners. Both pursuers were soaked to the skin, and Jess's feet were cut, since she had made the mistake of trying to run barefoot. Still, they must have looked formidable as they advanced on the figure that cowered against the chapel wall. Jess was too intent on their quarry, which had already demonstrated convincingly its ability to dematerialize, to spare a glance for David, but she could feel his fury, and knew that he must be glowering. She couldn't believe that they had almost caught the flitting, elusive shadow of a man; and David shared her doubts, for he said suddenly, "Keep an eye out behind us, Jess."

She whirled, half expecting to see Algernon's saturnine dark features at her shoulder. The long expanse of the chapel lay silent and untenanted; the moonlight left one wall in shadow but picked out every graceful detail of the interlaced arcade midway up the opposite wall.

David was now within ten feet of the fugitive, who had backed into the farthest corner, half-crouched, his draped arms up before his face. Step by slow step the pursuers closed in. David's outstretched arms were almost touching the shrouded heap of blackness when, with terrifying suddenness, it rose up—only on tiptoe, but at that time, and in that place, the effect was like something soaring up on flapping wings. The outstretched arms beat up and down, and the folds of the cloak flew. Then the figure darted at them, fingers clutching.

Jess tried to fall down. To his eternal credit, David stood firm; but he did flinch as the swooping blackness leaped at him, and the arms he had extended moved, quite involuntarily, into a position of defense. The black-draped arms embraced both him and Jessica, banged them together like cymbals, and let them fall.

Neither was hurt, but both were considerably amazed. For three short but decisive seconds they sprawled, motionless; it took another three seconds to untangle themselves from one another and from the cloak in which the fugitive had wrapped them.

David, the first on his feet, bolted for the doorway. Jess followed more leisurely, carrying the cloak. She found David outside, waving his fists.

"Gone?" she inquired.

"Damn, damn, damn, damn—whoops, there he goes!"

He ran off. Jess wrapped the cloak around herself; she was soaked with dew and perspiration, and the extra covering felt good. She was too tired to run, and too disgusted to try; from where she stood she had an excellent view of Glastonbury by moonlight, and also of the last scene of the second act of their little drama. Or was it the third act?

The running figure, now uncloaked, made no attempt to conceal itself; it moved as quickly as it could, as if heading for some definite goal. It made a slender, agile silhouette against the pale stone of the wall which bounded the Abbey grounds on the south. At the wall itself the figure stopped, and coursed up and down as if in search of something. David ran madly, but he was still some distance away when the black figure made its final move, and even after its earlier performances, this one left Jess gaping. He lifted his arms, hands together as if in an archaic incantation to pagan gods; then he swarmed up the wall as easily as if he had levitated.

David's lope slowed; then he threw himself forward. He was too late. The agile shape poised itself on top of the wall, flinging one arm out in what looked like a mocking salute. Then it vanished. A moment later David plowed to a halt at the base of the wall and began pounding on it with his fists.

Jess lifted up the trailing skirts of the cloak and broke into a slow trot. When she reached David he was leaning up against the wall, staring pensively at the sky.

"Shall we go home?" she asked tactfully.

"Yes, let's."

"How?"

David heaved a deep sigh.

"I shall lift you on top of the wall. You will then toss over to me the rope which you may—or you may not, but I rather think you may—find there."

"Is that how he got up? I thought he flew."

"So did I, for one frightful moment. If they took the rope with them, you'll have to locate the village bobby, and tell him your boyfriend got locked in."

The rope was there, still attached to the bole of a tree on the other side of the wall. Jess half expected to find something, or someone, else there; but the street was empty. The game was over for the evening. She was more confused than ever as to its purpose, and David grumpily refused to speculate. He pointed out, sharply, that they had missed dinner, and asked how long she thought he could go on like this, battling villains, without nourishment?

The first place they found was a Chinese restaurant, and David led the way in with the air of a man who is in no mood for argument. The chop suey fascinated Jess. It didn't taste at all like the chop suey she had had in the States. But it was filling and hot, and it seemed to soothe David. The restaurant was equally soothing, being warm and crowded and dim. The dimmer the lights, the better, she felt; she had removed the cloak when they reached the High Street, and her poor suit was slightly out of press.

David finished his chop suey, ordered egg foo yung, ate it, and ordered chow mein. By that time his expression was slightly less grim; and when his eye fell on the heap of black material on the bench beside Jessica, he looked almost human.

"I'd forgotten that. Let's have a look at it."

Held up in David's hand, the garment did not look particularly promising as a clue. It was black, made of some shiny cheap material, with a high collar.

"Looks like a stage costume," David said. "Yes, there's a label. Wells. He bought this, or hired it, yesterday."

"But why?"

"Can't imagine." David shook the garment angrily, and then cocked his head. "Wait a sec. Did you hear something rustle?"

"The whole thing rustles. It looks like taffeta."

"No, something else. Like paper. Wait, it's got a pocket."

"Cloaks don't have pockets."

"This one does. And . . ." David removed his hand. "There's something in the pocket."

They spread the paper out on the table, and both heads bent over it.

"Regent Hotel, Bath," Jess spelled out. She was reading upside down; by the time she had deciphered the larger letters of the heading, David had digested the body of the letter.

"Two single rooms booked for Friday night.

That's two days from now. He must have shoved this into the pocket and forgotten about it. I can't believe it—are we going to have one chunk of good luck, for a change?"

"I don't suppose he expected to lose the cloak," Jess said. "That's wonderful, David; it gives us time to do some planning. Hey—who's the letter addressed to?"

"Who do you think?" David folded the letter carefully and slipped it into his pocket. "I tell you, the lad ought to be on telly. It's addressed to a Mr. Arthur King."

SEVEN

It was raining next morning. Jess groaned as from under heaped bedclothes she blinked sleepily at the windows, streaked drearily with raindrops. She sneezed experimentally and decided that she wasn't going to catch a cold after all. It was a miracle she hadn't, crawling around up to her chin in damp grass, plodding through puddles, drenched with rain every alternate day. . . . Then she remembered the letter which had mentioned Bath—but not until Friday. Perhaps David would let her spend the extra day here, in a nice warm bed. How heavenly . . . The rain on the window made a gentle pattering sound. She drifted off to sleep again.

The second time she was awakened, less pleasantly, by David's eruption into her room and by his cries of anguish.

"Do you know what those—those—"

"Never mind the epithets," Jess croaked. She collapsed back onto her pillow, from which she had sprung at David's entrance, expecting fire, flood or murder. "What have they done now? Left their hotel? But we know where they're going to be."

"The motor's gone," David said. He sat down on the foot of the bed and looked as if he were about to burst into tears.

"The motor of what? Oh, no—not the car? David, you must be kidding; they couldn't walk out of the place carrying an entire six-cylinder—or is it an eight-cylinder—"

"Not the whole thing. Just every part that could be detached. Or pulled out. Or ripped away. Or—"

"Well, that's a shame. But can't it be fixed?"

"Oh, it can be *fixed*. Damn it, you don't understand; women never understand these things. It's like seeing your child mutilated—nose cut off, arms amputated—"

"Stop it, that's awful." Jess sat up and circled her bent knees with her arms. She made sure David got a censored view of her upper parts, and was pleased to see that his dull eye brightened. "Cheer up, darling, we can follow them on foot. All over Glastonbury. In the rain."

"They have left," David said. "I checked on that as soon as I found out about the car."

He was drenched, even to his hair, which dripped pathetically onto his nose. Jess had an inner vision of David rushing pell-mell down the street, teeth bared, coatless and wild—seeking vengeance. No wonder he was frustrated.

"Poor David. But we know where they'll be tomorrow night. Cheer up, things aren't so bad. Why don't you change clothes, and then we'll have a nice big breakfast together?"

"Here?" David asked hopefully.

"Certainly not." Jess pulled the blankets up to

her chin. "I'll meet you downstairs in fifteen minutes."

Jess spent one of the loveliest days she had had yet—reading in bed, sleeping in bed, and just lying in bed doing nothing. David was busy snarling at garagemen; he would no more leave the car than he would have left the hospital when his dear old mother was undergoing an operation.

His efforts paid off. The car was repaired in record time, and by noon the next day they were in Bath. The weather was beautiful; a radiant sun beamed down on Aquae Sulis of the Romans.

The Romans have been gone for a long time. Bath is Regency, even now, and Jess adored it. She babbled of Beau Nash and Jane Austen and demanded to see Laura Place, where "our cousins, Lady Dalrymple and Miss Carteret" had lived. David was learning her habits; he refused to stop and let her buy a guide to Bath, but he accepted without comment the rain of miscellaneous information she extracted from her general guidebook. As a result both of them were fairly happy, though their conversation might have sounded peculiar to an outsider.

"Beau Nash was the arbiter of society, whose dictates of amusements and polite behavior were slavishly obeyed."

"If the Regent Hotel is largish, we can stay there."

"He turned the city into a center of fashion. Everyone who was anyone went to Bath."

"Incognito, of course. If you can invent a new passport number you may as well invent a new name. Any ideas?"

"Ladies and gentlemen began their day in the

Pump Room, drinking in gossip along with the pre-scribed three glasses of the famous waters."

"Helen Broderick? Josephine Dubois?"

"Sam Weller . . ."

"Sam? That's a man's name. Ermingard Wilber-force?"

"Catherine Morland and Miss Tilney . . ."

"That's not bad. Catherine Morland."

It was perhaps just as well that Jess did not have to register as Miss Austen's heroine. The Regent Hotel was a charming old town house with an orna-mental façade, but it could not have boasted more than six bedrooms, and David abandoned his first plan after one glance. The hotel had one advantage, however: Across the street there was a group of small shops, including a secondhand bookstore. Af-ter they had registered in a larger hotel some blocks away, David led the way back to the bookstore.

Jess generally approved of bookstores and was glad to see that David shared the mania. This one was especially pretty, being an old shop with the double bow windows characteristic of Bath's hey-day. There were daffodils planted in boxes under each window.

"Bookshops, secondhand ones, are almost as good as pubs, for lookout points," David explained happily. "The owners don't care how long people browse. We'll browse at the front, where we can look out the windows."

He promptly disappeared into the rear of the shop and Jess, sighing, began to turn over a group of grubby volumes on a shelf marked "One Shilling."

The books were about what one might expect to

find on sale for a shilling. Though the shop assistant appeared to be asleep at his desk, Jess soon became self-conscious and began reading one of the books, which she selected more or less at random, just to be doing something. A red-backed volume called *In Darkest India*, it was not a travel book, as she had thought, but a very lurid novel. By page 54 she was deeply engrossed in the activities of Lady Valerie and Captain Smythe-Wilkins.

Lady Valerie was being pursued around a harem by a lustful rajah who had kidnaped her (Jess's inner mind inqured, Harem? Rajah?—and was promptly shushed). His hot breath was on Lady Valerie's face when a hand fell on Jessica's shoulder. She clutched the book to her bosom with a good imitation of Lady Valerie's terrified gasp.

"It's a good thing I was watching," David said mendaciously. "Why didn't you call me when they arrived?"

"Did they?"

"They must have come," David pointed out, with irreproachable logic, "because there they go."

"Oh. Both of them."

"Yes. Shall we?"

"Wait a minute." Jess fumbled in her purse and approached the desk. It seemed a shame to waken the clerk, so she left the shilling by his hand.

"You didn't have to buy that."

"I want to find out whether Captain Smythe-Wilkins will arrive in time."

"In time for what?"

"Never mind, they're turning the corner. Let's hurry."

They went down upper Church Street to Brock Street and around the Circus to Gay Street. On Milsom Street David had to take Jess firmly by the arm; she had come to a dead halt in front of a shop which might have been patronized by the immortal Jane herself. David's remarks on this occasion were pungent, and Jess forced herself to pay more attention to the quarry.

The villains were strolling, just like the tourists they always tried to ape. Jess was getting to know Cousin John's back quite well. Today he wore a dark-gray suit of irreproachable cut; he was bareheaded, and she felt sure that the brown locks were dyed, or tinted. His companion was half a head taller, but he slouched badly and his trousers were out of press. The crease in Cousin John's looked like a knife edge.

"They're heading for the Abbey," David muttered. "Damn."

"Why? I'd love to see the Abbey."

"I'm getting very tired of fiascoes in and around churches."

"You can't blame the churches for the fiascoes. But it is odd, the way they stick to the tourist places."

For a change, their destination was not Bath Abbey, which Jess would have called a cathedral if she hadn't dipped into her guidebook. Its lovely façade faced onto one of the most charming paved court-yards Jess had yet seen; the opposite side was an arcade opening onto a busy street, and the two long sides of the yard were lined with buildings out of the early nineteenth century. It was one of the tourist centers of town; both the ruins of the Roman baths and the famous Pump Room, as well as the

Abbey, could be reached from the courtyard. The two familiar, dissimilar figures crossed the court and disappeared into the entrance of the Pump Room.

Later Jess realized that one reason why the adversaries had selected this spot was because they knew it would throw her, at least, completely off guard. Apart from its historic and literary associations, it was a beautiful room, long and high, with a unique curved balcony at one end. The walls were tinted pale green, picked out with gold moldings on the capitals and pilasters between the high windows. There were red brocade drapes to match the red-figured carpet, and a huge crystal chandelier. The room was filled with little tables at which people were having tea, and a string trio played in the alcove under the balcony. A glass-enclosed bay on the side away from the windows held a complicated object which Jess recognized as the waters themselves, bubbling up in a many-spouted fountain.

David stopped in the doorway, his face a mixture of amusement and disbelief, his eyes intent on a table near the crimson-draped windows.

"Of all the gall!"

"They're having tea," Jess said. "What's so wicked about that?"

"For twopence I'd join them." David muttered; and then gulped. Cousin John had seen them. A smile of pleasure widened his mouth; he lifted one arm and waved vigorously.

David turned and looked around. There was a constant flow of tourists, in and out, but no one had responded to the greeting.

"He means us," Jess said. Cousin John's wave had turned into a beckoning gesture. He was nodding and beaming, and smirking and smiling as if he had just spotted two long-lost, rich relatives. "No—David! You can't—"

"Why not?" David's jaw squared in an expression that was oddly familiar. Jess identified it; the jaw of the hero of his most recent book, which she had perused during the leisurely day in Glastonbury, had been wont to square itself in just such a fashion.

"Why not?" she repeated indignantly. *"Timeo Danaos . . .* uh . . ." Even if her scanty high-school Latin hadn't failed, David probably would have paid no attention to the admirable warning conveyed in the quotation. He was already threading his way among the tables, and she followed, laden with foreboding.

Both men made the gesture of rising as she approached the table; but Algernon barely lifted his posterior from the chair, while Cousin John bounded airily to his feet and gave her a little bow.

"Marvelous to see you," he exclaimed, pumping David's limp hand. "We were so afraid you'd be delayed. Where are you staying? Not the Regent, we were sorry to find; it's a delightful little place, you should have stopped there."

The waitress arrived in the midst of this effusion and took Cousin John's order for another set of teas. He seated Jess with a flourish, and insisted that she take his cup. Algernon slid his cup toward David, who vigorously declined. His wary look brought a slight, unpleasant smile to Algernon's face. He took his cup back without comment and drank, long and ostentatiously.

Cousin John continued to burble, Algernon scowled, and David sat with his arms folded, trying to look menacing. Jess shrugged mentally and drank her tea. It was excellent tea.

David listened for five minutes to Cousin John's commentary on the beauties of Bath. During this time he consumed one eclair, one nut bun, and a sandwich. Fortified, he finally interrupted.

"Look here, it's time we had a showdown."

"I do admire your grasp of American slang," murmured Cousin John.

"Never mind that. What do you two want?"

The waitress arrived with the second order, and David assuaged his frustration with a second bun. He always ate in gulps; now, being quite angry, he barely chewed.

"I'd like a straight answer. Why are you following this lady?"

"Following her?" Cousin John thoughtfully sipped his tea. He put his cup in the saucer and smiled disarmingly at David. "Dear boy, I had the opposite impression. Isn't she following us?"

"Who hit whom over whose head?" Jess demanded angrily. "Who dragged whom into whose car? Who tied who up—"

"That doesn't come out quite right," Cousin John said critically. "Who tied up whom would perhaps—"

"Oh, stop talking like that! What do you want with me? It's possible, you know, that if you told me we might be able to make a deal." Meeting the fixed, black stare of the second man, she added, "And why doesn't he ever talk?"

"Let's go," said Algernon, rising, as if on cue.

"There, you see? You've hurt his feelings," said Cousin John sadly. "I'm afraid there's no use trying to talk to him now."

"Wait a second," David said thickly, through a sandwich. "You can't just—"

"I'll try to persuade him," Cousin John promised. "Perhaps in a day or two . . . But he's frightfully sensitive. Don't fret, we'll be in touch."

"Sit down." Jess caught David's sleeve. "It's no use, we can't chase them through the Pump Room. We haven't even paid for the tea!"

"Damnation." David subsided, blinking. "I'm so angry I'm weak in the knees."

"I know, he is maddening, isn't he? David, what was the point of all that?"

"Not to convey any information, certainly."

"Searching our rooms again?"

"That must be dull for them; they've done it so often."

"The car?"

"Not again, thank you. Why do you think I chose that hotel? It has its own garage, and I tipped the attendant specifically."

He yawned. "Too much food. It's made me sleepy."

"Let's go back to the hotel. I don't know why, but—I'm uneasy."

"I know why." David smothered another yawn. "Whenever Cousin John is on the prowl I'm uneasy. On general principles."

They got as far as the courtyard before he collapsed.

At first Jess thought he had stumbled, though the
manner of his fall was not characteristic; he folded
up like a stacked deck of cards which someone had
prodded with a forefinger. When he failed to rise,
she dropped down beside him and took his face between urgent hands. He blinked up at her like a
placid owl.

"What's wrong, David?"

"Nothin' wrong. Sleepy."

"Get up. Please!"

"Sleepy," David murmured. "Li'l nap . . ."

"Not here! David . . ."

A small crowd had collected, and one helpful by-
stander went in search of a doctor. David's eyes were
shut, but his face wore a gentle smile and he was
snoring. When the doctor arrived, he needed only
one look under David's heavy eyelids.

"A barbiturate of some sort. Is the young man in
the habit of taking sleeping medicine?"

"No, never. I can't imagine . . ."

"Hmmm. Well, I don't think he's had enough to
be in danger, but we'll just make certain." The doctor rose, fastidiously dusting his knees. "Can two of
you gentlemen carry him? My office is just there."

Jess stayed in the outer office while the doctor
made certain; from the sounds which issued from
the inner sanctum she was glad she was not present.
Eventually a green-faced, swaying David emerged,
supported by the doctor and his nurse.

"Shouldn't he go to the hospital?" Jess gasped.

"No, he'll do quite well now. Light diet, plenty of

coffee, then let him sleep off the remnants. And you, young man, be more careful in future."

David's bleary eyes focused in a glare of such malevolence that the nurse almost dropped him.

"Don't worry. I shall."

N o," Jess said for the third time, "I will not go around to their hotel. What do you expect me to do, challenge them to a duel?"

David sighed. Propped up on pillows, in the cold formality of the hotel room, he looked sad and misunderstood. Secretly Jess was relieved that he had recovered enough to be resentful. She had spent the night in his room, curled up in a chair; she had done nothing, really, except listen to his placid snores, but she had been afraid to leave him alone and helpless.

"I suppose," she said thoughtfully, "that the dope was in the tea."

"I think not." David looked sheepish. "I didn't give them a chance at my tea, if you recall. But—well—now that I look back, some of the nuts in that bun had a bitter taste."

"If you didn't gulp your food—"

"Let's not indulge in recriminations." David hoisted himself higher on the pillows. "Is there more coffee? Jess, I've been doing some thinking. There is something very odd about this."

"I'm glad you finally noticed." Jess poured the coffee.

"No, I mean about the last few days. It's degenerated into pure farce, Jess, this whole pursuit. From here to there and back again. All around the mulberry bush. We've been asking ourselves what the point of these incidents could be. Now what precisely have they succeeded in doing for the last three or four days?"

"Messing up your car," said Jess literally. "Drugging you. Getting us all wet and muddy crawling around in the grass. Stealing my—"

"Yes, but what does it all add up to? What, generally, have we been doing?"

"Wasting an awful lot of time," Jess said grumpily. "In—"

She stopped, staring, as the sense of what she had said finally penetrated. David nodded.

"Precisely. Do you suppose that, if the ring were really their goal, they couldn't have had it by now? That nasty-looking character we call Algernon has kept conspicuously out of our way. I hate to admit it, but if that lad wanted to put me out of commission he could do it with one hand."

"You mean it's not the ring they're after?"

"They may want the ring, but they want something else more. Delay and distraction, that's what they want. What is it they want to distract us from? What are they trying to keep us from doing?"

"There's only one possible answer," Jess said slowly. "It should have dawned on me before. From the moment I got off the boat they've been trying to head me off. There's only one place—"

"Cornwall," David finished. "And your loving grandparent."

"Then—then he isn't one of the villains."

"It's beginning to look that way. Another piece of the puzzle makes sense here, too. You said he asked

you to come to see him—'before he died,' or words
to that effect. Is he dying? Or seriously ill?"

"Why . . . I don't know. I thought it was a sort of
general, sentimental appeal; he's very old."

"It might have been an attack, or illness, a specific threat, that caused him to write to you. For all
you know, he could be breathing his last at this moment."

"I suppose he could. But—"

"But me no buts." David flung the bedclothes
back. "Hurry and pack. We're leaving for Cornwall
as fast as we can go."

The road to Cornwall—or rather the first part of
it—lay clear and straight ahead. David was driving a good deal faster than he should, and audibly
crowing over his cleverness in eluding the enemy.
Jess hunched over the road map, muttering.

"We have to go through Glastonbury. Maybe
we'll have time for another visit to—"

"Don't be a mutt." David overtook and passed a
Volkswagen. "We are heading for—where is this
house, anyhow?"

"Cornwall."

"Cornwall is a good-sized place. Where in Cornwall?"

"Near St. Ives. I remember that because of the
nursery rhyme."

"It would be; that's way down near the end of the
peninsula. Never mind, we'll do it nonstop, and you
can forget about the sights. You are the absolute
limit."

"One thing about Cousin John," Jess said nastily. "He did show me lots of nice places."

"And you know why."

"I don't care why. At least I'll have seen something of England before I die. Which—ow, look out!—which may be quite soon. I expect to be killed in an automobile accident."

David indicated offense by scowling and sticking out his jaw. They drove on for a while in silence, while Jess admired the peaceful meadows occupied by grazing sheep, and the clouds of apple trees in full blossom.

She was roused from her reverie by the intensity of David's curses; he had gotten stuck behind a procession of trucks, which were proceeding at a placid thirty miles per hour.

"Why the hurry?" she asked lazily. "We saw them go tearing out of Bath in the opposite direction."

David brightened.

"Yes, we were rather clever about that. Lurking conspicuously outside their hotel until they left, so that they would think we were going to follow them. I wonder where in Hades they were taking us this time? Gloucester? Oxford? Scotland?"

"I myself wonder how long it will take them to find that we aren't following them."

David's grin disappeared.

"There is that."

"And you shouldn't have stopped for gas at that town," Jess went on. Fast driving made her nervous, and when she was nervous she became critical.

"Radstock, that was the name of it. Once they know our general direction they'll be able to guess where we're going."

The trucks had turned off onto a construction site; David increased his speed until the wind lashed Jess's hair about her face. His own face was as long as that of the ruminating sheep that had stared, amazed, over the fence as they roared by.

"Jess, take another look at that map. Is there a smaller road out of Wells, that doesn't go through Glastonbury?"

"There's a little thin line," Jess reported, after a while. "To a town called Burnham."

"I know those little thin lines," David said pessimistically. "Hell. I haven't been this far west in years. I suppose we'd best stay on main roads; until we reach Taunton, or Bridgwater, we're more or less limited unless we go considerably out of our way. Cornwall itself is a maze; we can lose ourselves there."

He pulled out on a blind curve, as if any more delay would be intolerable; Jess covered her face with her hands and did not uncover it until the violent swerve of the car told her that they were back in their proper lane.

"Might be wise to disguise ourselves," David said, cheered by his narrow escape from annihilation. "How do you think I'd look in a beard?"

"Like the Matterhorn towering out of a forest of scrub pines."

"Spoilsport. Then you can be my prim, bespectacled companion and I'll be a nasty old lady—one of those fierce matriarchs with Roman noses."

"Driving a bright-red Jaguar?"

That ended the question of disguise. Jess knew that David would rather cut off his nose than abandon the car.

They reached Taunton without incident, though Jess's neck ached from looking back. David had settled down and was driving with skilled concentration; he displayed neither exhilaration nor anger, but she sensed, and shared, his frustration. It was maddening to have all that power under one's hands and be unable to use it. The roads were too narrow and too heavily trafficked for consistent speed.

Jess liked Taunton, and would have liked to have seen something of it. Having been a devoted reader of *Captain Blood* in her youth, she felt she knew all about the Monmouth Rebellion, the Bloody Assize, and Judge Jeffreys. But she knew better than to say anything to David, whose sober mood she had come to share; she only stared wistfully at the pretty black-timbered houses on the traffic circle in the center of town. It was while she was looking back at one such house that she saw another, more pertinent, sight—a pale-blue convertible.

The top was up, so that the occupants were not visible, but she knew that car as she knew their own.

"There they are," she said calmly.

"Doing what?" David did not take his eyes from the road.

"Just . . . there. Following."

He nodded, without commenting, and proceeded at a sedate pace through town, following the signs that read "Exeter." Jess leaned back and tightened her seat belt. She didn't know what he planned to do, but from the angle of his jaw she was sure he meant to do something, and she didn't want to distract him with inane questions.

They had left the town behind and were on a country road before David acted. Long ago Jess had decided that he was a reckless driver. Now she realized that she had underestimated him; she had never seen how reckless he could be. The car seemed to gather its haunches under it and leap off, like the animal it was named after. Jess's eyes were too blurred, with the pounding wind and with terror, to see the speedometer, but she knew that the speed remained constant; neither curves nor turns nor other vehicles slowed David one iota.

Jess looked back, partly out of curiosity, but mostly because she couldn't bear to watch what was coming at them. The blue car had fallen far behind; David's burst of speed had taken the pursuers by surprise. But the other driver was no amateur; as Jess watched, the blue car began weaving in and out, taking advantage of the consternation left in David's wake. It did not gain on them, but it did not lose appreciably either.

She knew David well enough by now to read his mind. He realized, he must realize, that he couldn't keep this pace up for long. He was simply trying to get far enough ahead of the other car so that he could take evasive action without being seen. A hill, or a curve, or a copse of trees between him and the pursuers, and a road or turnoff properly placed, that was all he needed. So far he had not found it; and Jess knew that it was simply a matter of luck as to whether he did find it before the inevitable disaster occurred.

The inevitable happened too soon. They were roaring up a hill, in the wrong lane, when a huge truck appeared at the crest. It hovered against the sky for a second and then seemed to fall straight down on them.

David tried to slide back into his own lane, but the driver he was passing had taken offense and refused to give way. The truck was so close that Jess could see the driver's face, fixed in horror as he roared toward them; his foot was surely on the brake, but the momentum of the heavy vehicle was too great.

David did the only thing he could do. Slamming down on the brake he went off onto the shoulder of the road. The truck skimmed by, missing them by inches, and the Jaguar slid, screaming, with David fighting the wheel.

Jess wasn't even frightened. She had resigned herself to death, and was only mildly surprised when it failed to materialize. They were still going at a good clip when they hit the treacherous surface alongside the road, and David played the car beautifully. He was a trifle white around the mouth, but his face was impassive; the only time he winced was when the side of the car scraped a stone wall. Then, miraculously, they were bouncing along, under control, with only a faint stench of scorched rubber to remind them of their brush with death. David didn't even stop. He glanced in the rearview mirror and swung the car back onto the road, picking up speed.

"That was stupid of me," he said evenly. "Sorry if I frightened you."

"You are," Jess said, through stiff lips, "a very good driver."

David glanced at her and grinned.

"That's the nicest thing anyone has ever said to me—under the circumstances. Will you marry me?"

"Probably," Jess said. "Ask me again sometime. If we survive. David—they've caught up. They're right behind us."

"I know."

For another mile they proceeded in line, the blue car a discreet distance behind the Jaguar. Then, as they rounded a curve and saw a long straight stretch ahead, free of other vehicles, the blue convertible made its move. It pulled out, and came up alongside. For several long seconds it hovered there. David increased his speed; so did the pursuers. There was a discordant note now in the Jaguar's smooth purr; something had been jarred by the rough handling, and it no longer responded so well. David lifted his foot, and the blue car moved ahead. In the distance Jess saw another car coming toward them, and the tightness in her throat slackened a trifle. Surely they wouldn't try anything now, with witnesses approaching. . . .

At first she thought the other driver had come to the same conclusion, for the blue car continued to pull ahead. She heard nothing over the roar of the motor and the rush of air; but all at once a neat little round hole appeared in the windshield, and David let out a startled exclamation. His foot went automatically to the brake, and just in time; a second shot must have hit one of the tires, for there was a loud report, and the car bucked and jolted to a stop.

David had just enough time to pull off the road. The blue convertible vanished around a curve, and the oncoming car, a small Austin, stopped in response to David's wave.

They spent the night in a field near Barnstaple. The Jaguar was one of the newer models, with a back seat, but neither of them slept well; Jess kept banging her head on the steering wheel, and David had to be extracted from the back by main force. It took five minutes of steady exercise to untwist him, and a hearty breakfast at Barnstaple's best hotel to restore his powers of speech.

"I'm sorry," he said, eyeing Jess's black-rimmed eyes and drooping mouth. "But from now on I'm taking no chances. Not with boys who carry guns."

"I'd almost begun to think they didn't intend to harm us."

"They didn't have to while we were trotting after them like good dogs. The shooting episode proves that we were right. They don't want us to go to Cornwall."

"We're going the long way around, at any rate," Jess said disagreeably.

"And we will continue to do so. I told you, I'm taking no chances."

"Oh, David, don't pretend. They don't have to chase us. They know where we're going. All they need to do is—wait."

David said nothing. There was nothing he could say. She was absolutely right.

* * *

They reached St. Ives in the middle of the afternoon. Jess, who knew the Cape Cod region well, realized why the Cornish immigrants had chosen to settle there, naming the new towns after the ones they had left behind—Truro, and Falmouth, and Plymouth. The scenery had a picture-postcard quality, with white beaches, and white gulls over pounding surf, and rocky cliffs sown with wildflowers. St. Ives had been a fishing town before the trippers took it over; it still huddled around its lovely harbor, with its little blue- and yellow- and salmon-trimmed cottages clinging to the sloping cobbled streets.

They had to stop in the town to ask for the Tregarth place, and they were directed back and up, on a road that looped across the cliff and then followed a wood-lined hollow toward the top of the plateau. David crawled along at about twenty; now that they had almost reached their destination, with no sign of the enemy, they were both convinced they would find a neat ambush waiting for them. There was enough traffic to relieve their minds, but when they reached the turnoff to the house, David came to a dead halt.

Heavy wrought-iron gates, rusted and sagging, filled the only gap in a high stone wall that seemed to run along for miles on either side. Two immense fir trees leaned over the gate, and cast a heavy shadow. There was no one in sight, but there was enough underbrush to conceal an army.

David took one look and put the car into reverse.

"What are you doing?" Jess asked. "This is the place."

"I'm taking you back to town."

"And coming back alone? Oh, no, you're not."

"Jess, we're asking for it—in spades."

"The gate isn't locked."

"That makes me even more suspicious. It's too inviting."

"I'm going to open them for you."

"No, you aren't. If anyone gets out of this car, it will be I."

"That's ridiculous. You can cover me better than I can cover you. Anyhow, they're less apt to shoot me."

David yelled and grabbed for her, but he was too slow. She moved quickly, to cover up the fact that she didn't feel as brave as she sounded; the back of her neck prickled when she left the doubtful protection of the car. The gate was heavy, but it moved; it took her only a few seconds to get it back far enough for the car to pass through.

The winding drive had been impressive, twenty or thirty years before. Now it was pitted with holes and overgrown with weeds which had been kept down below jungle size only by the passage of occasional cars over them. The trees lining the drive had not been pruned for decades; the vaulted branches had sagged and put out green tentacles which clawed at the roof and sides of the car. It was dark under the tunnel of foliage, dark and damp and very still. David wrestled with the wheel, trying to avoid the worst ruts.

"You know something?" Jess said slowly. "We won't be able to get away in a hurry. If we need to."

David started to reply, but the words caught in

his throat. They had emerged too suddenly, out of the overgrown tunnel of the drive, and the house lay before them.

The road had been a tattered ruin of a road; this was the ghost of what had once been a manor house. Built of stone, with a wide, elegant façade, it had towers on each corner and crenellations across the front. Architecturally it was not so much a nightmare as a rather vulgar joke. The towers had no business on a Georgian front, and the crenellations were pure fantasy. It was an explicit statement in stone of the old cliché, "I don't know much about art, but I know what I like"; and Jess, who had a hidden weakness for vulgarity herself, thought she would have enjoyed the house in its original state. But now the joke had gone sour. The humor had vanished and left only the vulgarity. Smeared with lichen and tattered ivy, its windows dull and its shrubbery overgrown, the house brooded sullenly like a neurotic urchin with a dirty face.

David had let the car jolt to a stop in the middle of a cleared space which had once been a circular carriage drive. He made a brief, pungent one-word comment.

If one could ignore the house, the prospect was magnificent. The site had been chosen to command a view for miles across the high upland and out toward the sea. In the distance the roofs of another house were visible, half hidden by trees; the land in between and all around was uncultivated parkland which had been let fall into ragged pasturage. From where they sat they could not see the ocean, but they could hear it crashing on the rocks far below.

Jess imagined that the view from the tower windows must be splendid. She said aloud, "Let's get out of here. Forget the whole thing."

"Too late. I'm captivated. I must see more."

"No ambush, David. Not yet."

"It's probably inside the house." David put the car in gear and they rolled across the remaining space up to the front steps. "Let's go and get it over with."

There was no doorbell, only a huge iron knocker in the shape of a short sword or dagger. The same symbol appeared above the door, set in a frame of scrolled stone. Jess looked at her companion. He gave her a shrug and an odd little half-smile. Then, bowing slightly, he indicated the knocker. Jess lifted it and let it fall.

EIGHT

She had expected to hear a reverberating echo dying hollowly away in the unseen interior. Too many thrillers, she told herself. The knocker produced a dull thunk, with no echoes at all. She banged it again.

"Do you suppose no one is home?" she asked hopefully.

"Dunno. I don't see the car, but it might be garaged. Try again."

Jessica tried again, several times. She was listening for the sound of approaching footsteps, but realized that this was absurd; the door looked heavy enough to cut off any sound from within. When it did swing open, she had no warning, and her upraised hand looked for a moment as if it were aimed at the nose of the man who had opened the door.

"Here, now," he said, raising his own hand as if to block a blow. Then a charming smile spread across his all-too familiar countenance.

"So you've finally arrived! No, you mustn't tell me; I'm sure you are—you can only be—my little long-lost cousin from the States. Dear Jessie: I may call you Jessie, mayn't I?"

Jess stepped back just in time to avoid a fraternal embrace, and the man's blue eyes narrowed in amusement. He was very little changed. The mustache had vanished, of course, and the hair was now flaxen, with the lusterless look which sometimes follows the hasty removal of hair coloring.

"You look better without the mustache," Jess said.

"I'm sure I do," her cousin said smoothly. "That's why I've never cultivated one."

"Splendid," David said approvingly. "Where did you get your experience? O.U.D.S.? Or the local dramatic society? That slight pause of surprise, and then the quick comeback, as they say in the States. . . ."

Cousin John drew himself up. He was of medium height; he wore an old shirt open at the neck under an out-at-elbows blazer; but as he examined David down the length of his elegantly chiseled nose, he was every inch the aristocrat viewing the canaille through a quizzing glass.

"I don't believe I've had the pleasure, Mr. ——— er?"

Jess fancied she was supposed to perform the introductions, but she was too flabbergasted by the sheer gall of the performance. While she hesitated, David took the problem out of her hands, snatching the other man's reluctant fingers and shaking them vigorously.

"David Randall. At long last I have the pleasure of meeting you formally, Cousin John. I may call you Cousin John, mayn't I? After all, we'll soon be related. Just call me Cousin David."

Cousin John's eyebrow lifted.

"You two are—engaged?"

David nodded bashfully.

"Isn't that just marvelous?" said Cousin John sweetly. "So you've brought your young man along to meet the family, have you, Jess? Well, well. But why are we all standing on the doorstep? Do come in; we must have a drink of something to celebrate."

He burbles, Jess thought wildly. Like the Jabberwock—was it that charming monster that burbled? Cousin John produced the same effect—menacing and ridiculous at the same time.

The hall was pitch-dark after the sunlit day; Jess banged her shins on something low and heavy. From somewhere in the nearby gloom she heard a muffled curse from David, and surmised that he had also encountered a piece of furniture.

"Devilish place," said her cousin's cheery voice. "No windows. Come on into the parlor," he chuckled. Grinding her teeth at the implications, Jess stumbled after him. Then a flood of daylight poured into the room as the heavy drapes were pulled back.

Jess understood, she thought, why they kept the drapes closed. If this was the main parlor, or drawing room, or whatever it was called, it looked best in a thick twilight. The interior of the house had the same air of decay which characterized the exterior, a neglect that suggested not so much lack of money as indifference. The furniture had never been particularly good, and now the upholstery was frayed and the wood was scratched. A thick coating of dust covered almost every object except the instrument that stood in one corner. In shocking contrast to the rest of the room, it looked like immaculately tended rosewood, and it was shaped like a miniature grand piano.

Cousin John followed her gaze, and misinterpreted her surprise.

"It's a harpsichord," he said kindly. "A precursor of the piano."

"Cool, man," said Jessica, giving him an equally kindly smile. "Like, Wanda Landowska."

For a moment his fair skin flushed. Then the smirk broadened into the first genuine smile she had seen on his face, and in spite of herself she found it attractive.

"*Touché*, fair cousin. Right through the liver and lights. Do you play?"

"No. I gather you do?"

"A bit," said Cousin John modestly.

David, who couldn't stand being left out of a conversation, spoke up.

"Mind if I open the other curtains? Still a trifle dim in here."

"Not at all. Silly to cling to these old customs, but . . ." He shrugged. "One does. Wouldn't want the neighbors to think we were lacking in respect."

David, his hand on the drapes, turned slowly. Jess knew, even before she asked the question, what the response would be.

"Respect for what?"

Cousin John's big blue eyes widened.

"Why," he said gently, "for the dead."

* * *

As soon as he had left the room, Jess and David flew together like metal onto a magnet. They stood hissing into one another's faces, like characters out of a television serial.

"It's him, all right."

"It certainly is he."

Jess ignored the snub.

"And he's dead!"

"Not the same he, I see. But equally correct."

"Now what do we do?"

"Where did you hide the ring?"

"I'm certainly not going to tell you here."

"For God's sake, do you think he's got the room bugged?"

"For all I know, he can hear through walls."

"He looks it," David agreed gloomily.

"Why did you tell him we're engaged?"

"Can't you stick to one subject?"

"No. I'm awfully confused. Why did you?"

"We've got to have a talk. The plot is so thick it feels like treacle."

"You don't think they killed him?"

"Who? Oh, I shouldn't think so."

"Why did you tell them we're engaged?"

"To keep him from tossing me out of here, you idiot. Why did you think?"

The were glaring at each other, faces only inches apart, when Cousin John returned, on little cat feet. Jess jumped when he said gaily, "I do hope I'm not interrupting anything."

"Not at all," David said, lowering the hands which had been hovering near Jess's throat.

"Good, good." Cousin John gave them a look of

bright-eyed malice. "If I didn't know better, I'd have thought you were having a jolly little lovers' quarrel. Shows how things can be misinterpreted. . . . Jessie, I know it's a bit early for stimulants, but I thought you could do with some sherry. You didn't know the dear old man, of course, but still, you looked a bit shocked."

Physically Cousin John might not be a formidable opponent, but verbally he was an adversary to be reckoned with, a D'Artagnan of the *mot juste*. Jess didn't even try to counter the most recent thrusts.

She had taken a seat with her back to the door, and now she learned where her cousin had inherited his silent walk. She did not see the new arrival until after the rising of the two men told her that someone else had entered the room.

"Well, Mother, here she is at last," said Cousin John. "A bit late, but . . ."

"Aunt—Guinevere," Jess said. The name did not come easily to her lips.

It was clear that her aunt did not mean to give her even the formal cheek-rubbing embrace appropriate to relatives. She shook hands, firmly but without warmth, and nodded brusquely at David. Then she sat down, accepted a glass of sherry, and stared at Jess, who returned the look with interest.

At first she thought that the reason why her aunt's face looked hauntingly familiar was because of a family resemblance; but as she inspected the hard features she found no trace of her father, or of Cousin John, who resembled his uncle more than he did any other relative. Aunt Guinevere had once been a handsome woman, but she had never been pretty; her good looks were masculine, the prominence of her features being accentuated by gray-streaked hair pulled back from her face and twisted into a bun on her neck. She wore a dark, simply cut dress. A stranger might easily have mistaken her for the housekeeper, and it was this word that gave Jess the clue. Aunt Guinevere looked just like the wicked housekeepers in half the Gothic novels Jess had read. From David's fascinated stare, she gathered that he felt the same.

She scowled at him, and he closed his mouth with a snap and took a sip of sherry. His expression changed, and he looked at the amber liquid with respect.

"Marvelous stuff, isn't it," Cousin John said. "The old gentleman was a connoisseur. Unfortunately. That's where a good half of his income went, on wine. The other half was devoted to his digging. So you see, old man, if you're marrying Jessie for her money you're going to be sadly deceived."

David's eyes brightened, and he returned a counterthrust.

"That is a blow. Sorry, darling, but I'll have to return your ring."

"Ring?" said Cousin John involuntarily.

"Yes, rather a sentimental touch, I thought. Old family heirloom." David divided a smile impartially among the audience. Aunt Guinevere didn't turn a hair and Cousin John, game to the core, recovered himself.

"Jessie, dear, you haven't given away Grandpapa's

ring? I suspect, you know, that he had other plans for it."

"What, for instance?" David asked.

"Oh, well." Cousin John looked vague. "One would have to wait for the reading of the will, wouldn't one? Do take good care of it, David. Just in case Grandfather had some last dying wish. . . ."

"As a matter of fact, I've come near losing it several times," David said casually. "Someone else seems to want it."

He sat back, and tried to raise one eyebrow. Both of them went up. Cousin John, scarcely bothering to conceal his amusement, raised his eyebrow. It slid up as if it had been oiled, while the other brow remained motionless.

"Really?"

"Yes, really. Oddly enough, the chap who twice tried to steal it looked amazingly like you."

This bombshell fell flat on the ground and failed to explode.

"Fascinating, these chance resemblances," said Cousin John.

Aunt Guinevere stirred and spoke.

"Johnny has barely left the house this past week," she intoned. "So concerned about his grandfather, the dear boy . . ."

Jess stood against the door of the tower room. Her back was pressed against the wooden panels, and her palms were damp with perspiration.

"All it needs is a few more cobwebs," she said aloud, and let out a stifled shriek as the door moved.

It opened despite her efforts and David's head appeared. He stepped in and closed the door.

"You shouldn't be here," Jess said, recovering herself. "The proprieties, you know."

"Yes, I observed that they've put me at the opposite end of the house. However, I doubt that it's the proprieties that they're thinking of."

David gave the gaunt, shabby room a comprehensive survey and let out a soft whistle.

"Cousin John must have worked hard to get this effect."

"It's got hangings," Jess said, gesturing toward the bed. "There must be armies of spiders in there!"

"That would be Aunt Guinevere's contribution. Probably spent all of yesterday catching them. I can see her now, leaping through the tall grasses, her spider net outstretched . . ."

"You're beginning to sound like Cousin John."

"I know. Damn the fellow."

"David, I really do want to get out of this place."

David walked gingerly across the floor to the window. In a different room it might have been a charming window; it was curved, to fit the shape of the wall, and under it was a deep window seat. But it was curtainless, and the panes were cracked, and when David put his knee on the cushions of the seat a cloud of dust billowed up from the faded chintz.

"Awk," he remarked, coughing. "Jess, don't do any star-gazing, will you?"

Jess joined him at the window. She knew why he had trodden lightly; the floorboards were quite solid, but somehow they managed to look as if they might collapse at the slightest pressure. She looked out the window, and straight on down, down without a break to the hard flagstones of a weedy terrace sixty feet below.

"David," she repeated. "I really do want—"

"I sympathize. But in all decency you can't leave before the funeral, and I expect you'll have to be present when the will is read. If we don't get a clue from that, and from what I can worm out of Cousin John—"

"What about his little alibi?"

"Balderdash. Aunt Guinevere's one of those doting mums who'd alibi him if he'd murdered eight little maidens and heaved them off the cliff into the sea."

"Six little maidens."

"I beg your pardon?"

"'Six little maidens you've drown-ded here, go keep them co-om-pany,'" Jess sang.

"Oh. So that's what I was thinking of. Wonder why."

"Because he's just that type." Jess sat down on the dusty cushions, fascinated by this new discovery. "'Take off, take off your golden gown, take off your gown,' said he; 'for though I am going to murder you, I could not spoil your fi-i-nery.' That's very clever of you, David."

"You have the most splendidly undisciplined mind." David sat down next to her. "Can't you concentrate on anything? I mean, the character of the villain is doubtless of interest, but—"

"I forget what we were talking about," said Jess.

"So do I," said David softly; and for the next few minutes there was no sound in the room except for muffled, hard breathing. Neither of them heard the soft tap on the door, and neither of them saw it open; the newcomer had to cough several times before they sprang apart.

"Sorry again," said Cousin John. "Frightful of me to keep interrupting . . ." His voice and his raised eyebrow implied volumes of unexpurgated material. "Thought you might like a stroll before dinner. Ancestral acres, and all that rot . . . I keep forgetting you two are engaged! So stupid of me!"

Dazzled as she was, Jess couldn't help being amused at David's expression. Caught off guard, and not quite in his normal senses, he couldn't have carried on a conversation about the weather, much less dealt with Cousin John. So she said demurely, "Well, it's new to us too. But we'd love to see the ancestral acres. Wouldn't we, darling?"

Jess had found the front of the house depressing, but the back regions verged on tragedy. What had once been a set of gardens, kitchen and flower, and a group of neat outbuildings, were now ruins overgrown with weeds. The stables had been converted, though not very well, into garages. One of the doors was not only closed but locked, with a new shiny padlock.

They fought their way through a small plantation of trees and found themselves on the cliff edge. The view was glorious. The sun was dipping below the flat horizon, whose pearly waterline blended almost imperceptibly into the flat silver of the sky and reflected the crimson streaks of the sunset. Below, surf creamed on a small secluded beach whose sand looked like white sugar. On either side of the small beach, rocks lifted jagged dark spears against which the sea leaped and bubbled.

Gripped by a sudden, unexpectedly strong emotion, Jess sank to the ground. The family homestead had not given her any sense of homecoming, nor had the others of her own blood made her welcome. Sea and rocks and setting sun and the cool salt breeze roughening her cheeks combined into an all-embracing sense of familiarity. She did not feel, she *knew*, that at some other time, in some other form, she had stood here and watched the sun set over the western ocean, where the sunken land of Lyonnesse still sends up from the depths faint-chiming echoes of its buried churches.

"Splendid view," David said, breaking the silence; and for a mad moment Jess resented his lack of understanding, an understanding which she felt, illogically, in the other man, who was in all else her declared enemy. She caught Cousin John's unwilling eye, and knew that he felt the kinship too; he didn't care for the feeling any more than she did. Momentarily his expression was unguarded, and his features, starkly lit by the sunset rays, held anxiety and distress. Then his mouth twisted in a sardonic smile.

"The call of the blood," he said, in a voice that only she could hear. "Still—it's the only part of the whole ramshackle place that's worth saving. And for what it's worth we've been here for a long time, Jess. That's hewn stone you're perched on. There was a castle here once."

"You talk as if you expect to lose it—all of it," Jess said.

"Oh, I shall." His voice was indifferent, but she

had seen through his defenses once, and now she recognized the underlying emotion. "There's not much left, and death duties will take the lot. Just as well, probably."

Jess stood up. Curiosity moved her, and so did discomfort; the rock was hard and sharp.

"A castle?" she said, poking at the turf. "Here?"

But she did not need his confirming nod to know that something man-made had once occupied the site. The block on which she had been sitting was roughhewn, and its shape was half obscured by weeds; but that shape was indubitably square. She walked along the cliff-edge and found other isolated blocks, then a line of them, as if they had fallen at the same time from a wall in a single earth spasm or battle.

Hands in his pockets, eyes on the glory in the west, David joined her. He kicked at a block.

"Not a very safe spot for a castle," he commented. "Right on the cliff edge."

"It wasn't so close to the edge five hundred years ago," John said. "The cliffs lose a few feet every year."

"Yes, but why do you think this was a castle? Probably one of the old tin mines. You see the towers all over Cornwall. About a century old."

"Anyone with half an eye can tell the difference," John said rudely. "Ever seen Tintagel? It's just up the coast. Same type of masonry as this."

Jessica was overcome by a basic human urge, the urge to dig. She squatted on her heels and dug her fingers into the turf.

"Wouldn't it be fun to find something?" she said,

scratching. "A lady's brooch, or a sword, or—why, David! I'll bet this is where the ring came from!"

The enchantment of the sunset and the site had made her unwary, or she would not have spoken; looking up, she was struck by the expressions on the two faces, so different and yet so alike in their surprised reserve.

As usual, Cousin John was the first to recover himself.

"Not likely," he said casually. "I've always suspected that the ring was one of the old man's fakes. Time we were getting back, don't you think?"

"It didn't come from a medieval castle," David said slowly. "It's not . . ." He caught himself, so obviously on the brink of a significant remark that the other two both stared hopefully at him. "You said Mr. Tregarth spent a lot of money on digging. Here? Was he an amateur archaeologist?"

Cousin John's not unhandsome face wore the look of bland innocence which meant, as Jess had learned, that he was about to tell a tall story.

"Amateur is right," he said wryly. "But not archaeologist. *De mortuis*, and all that, but the old boy was a bit of a nut. Didn't your father ever speak of his mania, Jessie?"

"You mean about being descended from King Arthur?" Jess's hands were hopelessly dirty by now; she abandoned herself in earnest, sitting down on the harsh grass.

"I thought he would. Poor old Uncle Gawain."

"He never told me much," Jess said vaguely; she had found something, a hard shape buried under inches of dirt. She broke a fingernail.

"The digging," David persisted. "He excavated here, trying to prove—what? That this—good God, of course! That this was Camelot."

"Completely mad," Cousin John agreed amiably.

"Not so mad at that . . . Jess, get out of that mud puddle."

"I've found something! Look—I've found . . ."

She pulled it out of its earthy grave, breaking two more nails in the process. In the pale, dimming light she held it up and stripped the disfiguring dirt from its elongated shape. It was glass. Thick, brown, opaque glass; crudely made, long, rounded . . .

"Beer bottle," Cousin John said with a grin. "That's the sort of thing he kept turning up, poor old soul. Not the bones of King Arthur."

Jess wiped her hands on the grass and stood up.

"Rats," she said.

Neither of the men answered. David was staring off across the pasture, his back to the view and a sea which was now pale gold and mother-of-pearl. John was staring at him.

"Time to go," John said abruptly, and started off without waiting for them.

"All the same, it wasn't so mad," David muttered. "Somewhere . . . Where did I read that article. . . ."

"Beer bottles," Jess said. "Bah. David, it's getting cold."

"Professional journal? Hardly. Newspaper? Book?"

"If you two don't hurry, you won't get any sherry," John called back. He had stopped some little distance away and was waiting for them, his slight figure outlined against the sky.

They walked half the distance back to the house in silence. In the failing light Jess had to concentrate on where she was walking. David, his gaze fixed vacantly on the horizon, kept stumbling. A turn in the path brought them around so that the sea cliff and the sunset were on their right, and David stopped.

"What's that?"

Jess followed his pointing hand and saw the object he indicated, outlined starkly against the darkening sky, its regularity of shape now visible—a long, low hill, like a giant grave.

"That?" Cousin John asked warily.

"Yes, the mound. Looks like a barrow."

"It is."

"Didn't Mr. Tregarth excavate there?"

"Matter of fact, he did. Burial chamber was empty. But it didn't interest him; too early for Arthur, you know."

They spent one of the most unpleasant evenings Jess could ever recall spending. David was abstracted to the point of rudeness; his lips kept twitching spasmodically, as if he were arguing with an invisible opponent.

After a poor dinner, served by a silent maid, they moved into the parlor. It was even less prepossessing at night, especially since John insisted on candlelight—for mood, he said. The dim light concealed the dust and shabbiness, but induced shadows and cast unpleasant lights on people's features. By candlelight Aunt Guinevere was something to behold; her hard, immobile features stood out like those of a corpse; her eyes were deep sockets of shadow and her mouth was a grim line.

The only pleasant interlude was when Cousin John consented to play. For an hour the tinny metallic notes of the harpsichord echoed in the big room. He played brilliantly—Scarlatti, Bach, and some strange stiff little pieces which he said were medieval dances.

"You could have played professionally," Jess exclaimed, forgetting antagonism in admiration.

"Not good enough," her cousin replied briefly. "That level of accomplishment requires more discipline than I've got."

He got his revenge for her induction of this admission later. At the end of the evening he lifted the candelabrum from the table and spoke to his mother.

"Jessie hasn't seen him yet, Mother. Are you going up now?"

His mother nodded, rising, and Jess realized to whom they were referring.

"You mean he's—he's still here?" she gasped.

"Where else would he be?" Her aunt studied her with unconcealed contempt. "We don't have your hypocritical, prettified approach to death. Of course he's here—in his home, where he would want to be."

The flickering candlelight shivered, as if the hand that held it—Cousin John's long musician's hand—were trembling. It made shadows dance wildly across her aunt's cold face, bringing out mad, shifting expressions. Then David's hand brushed hers, and David's voice said calmly, "The funeral is tomorrow?"

"Tomorrow," Aunt Guinevere said. "And tonight Jessica must see him. It is the custom."

The procession was headed by Cousin John, holding high his candelabrum. Her aunt followed with folded hands, pacing as solemnly as a priestess. As they passed through darkened halls and drafty rooms, Jess knew that this was all stagecraft, all for an effect, and, like many of her cousin's efforts, it went just a little too far. By the time they had climbed the great staircase and reached the room, she was calm and collected.

It was the master bedroom of the house—Arthur Tregarth's room. High-ceilinged and large, with high windows opening onto the sea view, it was sparsely furnished now except with shadows. Candles burned, their prayer-shaped flames unnaturally still in the airless chamber. They shone on the face of the old man who lay, not in his coffin, but on the bed where he had lain in life.

A heavy-set, middle-aged woman in black rose silently from her chair as they entered. She inclined her head and slipped out of the room; and Jessica took four steps and stood looking down, for the first and last time, on the face of her father's father.

The hard family features which his daughter alone of his two children had inherited were rendered even harder by his old age; sunken and yellowed by death, they were like those of a bird of prey, with a vast hooked nose, jutting chin, and massive forehead from which the white locks were neatly brushed.

She looked, and waited for some stir of emotion, and felt none. None at all, neither bitterness for a wrong which had never been hers, and whose truth she would never know, nor tenderness for a blood tie which was meaningless without love. She wondered if she was expected to touch him, or kiss his forehead; and decided that nothing on earth could make her do so. She stepped back, meeting her aunt's eyes squarely; and the older woman's features showed a certain distant respect.

"It is the custom here to sit with the dead. I don't suppose you'll want to."

"No, I do not," Jess said, and again got that odd flicker of respect.

"Good night, then," her aunt said.

Cousin John followed with alacrity.

"Ghoulish old custom," he whispered, as soon as the door had been closed. "Can't change them; easier to go along with them, avoid as much as one can. Well, here's your chamber, Jessie; want me to look for ghosts under the bed?"

While she was still trying to think of a suitable retort, John turned his weapons on David.

"By the by, old man, that ring of Grandfather's . . ."

"Yes?"

"Have you ever taken a close look at it? A really close look?"

"No. Why?"

"There's some old family tradition about it," John said dreamily. "All rot, probably, but since the will's going to be read tomorrow—"

"Did Mr. Tregarth leave the ring to you? Is that what you're trying to imply?"

"Not trying to imply anything, dear boy." Cousin John's eyes opened wider; in the light of the candle, which he was holding at chest level, the effect of the deepening eye sockets, with their inner shine, was distinctly unnerving. "I don't know what Grandfather meant to do with the ring. But I do know he asked Jessie to bring it along—didn't he, Cousin? So I presume he had something in mind."

Jess felt sorry for David; she could feel his brain spinning as he tried to discover the convolutions within convolutions which might be Cousin John's latest plot. She didn't know what he was up to either, but, like David, she felt sure he was up to something. After a brief pause David said, "This family tradition. What is it?"

"Just a silly old rhyme."

"What's the rhyme?" David persisted.

"The rhyme. Let's see, now; I think it goes something like this:

> *Tall knights and fair queens,*
> *Three and three;*
> *What left they on the highland*
> *Hard by the western sea?*
> *A king and a crown and a long sword,*
> *And a son for me."*

The two men contemplated one another across the candle flame like Druids over a fire; the blend of suspicion and duplicity in the two faces would have amused Jess at any other time.

"Very obscure," said David. "Well. We'll find out tomorrow, won't we?"

"Right, right, right. Nighty night, Jessie. Going my way, Dave?"

Jess watched them go off down the corridor side

by side, her cousin's slimmer shape beside David's ambling height. A turn in the corridor cut them off from her sight, and the retreating candle flame cast grotesque shadows back against the wall. Then it vanished; the hall went dark; and Jess felt with frantic fingers for her light switch.

It was not until she started to undress that she realized what should have been obvious much earlier— that the tower room boasted no private bath. However, there was a screen, formerly a handsome Japanese design on oiled silk, now tattered and torn. Behind it were several objects which she recognized with amazement, and then a giggle. There was even water in the pitcher, and she was glad to see it; not even for clean teeth would she have ventured out into the dark corridor that night.

She extracted from her bag the most exotic of her nightgowns, wondering what uncensored impulse had prompted her to buy it; it had yards of material in the skirt and practically none in the bodice, and the material was all sheer. She hadn't had the nerve to wear it before. But tonight her morale needed all the help it could get.

There was no mirror in the room, but she viewed all of herself that was visible to her with satisfaction. The tap on the door caught her by surprise and, naturally, she did not have her robe. The door opened before she had time to find it, or to say anything; she froze in the middle of the room, arms crossed over her top, while David sneaked in and closed the door. He turned, his fingers at his lips, and stayed in that position, staring.

"Well?" Jess said, after a while.

"Very well indeed," David replied, and came toward her.

Jess scuttled away and found her robe on the floor by the bed. She struggled into it.

"Now stop that," she snapped, evading his hands. "This is no time for—for that."

"Any time is the time for that."

"With that old man lying dead, practically next door—"

"For God's sake, don't be so Victorian."

"What did you come here for?"

"I forget," said David, reaching.

"David, don't. I mean it. I mean . . ."

The next few minutes were wordless, though not exactly silent. Eventually Jess freed her mouth long enough to say something about the lights; and David answered, indistinctly but with conviction, that he had no objection whatever to the lights. Presently the glaring ceiling bulb became only a mild distraction against her closed lids, then was not even noticed in the quivering darkness; and suddenly something brushed heavily against the leaded window sixty feet off the ground and a ghastly high screech shattered Jessica's mood. She sprang up with an echoing scream, banged her forehead sharply on something, and found herself upright and shaking in the middle of the floor.

David was sitting on the edge of the bed, staring at her over the fingers which were covering his mouth and nose. His eyes were enormous, luminous with what looked like tears.

"David—what happened?"

David removed his hands and very delicately

seized the tip of his nose between thumb and fore-finger. He wriggled it. Tears overflowed his eyes and ran down his cheeks.

"Oh, David, you're hurt. What was that awful thing?"

David swiped at his wet cheeks with his shirt tail.

"It was," he said, with enormous self-control, "an owl."

"It couldn't have been! Oh . . . Then what are you crying about?"

"Have you never received a sharp blow right on the end of your nose? You have the hardest head I've ever felt."

"I'm—I'm sorry."

"So am I," David made a dash for the window, flung it open, and hung out, breathing. When he pulled his head back in, his color had subsided.

"That should do it. Though if you don't get some clothes on . . ."

Jess groped for the discarded robe, and David went on resignedly, "I can see that the atmosphere in this place is not conductive to—er—that, as you phrase it. The next interruption may be a skeletal hand. I came for the ring, actually. Get it for me."

"David, are you thinking of that rhyme?" Jess reached for her purse. "You think it has some meaning?"

"The rhyme? He made it up, probably on the spur of the moment."

"What? How do you know?"

"Am I," David demanded of the air, "about to be wed to an illiterate? I thought America was full of Tolkien fans."

"What kind of fans?"

"Do, please, stop saying, 'What?' J. R. R. Tolkien, author of *The Hobbit* and *The Lord of the Rings*, one of the literary masterpieces of this century. I'll get you a copy; if you don't like it, I probably won't marry you after all. Cousin John's rhyme was inspired by one of the verses in the Ring trilogy. I expect that's what suggested it to him—*Ring*—ring, follow me?"

"Oh, no."

"Oh, yes. The original goes:

> *Tall ships and tall kings*
> *Three times three,*
> *What brought they from the foundered land,*
> *Over the flowing sea?*
> *Seven stars and seven stones,*
> *And one white tree.*

"The parallels are pretty obvious."

"Oh, gosh." Jess sat down on the bed. "Well, then, why do you want the ring?"

"I don't, especially. I just want to be sure you haven't it—or to be more precise, I want to be sure Cousin John is sure you haven't. His ambiguous remarks meant something; if I didn't know him so well, I'd think he was trying to warn us. Let me think; it's such an effort keeping one step ahead of that twister. . . ."

"But you told him already that you had the ring."

"I know, I know. Maybe he didn't believe me. Maybe he'd rather steal it from me than from you. Maybe he wants to save himself the trouble of searching for it. Wait a minute. . . ."

"Well, he's learned one thing, by your coming here," Jess said. She shivered.

"That up until now you had the ring. But then why—good God, Jess, that was a warning! Tomorrow the will's going to be read. If, as your jolly cousin implies, the old man left the ring to someone, or some institution, the villains know I'll meekly hand it over to the lawyer like a good little citizen. After tomorrow, the ring will be in a safe, or bank, or someplace less accessible."

"Good heavens! They'll try to steal it tonight!"

"I certainly would, if I were in their shoes." David paced, chewing his knuckles. "Why did he warn us? Or did he? The more I think about this, the less I like it. Give me the ring, will you?"

She held it out to him with cowardly alacrity; and as he studied her, perched on the edge of the bed, her hair in tousled curls and her eyes wide with alarm, David's worried look softened into a smile.

"Come over here and hand it to me," he said. "If I come to you, I may never leave."

She came, with a rush that ended in his arms; as he rocked her back and forth she felt his laughter against her hair.

"We are obviously made for each other," he said softly. "Mad, both of us, mad as hatters. Darling, in about three minutes I'm going to leave as conspicuously as possible. Cousin J. is undoubtedly peeping through his keyhole, and we want to be sure he sees . . . what we want him to see."

"And in the intervening three minutes?"

By actual count it was ten minutes later when David flung the door open and stamped off down the hall. Jess's mood was as feckless as his; she stood in the doorway trying not to laugh. At the corner he turned to blow her a kiss; then he bent over and dropped something that hit the floor with a musical ring; and David disappeared around the corner, cursing audibly. She heard him ringing and cursing all the way down the other hall—the hall that passed Cousin John's door. Jess grinned. Unable to resist, she tiptoed down her own corridor to the corner.

At first she saw nothing except blackness and heard only David's retreat; he was still in full theatrical bloom. Then she shrank back. A thin streak of yellow light had appeared on the wall of the corridor she faced.

The door that was opening opened toward her, so she could see nothing of the person within. But shortly the streak of light widened into a rectangle of yellow, with Cousin John's aristocratic features silhouetted, black and paper-sharp, upon it.

The explosion was not as loud as it seemed; it merely resounded through the silent house like an atomic bomb—the crash of something heavy onto a hard surface, and a loud, cut-off shout.

It was its unexpectedness rather than its violence that paralyzed Jess for the first, important seconds. She could still see her cousin's profile, outthrust and listening, and she couldn't understand how he could be in his room, while David was . . . David! Suddenly she was running, her bare feet pattering on the wooden floor. She ran mindlessly, straight into the waiting arms of her cousin. His grasp tightened as she struggled, and she heard him laugh softly.

"Let me go," she gasped.

"But you'll hurt yourself running round in the dark," he said reasonably. "Calm yourself; then we'll trot down there together and see what's happened. Not that I'm not enjoying this, mind you . . ."

This remark quieted her more quickly than any other method; and after a moment he let her go. His eyes moved speculatively up and down her body as she stood in the light from his doorway, and she realized, flushing from toes to hair, that she had forgotten her robe.

When he had finished his inspection, he put one hand on his shirt front and bowed genteelly.

"For the first time I am moved to regret the laws regarding consanguinity," he said. "Now, then, Coz, shall we see what obstacle your clumsy fiancé has encountered? I do think he might have been more discreet. Admittedly, moral standards have relaxed, but a lady's reputation—"

"Shut up," said Jess regrettably. She brushed past him, but he was right, she couldn't go quickly; once out of the light from his room, she couldn't see a thing. She heard his measured footsteps behind her; and then, as she stumbled over an object on the floor, his hands caught her shoulders and kept her erect.

"There's a light here somewhere," he said easily. "Stand still, you little fool, or you'll brain yourself."

The light went on, momentarily blinding her; then, with a cry, she fell to her knees beside David's prostrate body.

NINE

"Then shall the dust return to the earth as it was;
And the spirit shall return unto God who gave it."

Standing between her aunt and her cousin in the narrow pew, Jess was reminded of the last church service she had attended in England. The contrast was extreme. There were no angelic voices here, soaring up into vast vaults of stone; only the frail, reedy voice of the minister reading, without much conviction, the words of the ancient Service for the Dead.

Dark and small and heavy as it was, the parish church of St. Ives—one of the thousands of obscure virgin saints—had an austere beauty. The tracery of the old windows was splendid, though the newer glass looked like something out of a suburban hall of the 1920s; and the devout ladies of the parish had a real gift for flower arranging. Jess doubted that anyone in the family had bothered about special flowers; she certainly hadn't. So the white and purple clusters that overflowed the vases by the altar were probably the regular weekly arrangements.

They were all the more lovely for being ordinary, seasonal garden flowers, lilac of every imaginable shade for the most part; and the colors were certainly appropriate.

But the glory of the church, which would have redeemed uglier architecture than the sturdy fifteenth-century sandstone, was the wagon roof, with carved, painted beams and golden-haired angels.

Throughout the long day, with its depressing ceremonies, Jess's mind kept returning to those angels. They acted as a focal point on which her restless, worried imagination could settle, and find a kind of reassurance. They were ugly angels, really; stiff, badly carved, and recently repainted in colors as glaring as the original shades had been, cherry red, bright gold. What quality was it that redeemed this crude, local work and made it beautiful? For the angels were also beautiful angels. Beautiful, not because of the craftsmanship, but because of the certainty which had guided the craftsmen. Their belief formed their works: belief in God and in hell and in a specific devil, with horns and a tail—and in specific angels, whose golden hair was not yellow, nor flaxen, nor blonde—but gold.

Jess doubted whether the same sort of faith moved any of the members of their party. Aunt Guinevere looked like a nun in unrelieved black, with her set features hidden behind a veil. Cousin John, as usual, was a model of propriety. He wore formal morning clothes, and his fair head bent solicitously over his mother's shrouded form as he supported her from the church. But once during the service, when the minister referred to the deceased's virtues as father and husband, he had caught Jess's eye and let his right lid droop in an unmistakable wink.

Jess literally hadn't known what to wear. She owned one black dress, which was backless and three inches short of her kneecap; it would not have been appropriate even if it had been in her suitcase instead of in a closet three thousand miles to the west. Borrowing or buying a dress was both hypocritical and impractical, so, in the end, she had settled for white, a simple straight shift which, at least, possessed sleeves, and a white lace scarf which she had brought with vague ideas of Roman churches later that summer. Studying herself in the wavy mirror in the parlor, she saw her eyes enormous and shadowed under the soft folds of lace, and guiltily wiped off her bright lipstick. On second thought, she replaced it. She had no harsh feelings toward the old man who lay dead upstairs; neither did she feel grief, or guilt that she felt no grief. Let the villagers stare, and call her a cold, hard foreigner.

But the glances and murmured greetings were all friendly. There were many mourners, most of them contemporaries of her aunt's; there could not be many of the old man's friends still living. From the conglomerate of unfamiliar faces only one stood out: that of Mr. Simon Pendennis, who had a face like a wrinkled prune, a lean old body as straight as a lance, and a pair of wicked, lively, black eyes. He was a memorable figure; but she noticed him primarily because he was introduced as the family lawyer.

When they met at the church, Mr. Pendennis gave her a handclasp that made her flinch. She had barely had time to introduce David before they entered the building, and Mr. Pendennis's glance made it clear that he did not think much of David. Jess had to admit that her "fiancé" did not look prepossessing. The black band pinned around his arm did little to counteract the color of his bright-blue suit; sartorial elegance, as she had noted, was not one of David's strong points. His appearance was not improved by the fading bruises of his earlier encounters with Cousin John and Friend, and the clumsy bandage on his brow, fastened by her own fair and unskilled hands, completed the picture of a city tough.

When they settled down in the library after the funeral, Mr. Pendennis's eyes kept straying to David with fascinated distaste. Seating himself behind the heavy table, he drew a document from his breast pocket, slapped it down onto the mahogany, and announced that he had no intention of reading it.

"Sum it up, so you can all understand it," he said, glaring at them with a lawyer's contempt for the laity. Jess had heard about beetling brows, but this was the first time she had ever seen any. She was finding it hard to concentrate on the will, so intrigued was she by the thick white clumps of hair over the lawyer's eyes.

No one objected, so the lawyer went on.

"Legacies to the servants," he rumbled. "Fifty pounds. Not many servants left, heh? All debts to be paid, et cetera . . . The rest is simple enough. Perhaps too simple. I don't know how familiar you are with your grandfather's situation, Miss Tregarth—"

"I don't know anything about it," Jess said. "I don't care, either."

Mr. Pendennis put his fingers together.

"That is a most peculiar comment," he said bluntly. "Why do you say that?"

Jess looked at her aunt, who looked coldly back; at her cousin, whose smile held more than its usual share of malice; at David, rumpled and disreputable, paler than usual and altogether wonderful.

"He didn't owe me anything that he could give me now," she said steadily. "People owe children— all other people, but especially their children—some things. Love, perhaps, until they prove they don't deserve it. But not money. Not this way. I'd love to have had a grandfather; my mother's father died before I was born. I don't harbor any ill will at all. But I don't want his money. I'm sorry, I can't say it right. . . ."

Unexpectedly, it was the old lawyer who responded, and, though his rocky features did not change, there was a milder gleam in the black eyes.

"I understand quite well. And, may I say, I respect you for your sentiments."

Jess was so surprised and grateful that tears came to her eyes. It was the first softening emotion she had felt that day, and she was grateful to the lawyer for evoking it.

"Arthur Tregarth was a hard man," the lawyer went on. "He was my old friend and my old enemy, but no one could call him sentimental. And your father, my dear, was an impetuous, weak fool. We need not resurrect that long-past quarrel, but it was

not to the credit of either participant. Your grandfather despised his son; but he did come to regret not
knowing his granddaughter. That was why, with my
knowledge and at my suggestion, he wrote to you.
But his intention was to meet you, nothing more.
There was no restitution he could have made, if he
had wanted to. Do I make myself clear?"

"You mean there isn't any money," Jess said. She
was beginning to like Mr. Pendennis; he, too, believed in calling a spade a spade.

"Precisely," the lawyer said calmly. "He left to you
some small investments, which were his sole source
of income except for an annuity which dies with
him. They will not bring in more than two hundred
pounds a year. The rest of the property goes to your
cousin, who is the residuary legatee. That means—"

"I know. It means he gets everything that isn't
specifically left to someone else."

"In nonlegal language, that is approximately
correct."

The short silence was broken by Cousin John,
who rose with his customary grace.

"Thank you, Mr. Pendennis. May I offer you a
glass of sherry before you go?"

The lawyer grunted.

"At least you inherit some noble vintages," he
said, holding the slim glass up to the light.

"Four bottles of this left," said Cousin John
wryly. "The old gentleman—God rest his soul—
calculated his demise quite accurately."

"Drank most of it himself, did he?" Pendennis
made an abrupt barking sound which was evidently
meant to be a laugh. "Quite in character."

Her cousin smiled; catching Jess's eye, he said, "Shocked, dear Coz, by our disrespect? Thought you Americans were more realistic. Darling Jess, why pretend? Our mutual ancestor was something of a bounder. When he inherited, the place was in flourishing condition. He sold most of the land and spent the capital in riotous living. Correct, Mr. Pendennis?"

"Quite accurate," the old lawyer said calmly.

"Which means," John continued, "that there's nothing left. I probably won't even be able to keep the house."

David stirred.

"Will you have to sell the house to pay the death duties?"

"No," the lawyer answered. "Mr. Tregarth made provision for that outlay. But there is, literally, nothing left. I would myself advise John to sell, if he can find a buyer; the house is in need of repairs, and there is not enough land remaining to be productive."

"No one would buy a moldering pile like this," John said carelessly.

"No private individual, perhaps; but it might do as a hotel or institution of some sort."

This optimistic suggestion seemed to annoy Cousin John; he scowled, and Jess, thinking she had seen another sign of his family feeling which he was embarrassed to own, said gently, "This seems to be a popular vacation area. Would it be possible for you to run the house as a hotel yourself?"

That was the wrong thing to say. Cousin John transferred his scowl to Jess and said curtly, "It would require a great deal of money to finance such a thing. Even supposing that I wanted to see the house so degraded."

Jess caught the old lawyer's eye, and saw a gleam of frosty amusement which made her refrain from further comment. Suddenly she was aware, not of fear, but of a vast distaste. The dark, dusty library and the unspoken antagonism of her relatives repelled her; she felt a need for sunshine and fresh air.

"That seems to conclude our business," Mr. Pendennis said. "John, I'll just take that box with me, if you will put it into my car."

"Box?" Cousin John repeated guilelessly.

"The box of artifacts. I'm sure your grandfather must have spoken of it. He told me years ago that he was leaving it to me."

"Oh, of course. The objects he found in his digs."

"The box is mentioned specifically in the will," said Mr. Pendennis coldly.

"Of course, sir. Let me think. . . . Mother, what did we do with that box?"

Without speaking, Aunt Guinevere inclined her head and John went to the bookshelves on that side of the room.

The library was lined with bookshelves on three of its four sides, except for the spaces occupied by doors and by a cavernous fireplace. One section of shelving held, not books, but a miscellaneous collection of objects of stone and pottery. From the lowest shelf Cousin John lifted a large box, made of dullish metal. It was two feet long and about a foot deep, and Cousin John carried it as if it were heavy.

He deposited the box on the table in front of the

lawyer, who had risen to his feet, and who now bent over the box with undisguised curiosity and eagerness.

"Have a look, sir," said Cousin John gravely. "Make sure nothing is missing."

The old lawyer glared at him.

"Nothing worth stealing, I daresay," he mumbled. "Arthur always was a braggart. The prizes of his collection, indeed. . . . Still, we may as well have a look."

The box was unlocked; its lid fell back at a touch of the old man's hand. The hand was actually trembling as it removed the first object and placed it tenderly on the table; Jess found the elderly lawyer's excitement rather pathetic.

The objects, as they came out of the box, did not seem like the sort of thing that would produce such rapt attention. Several chunks of broken pottery; a large scrap of rusted, blackened metal; three greenish lumps; a collection of bones; a bronze arrowhead.

When Jess looked up in some disgust from the collection, she was amazed to see that Mr. Pendennis had gone pale. She stood up and walked over to the table. At close range the miscellaneous collection looked even worse, but the lawyer stood staring at it with the expression of a man who has been dealt a stunning blow.

"So he did find something," he muttered. "It's impossible! All these years. . . . But where?"

"What is it?" Jess asked. "What are these things?"

Pendennis merely shook his head dazedly. David, who had joined them at the table, picked up one of the chunks of metal which glowed with a brighter gleam than the rest.

"That looks like gold."

"Yes." The lawyer spoke carelessly, but his long gnarled fingers twitched, as if he were aching to snatch the fragment away from David. "A scrap, no more. Meaningless. . . . Ah—do you know anything about archaeology, Mr. er—um?"

"Not a thing," David said guilelessly. "But I've got a pal who lectures on British prehistory at Cardiff."

"I take it that these are the results of Grandfather's excavations," Jess persisted. "They don't look very exciting, I must say. Are they worth anything?"

"Completely worthless," said the lawyer firmly. "Although in a sense they did cost a great deal of money—thousands of pounds of what might have been your inheritance, Miss Tregarth."

"Thousands of pounds! I didn't know digging up a lot of dirt could be so expensive."

"You have the usual layman's ignorance," said Pendennis. "One doesn't simply go out with a spade and plunge in, you know. Nowadays all sorts of technical equipment is necessary, not only for the actual removal of the soil, but for treating and preserving the objects one finds, and for surveying preparatory to digging. Why, last year Arthur purchased one of these soil anomaly detectors, instruments which can indicate the existence of metal, or of filled-in trenches and postholes, under the soil. That alone cost—"

"Two thousand five hundred pounds," said Cousin John. "Know anyone who'd like to purchase a used soil anomaly detector?"

He spoke lightly; but his eye was on Mr. Pendennis, and Jess saw a spark, cannily suppressed, appear in the old man's own eyes.

"Don't blame me for your grandfather's folly, my boy. I did my best to dissuade him."

"But I get the impression that you are also interested in archaeology," David said. "Why did you try to discourage him?"

Pendennis snorted.

"Because he was quite unreasonable about his researches. Oh, he discovered some interesting material—beaker fragments, Roman weapons, medieval artifacts. But he was not interested in scientific archaeology. He was obsessed with his—er—obsession. Just fancy, Mr. er—um—the old fool thought he was going to find the site of Camelot!"

"That is a shame." David shook his head. "Even I know that the real Camelot is in Somerset. It's been in the news lately. What's the name of the place? Oh, like the chocolates. Cadbury."

"Nonsense," Mr. Pendennis exclaimed. "You've been taken in by all the sensationalism too. There are solid traditions which place Camelot in Cornwall. No, my dear fellow; I have a much sounder reason for knowing that Arthur would never find Camelot here. You see, Camelot is on my property."

David took the curve at sixty, and Jess sat on her hands to keep from grabbing the wheel.

"I share your urge to leave that place," she shouted over the roar of the wind. "But let's do it alive, can't we?"

David took his foot off the accelerator and the

car slowed to a pace more suited to the narrow road
and the negligible visibility. It was the most dangerous time of day for driving, near dusk, and a fog
hovered over the pastures of Cornwall. Or was it
still Cornwall? Jess tried to catch a sign, but there
were no markers on this lonely road.

They had been driving for two hours, after a departure whose abruptness had left even Jess gasping. David had turned down the invitation of Mr.
Pendennis to come to his place, which adjoined the
Tregarth land, and have a look at Camelot. He had
refused Cousin John's halfhearted invitation to stay,
at least, overnight. He had wanted out, and he had
gotten out, without finesse or good manners.

Jess thought it might be nice, for once, to know
where she was going, but she was not deeply concerned. Even a foggy dark English road, on a rainy
night, with a mad stranger at the wheel of the car,
was more restful than what she had been through.
She had not forgotten the threats of the last week,
nor the still unsolved questions she and David had
argued so often; she had simply dismissed them.
Probably she would never know what had been behind her cousin's actions. She didn't want to know.

She glanced at her companion's intent profile,
with the rakish white bandage and the nose jutting
forward like the prow of a ship; and an unaccustomed shyness came over her as she remembered
certain episodes. One good thing, at least, had come
out of all the confusion—assuming that David felt
as she did, and she was sure he must. Most of the
relief she felt was on his account. The ridiculous

bandage reminded her that, although they had lost the ring, they had kept something more important—their lives. And the danger must be over now; with the ring gone, and her grandfather dead, there could be no reason to harass them further.

Odd about the ring, though, she thought lazily. All the plotting and pursuit and bloodshed, for an ugly chunk of meaningless jewelry which her grandfather had not even bothered to mention in his will. Yet the plotters had wanted it badly enough to attack David within the house itself. The attacker must have been Algernon; but where had he been the rest of the time? Well, it was a big house. Yet Cousin John had . . .

With a surge of annoyance she made herself stop thinking. It was over, over and done with. There were more attractive matters to contemplate now. They would be stopping soon, for the night—the first night they would be together without fear or suspicion since they had met. Her mind wandered into primrose paths. . . .

Then David said, "Mind driving all night?"

Jess felt as if he had poured a pail of ice water over her.

"Yes, I do," she said in a strangled voice.

"Really?" He glanced at her casually. "Tired?"

"Yes."

"Oh. In that case . . . I suppose it's just as well. I must ring Cliff."

"David."

"Mmm?"

"Where are we going now?"

"Where? Oh. Why, Cadbury, of course."

He began to whistle. Jess ground her teeth together. The gesture failed to relieve her feelings, much less enlighten her as to the significance of that name. It sounded vaguely familiar; but try as she might she could not remember where she had heard it, nor what its significance might be for the quest which David had, clearly, never abandoned.

Two days later she was none the wiser, though she stood on the heights of Cadbury Castle itself. It did not resemble a castle. It looked like, and was, a cow pasture on a hill. Rough high grass covered all of the plateau except for a section in the center of the area which was enclosed by a fence. The grass inside the enclosure was even higher.

From the little village of South Cadbury, with its gray stone houses and thatched roofs, they had climbed a steep, muddy lane which got steeper and muddier the higher they went, between thickly massed trees and bushes, until they reached the cleared crest.

It had rained all the previous day and this afternoon was still partially overcast; the shapely clouds and moving shadows on the plain below gave a sense of drama to the placid beauty of the landscape. Another high rise, greenly wooded, raised itself up across the valley. Except for that, the countryside for miles around was flat, spotted with peaceful villages and with the pale puffy shapes of fruit trees in bloom. In the distance, clear to the imagination, if not to the sight, was the towering height of Glastonbury Tor, where the Cup of the Last Supper had been hidden; Glastonbury, in the Island of Avalon, the last resting place of Arthur and his guilty queen.

None of the Tennysonian Romanticism of Glastonbury haunted Cadbury Hill. Jess glanced from the red-and-white cow which was trying to look over her shoulder to the irate, bearded youth who was expostulating with David.

"Dragging me all the way down here," he bellowed. "Right in the middle of a lecture series! I could have written you a letter!"

Not only was he bearded; he was thickly thatched—like the cottages, Jess thought, eyeing the furious youth's uncombed head. At least he was sensibly attired for the site; his unpressed trousers were tucked into high boots which were thick with mud. Though there was a stiff breeze on the height, he was in shirt sleeves, his jacket slung over his shoulder and held by one hand. The other hand, shaped into a fist, was at present just under David's nose.

"I was in a hurry," David said mildly. His own black locks were blowing in the breeze, and his attire was only slightly more formal than his friend's. He wore a jacket, but no tie, and in his haste to climb the mysterious hill he had tramped through mud up to his knees. "Stop raving, you maniac," he went on. "You're here now, so you may as well talk."

The maniac tugged at his beard. Then he glanced at Jess, and after a moment the beard split in two and a set of even white teeth appeared in the middle of it.

"Where did you meet this fellow, Miss Tregarth?

You look like such a nice girl, too. . . . Ah, well. Precisely what is it you want to know?"

"Precisely," said David precisely, "what details define, identify, or characterize, an Arthurian site?"

For a second Jess was afraid the bearded youth was going to explode. He calmed himself with a visible effort.

"First, get one thing clear. There is no such thing as an Arthurian site. There may not have been any such person as Arthur. Wait!" He raised a long, peremptory finger. "What you probably mean to ask about is a site dated to the period which would be the right period for a character such as the historical Arthur might have been if there had ever been such a character."

David opened his mouth, closed it, and looked blank.

"I haven't the faintest idea what you're talking about," Jess said.

The young man looked at her and seemed to find the sight soothing.

"Well, see here. You know that the Arthur of Malory and Tennyson, the chivalrous king in clanking armor, is impossible. Or do you? Oh, God. Let's start from the beginning. Alfred, Lord Tennyson, was a poet."

Jess couldn't resist. She struck an attitude, swept her hand across her brow, and remarked,

> *"That grey king, a ghost, whose name,*
> *Streams like a cloud, man shaped,*
> *from mountain peak,*
> *And cleaves to cairn and cromlech . . ."*

"Close enough," said Cliff wanly. "Thank you, love, for putting me in my place. How are you on Nennius?"

"You've got me there."

"What a beautiful thought."

"Don't encourage him," David said.

"Nennius, monkish chronicler of the ninth century. Mentions Arthur. Then there are Welsh sources. . . . Ah, Hell, what's the use of talking to you people? Point is, after the Romans left Britain, in 411 A.D., the southern part of the country was partially Romanized—villas and towns, old retired legionnaires, an upper class who spoke Latin and took baths and wore togas. When the Saxons invaded, these people appealed to Rome for help. They didn't get it. The Saxons came on. According to the exceedingly unreliable contemporary sources, the Saxons encountered opposition from a general of the combined British forces, whose name was Arthur, or Artos, or something. We're in the fifth century, the so-called Dark Ages; very little is known about this period. But . . . a Romanized Briton, trained in Roman methods of warfare, might have led a troop of mounted soldiers—knights in armor, if you want to call 'em that, but not blokes wearing sheets of tinware, just local boys equipped with the weapons of Celtic and Roman Britain.

"All this nonsense about Camelot is . . ." He glanced at Jess, and said mildly, "nonsense. Cadbury—this here—is a hill fort, one of about seventy such sites, which were fortified in the Iron Age. Prehistoric earthworks, that's all they were. The Romans took them when they overran Britain, and they were still here when the Romans left. Such sites would be logical places to refortify against later invaders such as the Saxons. And at Cadbury, as well as at other places, we've found evidence of fifth-century occupation. That's what the newspapers are going on about, that and an old tradition which identifies Cadbury with Camelot. Or do I mean vice versa?"

"That's all?" David looked slightly dazed by this spate of information.

"Well, Cadbury's the biggest of the fifth-century sites," Cliff admitted. "Then there's the Tintagel pottery—found at Tintagel, as you might guess, and other places, as well as Cadbury. It's related to pottery from the Mediterranean area—we date the site from these scraps—and it suggests that the man who was in charge here was rich enough to enjoy and afford imported wine."

"Pots," David muttered.

"Potsherds," Cliff corrected. "Meat bones. A cloak pin or two. Rusty scraps of knife and sword blades. No coins, no inscriptions. And some holes in the ground." He swept one arm out in an inclusive gesture which took in the mild-faced cows, the tall grass, and the circle of raised turf which surrounded the brow of the hill. "That's the fortification, that raised section. Part is Roman wall, part is Saxon; the middle bit, the one the Arthurians are so hysterical about, could be fifth century. Or early Saxon. Or late Roman. There are some postholes, trenches—no buildings, most of the structures of that period would be of wood and thatch. Perishable." His voice broke. "I don't know why the *hell* you dragged me all the way down here for this."

A friendly cow, moved by his distress, wandered up and leaned on him. He staggered. "Get away, you brute," he said, and hit the cow. It lowed irritably and left.

Jess was struck with a brilliant idea.

"Didn't I see a pub in the village?"

The melancholy searcher for Camelot looked at her.

"That's the first intelligent question I've heard today," he said, and led the way down the hill.

Much later they dropped him off in Glastonbury, where he could catch a bus that would eventually take him home; and on his way out of town David parked the car, suddenly and illegally, in front of the prosaic wooden gates that led to the Abbey ruins. Jess followed him along the alley and through the turnstile; they stood at one end of the green park and looked at the noble walls, glowing in the sunset. The flowering thorns of Glastonbury looked like fallen clouds.

David stood with hands in his pockets and lips pursed, but his expression was sober.

"You've figured it out, haven't you," Jess said.

"I think so. It's mad—completely mad—and comic—and, in an odd fashion, rather beautiful! All based on another insanity, an old man's senile dream . . ."

"Dreams have their beauty, too. Even senile dreams, I guess."

"We'll know, in the due course of time. Shall we dream our senile dreams together, Jess?"

He took one hand out of his pocket and put his arm around her shoulders. Her head against the hard muscle of his upper arm, Jess looked up at him.

"That's the most romantic proposal I've ever had," she said, and saw his face change, the mouth taking on an expression that made her knees go weak.

"We'd better get out of here," he said. "I don't think the ghosts of Glastonbury would object, but we may shock the tourists. And I may be collecting a summons for illegal parking."

"Aren't you going to tell me?" Jess trotted meekly at his heels.

A slow, catlike smile replaced David's sobriety.

"No, I think I'll show you instead. Would you mind . . ."

"Driving all night."

"Poor girl." He laughed exuberantly. "No; I've a fancy to spend the night in Glastonbury. At the pilgrims' inn. It seems appropriate. Just how appropriate, you shall see, tomorrow night."

They came into Cornwall by night, under a wayward moon that raced across the sky behind threatening clouds. It was well past midnight when David turned up the steep lane. By the rusted iron gates he stopped the car and switched off the engine.

"From here on we go like little mice," he said. "If you must talk, whisper. But don't talk."

"I'm going crazy with curiosity," Jess complained. "Can't you tell me a little something? What are we going to find? What makes you so sure we'll find anything? I'm scared."

David had cuddled the car close up against the

stone wall, so close he couldn't open his door. He shoved her over and slid across the seat.

"I'm not absolutely sure we'll find what I'm looking for, but I suspect they won't waste time now that they believe we've gone for good. And it would take far too long to tell you what I suspect. You wouldn't believe me; this is so far out that it must be seen to be believed. So—let's go along and see it."

They were both dressed for prowling, David in a dark sweater and slacks, Jess in a similar costume, with a scarf flattening her curls. David took her by the shoulders and looked her over. Jess tilted her head back and batted her eyelids at him. His mouth curved up and he gave her a quick hard kiss and let her go.

"None of that, now. Let's conceal your distracting beauty."

He stooped and came up with a handful of dirt which he applied to Jess's cheeks. Then he smeared his hands over his own face.

"That should do it. We don't want to be seen, though I don't think there's any real danger. Remember, no talking."

They met their first block at once. The gates were locked this time, with a rusted chain and a very new, shiny padlock. David climbed the wall, at the cost of ripped trousers and scraped knuckles. Lying flat across the top, he dragged Jess up, and then lowered her down inside. They set off across the grounds.

The softness of the soil, after the recent rains, made their progress almost inaudible. Jess felt sure it was also invisible; the overgrown state of the landscaping provided ample cover, and the moon-light, flickering on and off like a bad light bulb, was confusing to vision. She trotted along after David, obeying his peremptory hand signals, stopping, crawling, and running as he did. She was damp and breathless before they came in sight of the house.

It crouched on its rise of ground, a humped heap of darkness against the mottled sky. Lit by pallid moonlight, the towers looked like ivory horns on a massive beast's head. The house was dark, except for one square of light high up in the façade; it looked like the cover of one of Jessica's favorite books.

David crouched in the shadow of a gnarled lilac bush. One of the heavy, hanging sprays of blossom brushed Jess's cheek and she turned her face into the perfumed wetness.

To her relief, and her surprise, David did not head for the house. She had never seen anything, not even the dentist's office, that she wanted less to enter. But she was completely baffled when her guide cut off toward the back of the house and the sea cliff. It took another half hour of slow, hard go-ing before she realized where they were going, and still she did not know why.

Under the shadow of the belt of trees which fringed the far pasture David stood upright and pro-ceeded less cautiously. Any noises they made, snap-ping twigs, or rustling leaves, would be taken for the movements of night animals. It was very dark under the trees; the moonlight sifted through the branches to shape silver lace patterns on the damp ground, but gave little illumination. Jess could hear the sea now, but the muted crash of water far below was almost lost in the keening of the wind in the branches overhead.

"It's going to rain," she whispered.

David made no response to this irrelevant comment. He had reached the edge of the little wood and peered out from behind the shelter of a thick bole. Jess peered out from behind the shelter of his shoulder. There was nothing to be seen except the pasture, and the ragged slope of a slight rise just ahead. But she heard sounds which were not made by night animals, nor surf, nor wind. They were strange sounds, like little bells ringing softly. Like metal sounding on metal or stone . . .

To her disgust, David dropped flat on his stomach and began to crawl. She tried to cheat, bending over as she walked, but David caught her at it and made threatening gestures. Jess groaned as she lowered herself to the ground, which seemed to contain every undesirable feature ground could contain— patches of mud, sharp stones, prickly weeds.

They inched along, one after the other, up the slight slope and over it. David's hand in her hair stopped Jess, who was concentrating on prickly weeds and could see nothing farther away than two inches ahead of her nose. David was now squatting on his heels, and she lifted herself up to a similar position.

In front of her was a low stone wall which surrounded the pasture where her grandfather had carried on his expensive archaeological activities. And someone seemed to be archaeologizing, if that was the word, now. The semimusical clinking sounds made sense to her, now that she had that identification in mind; they were the sounds of shovels or picks, or some metal implements, on stone.

David need not have bothered to blacken his face; the muddy countenance he turned toward her had picked up so much additional disguise that he was barely recognizable. Jess was admiring the rare collection of botanical specimens that adorned his hair when she realized that she must look just as bad. Thoughts of this sort do very little for a woman's morale, even when she is supposed to be thinking of more important matters, and for a few seconds she missed the meaning of David's dumb show. Finally he grabbed her by the neck and pulled her face up to his.

"Take a look," he hissed, like a stage villain. "But be careful. They're out there, all right."

Their two black faces rose, like spouting mud pots, over the top of the wall. Then Jess forgot dishevelment and discomfort, and stared in utter amazement.

The light was now very poor; the clouds had gathered to hide most of the sky, and only a frail sliver of sly moon peeped through. She made out the workers as two dark shapes, and could see nothing, at first, of what they were working at. Then the moon found an opening in the clouds and the shadows took on form.

The ground was broken by a deep ragged trench, and one of the figures was working in it. As she watched, Jess's brows drew together in a frown of bewilderment.

She had always thought that archaeologists dug things up out of the ground. These men were putting things into it. Not treasure chests, nor dead bodies, nor anything else so *outré*, but—stones. From a pile on one side of the field one figure staggered to the trench carrying a big, shaped stone. He lowered it to the man inside the trench, and went back for more.

This weird procedure went on for ten minutes, while Jess tried to make sense of it. Obviously she was missing something; the two men couldn't possibly be building a wall under the ground, though that was what it looked like.

One of the men was her cousin, and again Jess was moved to something resembling pity, for John had, as usual, the hardest part of the job. He was the stone carrier. The activities of his partner—who must be the objectionable Algernon—were hidden from her, but she was willing to bet they were easier than stone carrying. The blocks were massive things; after ten minutes her cousin was staggering and clutching the stones to his manly chest as if he were afraid of dropping them—which he probably was; if one had landed on his foot it would have smashed half the bones. Yet even in his gasping exhaustion and general misery, he had not lost all his insouciance; dropping the last block on the edge of the trench, he wiped perspiration from his face with his sleeve, and did two steps of a popular dance.

"That's the lot," he said, without troubling to lower his normally low-pitched voice. "Think it's enough?"

"For now. Tomorrow night we'll start on the gate."

Jess heard a suppressed snort from David. The expression on her cousin's face when he heard this depressing news was so disgusted that she wanted to laugh too. He contemplated his muddy, bleeding hands with fastidious disgust, wiped them on the seat of his trousers, and sat down on the ground.

"For the love of God, Freddie, must we have a gate? I thought you said archaeologists never have enough money to dig everything up."

"You ass, we don't know what parts they'll want to dig, and we can hardly limit them without arousing suspicion." A head appeared at the lip of the trench; it was followed by the rest of Freddie. He was the second man, Algernon—the one who had twice flattened David. Jessica's amusement went up in smoke. She never had liked Algernon, and she didn't like Freddie—what a name, almost as bad as Algernon—any better.

Her cousin had collapsed at full length on the ground, and did not see his ally's face; which, Jess thought, was perhaps just as well, for Freddie gave his sensitive associate a look which could have scorched rock.

"You know I've been against this from the start," he grunted, sitting down cross-legged. "Give me a fag, will you?"

An arm and hand, graceful even in their battered state, rose up from the grass and extended a cigarette. Freddie took it and went on with what was evidently a long-standing argument.

"We can drop the whole damned business so far as I'm concerned. It's not too late to go back to my scheme."

"But, dear old boy," said Cousin John's lazy voice from the grasses, "we lose so much lovely, lovely money that way. You don't think the professionals will detect any little errors in our wall, do you?"

The other man shrugged and blew out smoke.

"Some may do. But their criticisms will be denounced by other experts, who will defend us for the sheer fun of attacking their professional rivals. That's precisely the trouble with the lot of them, none of the old fools ever agrees with one another. They're petty-minded, jealous old devils. And gullible! They can make themselves believe anything they want to believe. Look at Piltdown man; the whole bloody scientific world fell hook, line and sinker for a bad fake."

"You ought to know," said Cousin John, in that tone of sweet malice which Jess knew so well.

The comment stung, as he had known it would; Freddie looked at him with a face so ugly that Jess recoiled, even behind the shelter of the wall.

"I've told you that was a lie. That swine Barton kept me from my degree out of pure professional jealousy."

"Professional?" murmured the sly, sweet voice. "Dear Mrs. Barton; how charmingly she administered tea and sympathy. But the rest of us were courteous enough to be discreet."

Jess bit back an exclamation as Freddie's hand darted toward the handle of the pickax which lay next to the ditch. She knew her cousin must have seen the gesture; but his long limbs never moved, and after a second or two, Freddie's fingers loosed their hold.

"You're going to bait someone into murdering you one day," he said.

"Not while I can give that someone his share of half a million pounds," was the contemptuous reply. "Freddie, you have absolutely no sense of humor. You must learn to laugh at yourself, old boy. Now, then, how much more is there to be done here? We've got to let it cook for months, perhaps a year; the sooner we finish the sooner it begins to pay off."

There was another, louder snort of amusement from David, and Jess popped her head down out of sight, poking at him warningly.

"What was that?" asked Freddie; Jess heard a rustle of grass.

"An owl. Sit down, you exhaust me."

"Couldn't be anything else, I suppose." Freddie sat down, producing more rustling noises. "Well, I think we'll stop when we've built the gate. And the grave, of course."

"Look here, damn it all, I thought we'd decided not to have a grave. I mean—one can't have a grave without a body."

"We can have a skeleton easily enough," said his ally contemptuously. "But bones are difficult to fake properly, with the new scientific tests. And they'd have to fit the traditional descriptions—size, age, and that. No, we shan't have a body, but we must have a grave if we're to explain the treasure. I've got it all worked out. An empty grave, robbed in antiquity—a cache of objects, secreted by the thieves in panic as their crime is detected. . . . It makes a lovely tale."

A weary groan from Cousin John was the only

response, and Jess felt that it was safe to take another look. She was beginning to understand now; but she still couldn't believe it.

"We'll finish up tonight by planting the ring," Freddie said briskly. "Before you lose it again."

"That's not fair, I've never actually lost it." Cousin John rose up, stiffly, like a warrior's effigy from a tomb. "The ring, yes. What did I do with it?"

"I shouldn't have given it to you," said Freddie. "After all, I was the one who took the risk of retrieving it."

"Yes, and I have a smallish bone to pick with you on that," Cousin John said. He stood up and began to investigate his pockets.

"That bone's been overly picked. You're too squeamish, Johnny boy. At your insistence, I didn't even damage the fellow much."

"All that blood," said Cousin John. "Nasty. Ah, here it is."

Freddie took the ring and dropped back into the trench. Muffled scrapes and bangs issued from the depths. Standing on the edge, Cousin John balanced himself and peered down.

"I say, don't plant it too far down. That's one item we do want them to find."

"They'll find it." Freddie's head reappeared. "We're going to leave our bits of stone protruding here, remember? The ring will be found at the base of the wall, where it might have been dropped by a panicky thief climbing over."

"Very nice," said John appreciatively. "I can see the *Observer* pulling out all the stops on that one."

For some minutes Jess had been seriously alarmed

by the ominous quaking movements her companion
was making. The last comment was too much. He
burst into a shout of laughter.

Jess couldn't have run if she had wanted to; her
muscles were too stiff from squatting in the damp.
And she had come to share David's unworried as-
sessment of the situation; it was too ludicrous to be
frightening. She began to suspect that they had
both misjudged the problem when Freddie's hand
dived into his pocket and came out with a small
black object. The sight of it alarmed John as much
as it did Jess.

"Here, now," he exclaimed, snatching at it.

Freddie hopped nimbly to one side.

"Stop it, you bloody fool, or I'll shoot you as well.
Come out from behind that wall, whoever you are."

David straightened himself to his full height; he
was grinning broadly, and both hands were in his
pockets.

"It's all right, Jess, he's just playing villain. He
wouldn't dare use that gun."

He leaned negligently against the wall, which
was about waist high. Jess had to admit that his casual pose and his grin were probably annoying. But
the reaction was far more violent than she had cause
to expect; she didn't believe what was happening
even after she saw the spurt of flame from the muzzle of the gun and heard the report.

The sharp short sound was like the snap of a ma-
gician's fingers, that turned them all to stone. Jess
saw the two men through a sudden fog that dimmed
her eyes: Freddie with his dark face twisted in a
snarl and his arm half extended; John frozen in the

middle of an abortive attempt to snatch at the weapon.

David too stood motionless, leaning slightly forward against the wall's support. Very slowly his head fell back. His elbows slid out across the top of the wall. Then he fell.

TEN

The affair had turned from farce to tragedy too quickly for Jess to accept its reality. She didn't need to look at David, sprawled face down in the weeds, to be convinced that he was dead; but the thought short-circuited her brain, and for the following minutes she operated on sheer, unreasoning instinct. She got over the wall with the neat movements of an experienced climber, and ran toward Freddie and his gun.

She probably would have ended her brief career then and there if it had not been for her cousin, who came out of his horrified paralysis in time to complete the movement he had begun. The bullet struck the ground, not too far from Freddie's foot, and Freddie made a brief, pungent remark. He added viciously, "Grab her, then, you fool. If she goes haring off into the night screaming, I swear I will plug her."

Cousin John made a lunge for Jess and caught her just before she could claw at Freddie's face. They wrestled. Jess's strength was intensified by extreme mental anguish and John was restrained by the code of his class from clobbering a lady, though she was in no state to appreciate his forbearance. Freddie, watching the struggle with cynical amusement, suggested, "Slug her. Or I shall."

"If you must talk . . . like an American gangster film," said Cousin John, between gasps, "please try to . . . ugh! . . . bring your slang . . . up to date. Jess, stop it. I don't want . . . ooooh, you nasty young woman!"

The comment ended in a howl of pain as Jess sank her teeth into his hand. Carried away, he swung a useful fist, and Jess saw stars. Draped limply over her cousin's arm, she heard him say, "Take a look at him, Fred. If you've killed the fellow . . ."

"I haven't," said Freddie. He sounded regretful. "He's breathing."

"Thank God. Is he badly hurt?"

"Can't tell," said Freddie, with supreme indifference.

"Well, find out! If he needs a doctor . . ."

"He's not going to get a doctor."

Jess was in a peculiar state, not so much from the effect of her cousin's sock on the jaw, which had not been very hard, but from shock. Her numbed brain had accepted the fact of David's breathing with the same lack of reaction with which it had accepted his supposed demise; she could feel her heart banging frantically around inside her rib cage, and knew that she was incapable of resistance or flight. In her confusion she missed part of the discussion, and only stirred feebly when she felt herself being lifted.

"It's a good job she's small," her cousin remarked.

"Even so, I'm not sure I can carry her the whole distance."

"You'll have to. I can't leave him, he might wake up. Bring a mattress, or stretcher, or something to carry him on."

Jess had been carried before, but only by male acquaintances anxious to show off their muscles. The position was surprisingly uncomfortable when head and limbs were left dangling. She made croaking noises, and tried to lift her head.

"She's coming round," said Cousin John, alarmed.

"Then put her out again, you incompetent ass," said Freddie. "Oh, Christ, you're hopeless. Here . . ."

Incompetence was not one of Freddie's vices. What he did, he did well. She felt a brief, sharp flash of pain, and then nothing.

Waking up was far more painful. Noises beat at her head; rough hands jabbed her face and neck. There was light somewhere, nasty dirty gray light like the pale luminosity of fungi grown in a damp cellar. . . .

The first thing she saw was David's face, enormous, and out of focus, hovering inches from her eyes. The upper part of his face was disfigured by dried blood; the lower part by a dark growth of beard. His eyes were bloodshot and his lips were cracked. A more beautiful sight she had never seen.

Jess sat up, ignoring the twinge of pain that shot through her head. She had been lying on a pile of dusty rags laid on a bare wooden floor. The light was not as intense as she had thought; it filtered through glass panes so black with dust that they looked translucent, and the bars set across them further obscured the light. The windows were small and high, set in cold stone walls whose austerity was softened only by enormous swinging swaths of gray spiderwebs. The walls were curved. That fact, she knew, ought to mean something, but at the moment she could not think what. She could comprehend only basic ideas—stone walls, bars—a prison, and nuts to Lovelace's definition. And David—still alive, and conscious, but not being very convincing about either one.

"They shot you," she exclaimed, clutching at him. "Where did they shoot you?"

"Shoulder, of course. Where else do heroes get shot?" He grinned at her. The effect was indescribably horrible.

"Leg," Jess said.

"My legs weren't exposed. When you stop to think about it, shoulders are logical places in which to be shot. They take up quite a lot of area. With a hand weapon, at any distance, it's not easy to hit—"

"Oh, David, you fool, can't you ever stop talking?"

Her embrace was, under the circumstances, too fervent. Still smiling, David folded up and fell over backward. She snatched at him, trying to keep his head from banging on the floor; and found herself down, hands pinned between black hair and dusty wood, body hard against what had to be his injured shoulder.

She looked down into his face, which was sickeningly white under its varied scars, and took a grip on herself.

"So long as I've got you helpless," she said, and kissed him thoroughly. Then she untangled herself, sat up, and inspected their quarters.

She had already absorbed most of the information in that first glance; there was very little in the room. A cot, made up with rough blankets, which had, from its relative cleanliness, been recently moved into the abandoned chamber; a small inlaid table, whose polished elegance was distinctly out of place—these were the only articles of furniture. There was a single wooden door, which Jess didn't even bother to try. On the table stood a thermos, a pitcher of water, and two glasses, long-stemmed, fragile crystal wine glasses. Jess recognized the touch. It was apparent as well in the only other article the room contained, besides cobwebs: a round white vessel, placed discreetly behind the cot and painted, chastely, with blue forget-me-nots.

"I'm going to put you on that cot," said Jess. First things first, she thought.

"I've been on it." David tried to help; it took their combined efforts to land him on the cot, with a jolt that left him limp.

"What happened? Do you remember anything?" Jess searched her pockets. She had no handkerchief. She took off her sweater and her blouse, replaced the sweater—the room was dank and chilly—and tore a piece out of the blouse. She soaked it in the water and mopped David's brow.

"Not a thing, between the time that crook shot me and the moment when I woke up in this chamber of horrors with you flat on the floor beside me. I thought the worst; that's why you caught me babbling and pawing at you. I'm not my usual phlegmatic self."

"You certainly aren't yourself. Didn't they even try to bandage you? Damn them. What a pair of cold-blooded—"

"They probably had other things on their minds," David said reasonably. "No, Jess, leave it alone. At least it's stopped bleeding, and if you start mucking around with it . . . Do you know where we are?"

"Only one place we can be. The house."

"Right. One of the tower rooms, obviously. I know you feel pretty rotten yourself, but do you think you can reach that window?"

She could, by standing on tiptoe, but she could see very little. The bars were several inches from the glass and too closely set to permit the insertion of anything larger than a finger, so she couldn't wipe any of the encrusted grime from the glass.

"I can see the courtyard," she reported, squinting. "It's one of the back towers. David, it's dawn. We've been here all night."

"No way out through the windows?"

Jess tried to shake the bars. They didn't stir.

"Well, try the door, just for laughs."

The door was definitely locked. Jess couldn't hear a sound outside, even when she put her ear against the panels. The floor, though old, was equally impervious to attack, and the stone walls she didn't even try.

She went back to the cot, wrung out her shirttail, and wiped David's face again. He made no sound, but the relaxation of his tight mouth as the cool water touched his face made Jess sick with rage and pity.

"We may as well face the facts," he muttered. "We're caught good and proper, darling. Even if you could break the glass in those windows, we're at the back of the house, where visitors never come; no use yelling for help. And I'm in no condition to over-power the villains when they enter. I rather doubt if I can stand up."

"But they can't just leave us here! You need a doctor. . . ."

"I don't think they will just—leave us here."

She stared at him wide-eyed, her hand at her mouth.

"I'm sorry, I don't mean to frighten you," he said gently. "But the prospect's rather grim. They've gone further than they intended already; in for a penny, in for a pound, you know. And your suave cousin is not the man to—"

The hideous room needed only the rattling of chains to complete its Gothic air; now the rattling was supplied. Jess bounded to her feet and glared, first at the door, whence the rattling came, then around the room for a possible weapon. Her wild eyes lit on the convenience standing demurely in the corner, and in one leap she had gathered it up into her hands. A second leap carried her to the door, chamber pot raised for action.

The door grated and groaned in traditional fash-ion as it swung slowly open. Jess saw David, raised painfully on one elbow, regarding her with alarm; she waved the chamber pot at him and he subsided, whether in response to her warning or in shocked unconsciousness she could not be sure. Then the opening door cut off her view of the bed.

It opened about halfway and stopped. There was a pause, during which she heard only the sound of even breathing. Then in a sudden rush the door finished its swing and pinned her flat as a beetle against the wall. A hand curved around the edge of the door, caught her wrist, and shook; the pot fell, sending sprays of forget-me-nots into the air.

Released, Jess slumped against the wall, fighting tears of rage and frustration. She didn't move, even when the door closed, exposing her to the quizzical gaze of her cousin.

"Freddie's down below, in case you're thinking of bolting," he remarked, and bent to pick up a heavy tray which he had put carefully off to one side before frustrating her attempt to brain him. He looked around for a spot on which to deposit his tray, found the ormolu table inadequate, and, with a shrug, put the tray back on the floor and sat down, crosslegged, beside it. Characteristically, he retained his aplomb even in this unorthodox position; but Jess thought his gaze tended to shy away from hers.

"Thought you might like a spot of tea," he explained ingenuously.

"That's not all I'd like," Jess said curtly, advancing on him. "No, don't give him that cup, he can't hold it. He can't even sit up. Hold his head and I'll take the cup."

"Hmmm." Cousin John contemplated David, whose head was on the same level as his. He lifted a bottle from the tray and poured a stiff dose into the tea. "This may help."

Between them they got the spiked tea into David without spilling more than half onto his chest, and Jess was relieved to see a tinge of color seep into his cheeks. He sank back without speaking, and though Jess knew he might be pretending greater weakness than he felt, he didn't have to pretend very hard. She fixed her cousin with a contemptuous stare, and was glad to see that his eyes fell before hers.

"Band-Aids and iodine?" she inquired, indicating the tray. "That's a lot of help. He needs a doctor, you—you murderer."

"Well, he can't have one. Not immediately. Jess, not to worry—"

"Not to worry!" She leaped to her feet, fists clenched. "To think that I'm related to you! I'd rather have the Boston strangler for a cousin! I'd rather share grandparents with a sex maniac! The Marquis de Sade would be—"

"Now, he wouldn't be, not really. For goodness' sake, girl, calm yourself. At least we can make him more comfortable now; I'll help you, I know a bit about first aid. Then, tomorrow—"

"The execution?"

Cousin John looked shocked.

"Would I be going to all this trouble if we were planning to be so drastic? Why wouldn't we have killed you at once if that had been the idea?"

"I can think of several good reasons, John . . ." She called him by name, almost for the first time since she had met him. The result surprised both of them; it was incredible how much intimacy could be conveyed in a formal, personal name.

"You are my cousin," Jess went on, after that

brief, demoralizing pause. "And basically not such a bad human being. I think . . ."

"Thanks so much."

"I'm sorry if I'm expressing myself badly. I don't even know for sure what you want out of all this. I don't care, so long as it's not something filthy like drugs or kidnaping. I just want—to keep on being alive. With David."

"You are in love with the fellow, aren't you?"

Jess looked down at her recumbent lover. He was pathetic enough to disarm many a villain, with his dark lashes—she had already had occasion to note their unexpected length—lying on his pale cheek, his mouth curved down in a line of pain. The black hair on his forehead, under the filthy bandage, was tumbled, and even the arrogant nose looked smaller.

"Yes, I am."

"And he's keen on you, too; that was obvious. Jess . . ."

He was kneeling beside the bed, so that she had to look down at him. The light outside had been steadily growing stronger. Enough of it filtered through the grimy panes to enable her to see him clearly, and his expression weakened her anger. She found it hard to believe that this man, whose well-cut features and keen blue eyes reminded her so strongly of her father, could be a murderer. The reasoning was faulty, but hard to fight.

"Jess," her cousin said again, in a conspiratorial whisper. "I want to—"

She had occasion, then, to be grateful for the horrid creak of the door. No other warning of the man's approach had been audible. The shriek of rusted hinges cut through Cousin John's speech like a knife, and he swiveled on his heels to stare at Freddie, framed by the open doorway, smiling like a tiger.

"Not through yet, Johnny?"

"Barely begun," said Cousin John, in a voice that was almost steady. "Jessie needed to be reassured."

"What a lovely job." Freddie's flat black eyes went over Jess with a clinical interest; she didn't know whether to blush or turn pale with fear. "Get on with it, then."

His face again under control, John produced a pocketknife and cut away David's sweater and shirt from the wound. They had to soak the crusty, hardened linen from his shoulder, and the water in the pitcher was red when they finished.

"We'll need more water," said John to his ally.

Freddie's mouth widened into an expression which could not, by any stretch of the imagination, be called a smile.

"Here," he said, producing a bucket from outside the door.

This was almost the last word spoken.

To Jess's inexperienced eye the puffed, reddened skin around the bullet hole looked bad, and her cousin's silently pursed lips confirmed her fears. However, he proceeded to paint the area with some sort of antiseptic, and bandaged it quite skillfully.

"It's not too bad," he said, avoiding her eyes. "Clean through, no bones broken. Don't try to get that arm into a shirt or jacket, just keep him covered."

Jess said nothing. The presence of Freddie affected her the way a snake affects some people; it paralyzed even her well-exercised vocal muscles. She was relieved when the pair left the room and the heavy door swung shut. She heard the rattle of keys and chains and bolts; then silence.

The day dragged interminably. The sunlight strengthened, and began to fade. Jess finally fell asleep, through sheer boredom; she awoke at the touch of David's hand, shocked and groggy; but her first glance at his face reassured her.

"You're feeling better."

"Better than what?" David inquired disagreeably. "Damn it, I've slept like a log and so have you. Time's awastin', as one of your national poets puts it."

"You talk too much. I know you're feeling better. See what my dear coz left. How about a slug of cold tea?"

"I'd like a slug of whatever's in the bottle even more. Jess, what was Cousin J. about to say when you were interrupted by the advent of Freddie?"

"Were you awake?"

"Most of the time." David gulped brandy and cold tea. "I needed that. False courage."

"He started, at one point, to say something about tomorrow."

David slumped back against the pillows she had arranged behind him.

"I rather think that should read 'tonight.' "

"Why?"

"Because, whatever they mean to do, they'll need darkness in which to do it."

Jess looked at him, and found him studiously

contemplating the rough blanket and the shape of his lax hands which lay upon it. The implications were clear; nor were they new to her. In a way it was almost a relief to hear them spoken.

"It's getting dark now," she said in a small voice; and her hand crept across the blanket to touch David's.

Both his hands closed over hers, in a quick movement that came close to unnerving her; but his need steadied her; she felt the fury of frustration that seethed beneath his calm.

"It's not very late," he said. "Dark in this filthy hole, that's all."

"Is there anything—anything at all—we can do?"

"We can talk." David gave a sudden laugh; to her relief there was no bitterness in it. "I can always talk. Jess, the picture isn't all that black."

"Then show me the little rays of sunshine. At the moment I can't see any."

"Well, we still live, as one of the heroes of my youth kept monotonously repeating. If they mean to do us in, they're wasting a lot of good brandy."

"That's a small bright ray." Jess slid down onto the floor and curled up, her head against the edge of the bed, her hand still warm in his. "Tell me more."

"This isn't a fact, but it's a fairly solid hunch. Remember, I've had altercations with both of the boys, and believe me, there's no better way of evaluating a man's capacity for committing murder than fighting him. Freddie's a bad lot; he fights like a killer, with no scruples and no notion of fair play. John holds back. He doesn't like being hurt, and he doesn't like to deal it out. He could kill, if he had to; but only in a fit of rage, and it would take a hell of a lot to make him that angry. He's a civilized coward, like me."

"You think Freddie wants to kill us, and John doesn't?"

"A number of subtle clues point to that conclusion. After all, Cousin John reads Tolkien. No man who does that can be wholly evil."

"I question your reasons, but agree with the conclusion. I wonder which of the boys is going to win."

"So do I," David muttered. "I'd hate to be dependent on Freddie's goodwill."

"Which of them is the boss?"

"Oh, John, most certainly."

There was a pause, during which Jess noted, against her will, the grayness of the remaining light.

"Why?" she asked.

"He must be the instigator; it's his plot, and his property."

The objection was clear to both of them: Cousin John might have instigated the scheme, but was he still in control of a more violent, less scrupulous, personality? Neither voiced the question; the rest of the conversation skirted delicately around it, as two people might circle a nasty patch of quicksand or smelly corpse.

"What about Aunt Guinevere? Does she know we're up here, freezing to death and starving and dying of thirst and—"

"Rotting? Sorry . . . I don't know. She must know of the original plot; but I can't see her approving of murder either. If that's any consolation."

"No, it isn't. David, I still don't know what this is all about. What is the original plot?"

"But it's so obvious."

"Only to a writer of Gothic thrillers." Jess smiled at him. It was harder now to distinguish his features. The light was definitely failing.

"Well, maybe I'm mental. But I can't see what else it can be. Would you like a résumé? We've nothing else to do."

"Except—wait."

"Yes. Well," David said quickly, "it all began with your grandfather's Arthurian mania—that, and the recent discoveries which have brought Camelot into the news. Plus a third event, which I can't actually prove, but which I postulate in order to fill an otherwise gaping hole in the motive."

"Go on."

"You told me, some days ago, about your grandfather's belief that the family was descended from Arthur. I didn't take it seriously, any more than you did. Even if it could be proved—so what? But people who get hung up on genealogy go all out to prove their point. Your grandfather went into archaeology, hoping to find evidence of Arthurian occupation on his land. He was looking for Camelot.

"It sounds mad. But in the last couple of years quite a number of solid, unimaginative academicians have been doing precisely the same thing— looking for Camelot. I read the stories about the Cadbury dig more or less in passing, paid no particular attention to them at the time, but a few odd facts did stick in my mind. Grandpapa wasn't completely bonkers. Cadbury isn't the only place connected with Camelot by good local tradition; there are other such sites in Wales, Cornwall, even Scotland. Tintagel, up the coast from St. Ives, is the place where Arthur is supposed to have been conceived, and they've found objects there which date to the right period.

"All right. These odds and ends were sloshing around in my mind when we arrived here. Naturally I wasn't really concentrating on them; I had no reason to suppose they were relevant. Then we met Mr. Pendennis."

"But he thinks he's found Camelot," Jess said. "Doesn't that make him some kind of a nut too?"

"No, actually it's the other way around; it makes your esteemed old ancestor something less of a nut. Pendennis is no fool, for all his age; he might exaggerate or misinterpret evidence, but he wouldn't invent nonexistent evidence. If he says that he succeeded where your grandfather failed, I'm inclined to believe that he did find something—something from the period of Arthur, on his own land.

"Now we come to the mysterious box, which your grandfather left his old friend and rival. That's unlikely, to begin with. Collectors don't leave collections to rival collectors; they bequeath them to museums for the admiration of posterity, with little tags reading 'Donated by.' And you saw Pendennis's face when he opened that box. He was thunderstruck. He was seeing not only something totally unexpected, but something he didn't want to see. After I talked to Cliff, I knew what that something was. The objects in the box were typical of fifth-century sites. The period of Arthur."

"Then—then Grandfather did find it! Camelot."

"Wait, wait; you're jumping to conclusions. This is a lot more complicated than it seems." Jess could hardly see him now, but he sounded almost like his old self. Wrapped up in his theories, he had forgotten about night-fall and what might come with night.

"All right, continue," she encouraged.

"One further point about the box. Did you notice how those paltry odds and ends rattled around in it? Why put them in a container much too large?"

"Oh? Oh! I think I'm beginning to get it. There was something else in that box!"

"Must have been several somethings. And one of them, at least, was gold; that fragment had been recently broken, the edges were clean."

"Wow. David . . . David—remember what John said? In the pasture? About the treasure? That's what he said, treasure. . . ."

"He did, he did indeed. That's what he's after, Jess. That's why he chased you all over England."

"Then the ring must be part of the treasure. Gosh, David, if the rest of it isn't any more exciting than the ring—"

"Exciting, hell. Didn't you listen to Cliff the other day? Scraps of metal, bones, holes— that's all they've found from that whole period. There was gold in that box, Jess. Can you imagine what a collection of fifth-century jewelry would be worth? It would be absolutely unique; the British Museum would probably hire killers to get it. But that's not all. Think of the other implications."

"What do you mean?"

"Think! Fifth century . . . fortified castle site . . . chieftain . . . jewels . . . royal regalia . . ."

"Oh, David, no! Not King Arthur's crown!"

"I'll lay you odds that that's what Cousin John has in mind. He and his hired hatchet man. They wanted the ring back, it's part of the loot. But the ring was not the reason why they were after you. They wanted to prevent your reaching your grandfather before he died. There was no ambush waiting for us at the gate, was there? Up to that point they had tried every means up to and including murder to prevent our reaching Cornwall. But we walked in as peacefully as lambs. Why? The old man had died in the meantime."

"He might have told me about the treasure," Jess muttered. "Hmmph. I doubt that he would have. He wasn't sentimental, they all said that. Something about inheritance . . . Wait a minute. John is the residuary legatee. He'd get the treasure anyhow. Why steal it?"

"Because," said David patiently, "the treasure was in the box, and the box was left—to whom? You're getting there, Jess. Keep thinking."

"To Mr. Pendennis. Why, David? You're right, that isn't logical. Either to a museum—gosh, they'd probably name it after him—the Tregarth Treasure—or to his heir, the last male of the line of King Arthur. Why didn't he leave it to John?"

"Keep thinking, you're doing splendidly. Why did your grandfather ask you to bring the ring back to him? Why didn't he make public his discoveries of fifth-century material—particularly such material as the treasure?"

"To Mr. Pendennis. The ring to Mr. Pendennis, he must have meant it to go into the box as well. David! He stole it. Grandfather. It never was his treasure."

"That's it."

"Why, the old crook!"

"Don't be too hard on him. Collectors suffer. Imagine his feelings all those years, with Pendennis gloating over him as he produced one more lovely scrap of dirty fifth-century pottery after another. He couldn't stand it. I imagine we'd find, if we inquired, that Mr. Pendennis went off one year, on holiday or on business, for an extended period, and during that time your granddad did some illicit digging. He found the treasure—and he couldn't bear to give it back. But he was no criminal, Jess; I imagine he kept telling himself that he was just borrowing the stuff, playing a practical joke. He never admitted what he'd done, but made sure, when he died, that it would be restored to its rightful owner. Even the ring, which your father walked off with in a fit of pique."

"I wonder if Father knew."

"Probably. He must have known how important the ring was to your grandfather. Maybe he helped with the digging."

"Maybe. He hated the whole Arthurian business. But if it happened that long ago, before Father left home—why, John wasn't even born. How did he find out about the treasure?"

"That one's easy. Snooping. He's a born snooper. Or did he pretend sympathy for Grandpa's hobby, hoping to control some of the expenditures?"

Only the clasp of his hands kept Jess anchored in time and space; the gloom was so complete that she saw him only as a featureless shadow.

"It's weak, though, David," Jess said, sobered. "There are a lot of flaws. We've invented a treasure on the basis of one word, and a scrap of gold, and we've explained a lot of peculiar behavior on flimsy theories. So much violence . . ."

"The violence is my strongest point," David said, in a voice which had become slightly husky. "Your cousin isn't the man to risk it unless the rewards are great."

"But David—supposing I had gotten to Grandfather before he died. Supposing he told me about the treasure. What could I have done? It would be my version—of an old man's delirium—against my aunt and cousin, both respected members of society. It doesn't make sense."

"Don't forget Mr. Pendennis. A story such as you could tell might arouse his suspicions, together with the other evidence."

"All they need to do is wait till he dies; he's old. If the treasure belongs to him . . ."

"Ah, but it doesn't." David chortled triumphantly. "There's the rub, Jess—the missing piece of the puzzle. The treasure doesn't belong to Mr. Pendennis."

"But—if it was found on his property—"

"Then it is treasure trove. Do you know what that means?"

"Well—no. I guess I don't. Or is that when the finder gets half?"

"Some places, yes. Not here. Treasure trove belongs to the Crown."

"Oh. Then what difference does it make whether it was found here or on Mr. Pendennis's land? The Crown gets it anyhow."

"Wait, let me finish. I'm proud of this. Mind you, I haven't checked it out with a barrister, but I think I'm right. Treasure trove is defined as objects found *in the ground* which cannot be legally claimed as the property of any living person. If you dug up your grandfather's watch, it wouldn't be treasure trove; you'd be his legitimate heir, even if he left no will. But this treasure, if we're correct about it, dates from the fifth or sixth century. No one living can prove descent from the original owner—except, possibly, an old Cornish family which has records going back centuries in the same place."

David's voice, flat with suppressed excitement, seemed to light the blackness with a burst of illumination, like sunlight flashing off a heap of piled jewels. Jess gasped.

"You don't think that's what John is planning!"

"Jess, I don't care for your elegant cousin, but he and I are alike in more ways than I care to admit. That is precisely the kind of magnificent mad plot he would think up. It's straight out of an old Alec Guinness film; and I spotted it because I've got that kind of mind myself."

"Then his digging, out in the pasture—"

"He's building Camelot." David burst out laughing. "Damn the fellow, I can't help admiring him. Even that absurd rhyme—remember it? 'A king and a crown and a sword'—something like that—'and a son for me.' 'Me' being the local Cornish lady Arthur befriended. Five will get you ten that John plans to produce that doggerel, carefully forged onto a crabbed old parchment, as part of the claim. Out there in the pasture he's building a site into which to plant his treasure—and if I know him, he'll plant it somewhere *above* ground, in case the law can be literally interpreted. Objects found above ground are flotsam and jetsam, or missing property, or something; finders keepers, in other words."

"But it's—it's crazy! It can't work."

"I'm not at all sure it can't. Life is crazy too, you know, and the law is the craziest thing of all. It would certainly be worth a try. Peddling stolen valuables, especially antiques, on the black market, means going to a fence, an illegal dealer. You'd lose half the value, maybe more, that way."

"How do you know so much about all this?"

"Thrillers. I write 'em, remember? In my next before last, *The Carruthers Caper*, I had a jewel robbery. The heroine—"

"Never mind her. This is—this is the wildest—"

"And that's not all," David went on gleefully. "The scheme is capable of infinite variations. I can think of three beauties myself, just offhand."

"Save them for Cousin John," Jess said; she was glad to find that her voice was steady. "I hear him coming."

David's hand tightened over hers, and they sat staring through the darkness towards the invisible door, from which came the now-familiar rattle and clank of bolts being unbolted.

They heard the door open; there was no mistaking the ghastly creak. But they still saw nothing, for the person carried no light. Their hands parted as

Jess forced her stiffened muscles to move. She got to her knees, groping for something she could use as a weapon; she heard David's feeble thrashing among the blankets.

There were cautious sounds near the door; then it creaked a second time. Had the intruder gone, leaving some deadly device inside; or were they now shut into the lightless room with their murderer?

Jess's fumbling hands found the tray, too abruptly, and sent the teapot crashing to the floor. Since silence was no longer necessary, she relieved some of her feeling by swearing, and then snatched at the tray, sending the rest of the crockery to noisy ruin on the floor.

"Wait, wait," said an alarmed voice from the direction of the doorway. "Must you break all the china?"

A light flashed on, catching Jess with the tray lifted. It jittered nervously from her to David, who was still struggling, half in and half out of bed. As soon as the light left her eyes Jess was able to see fairly well. It was only a flashlight beam.

"Sssh!" Now she made out her cousin's features, contorted in an agony of alarm. "Can't you two shut up? I'm trying to save your lives and you make enough noise to rouse the dead, let alone Freddie."

"Relax, Jess," said David. He slumped back against the pillows and mopped his brow. "I think we're all right."

"I'm not so sure," John said grimly. He put the flashlight onto the floor, so that its beam shot crazily up to illumine the cobwebby ceiling; enough side light remained to give a dim glow to the scene, and by it Jess saw that he had brought another tray.

"Here, get started on the food. I'm sorry I couldn't get it to you earlier, but it wasn't safe."

"I could do better with some of that brandy," David said.

"Not on an empty stomach. You've got to move quickly, and soon. Stop talking and eat."

David bit into a sandwich, but not with his usual enthusiasm.

"Why must we move?" Jess asked.

"Don't worry, I've got it worked out." Despite the tenseness of his voice, there was an undertone of satisfaction; it was clear that Cousin John enjoyed working things out, but having just heard a synopsis of one of his schemes, Jess was not impressed with his practicality.

She said so, emphatically.

"You solved it, did you?" John grinned at David. "And I thought I was being so frightfully devious."

"You were that." David chewed doggedly. "I'm not at all sure it would have succeeded."

"Neither am I," John said cheerfully. "But planning it was half the fun. And what a hoax! It would have made Chatterton look like an amateur."

"Was it worth it?" Jess asked, through a mouthful of bread and cheese. She was limp with relief, now that rescue had appeared, but the removal of fear left ample room for indignation. "After all the things you did to us . . ."

"One must define 'it,'" her cousin said pedantically. "Your first indefinite pronoun refers, one presumes, to the treasure. My dear, it definitely is worth it! Whatever your second 'it' may mean . . . Wait until you see the stuff—alas, I forgot. You won't see it, I don't imagine; collectors who acquire objects illegally aren't frightfully keen on admitting that they have them. Ah, well, life does have its disappointments. Don't cavil; you could be—believe me!—far less fortunate."

His light tone hardened on the last sentence, and Jess choked on a mouthful of food which seemed to have swelled.

"Freddie?" she asked.

Cousin John held out his right hand and shook his head, sadly.

"Just as well we abandoned the digging, I suppose. My hands were getting so stiff I couldn't play. Freddie? Yes, Freddie is getting a bit out of hand. He never was a conformist; however, if I'd realized how thoroughly nonconformist he has become since our under-graduate days—"

"What was Freddie's subject?" David asked.

"But, my dear fellow!" Cousin John gave him a winning smile. "Archaeology, of course."

"But that wasn't the only reason why you invited him to join you," Jess said.

"Well, I needed professional advice after I stumbled across Grandfather's little hoard. I suspected from the first he'd gotten it illegally; he wasn't the man to hide any lights under bushels. Freddie confirmed that there were no proper fifth-century sites where he'd done his digging. And there's no doubt that Freddie does have a certain talent for matters which more fastidious people prefer to ignore."

"Too bad you didn't study history," David said dryly. "There are parallel cases which are applicable."

"You mean like the jolly old Romans inviting the barbarians in to protect them? I assure you, that parallel has occurred to me since. Freddie is really too much."

"Then it was Freddie's plans for us that made you decide to double-cross him?" David poured himself a generous shot of brandy and tossed it off. "Come, now, John."

John made a wry face.

"What a vulgar phrase. Double-cross, indeed. Naturally I don't care for murder, particularly the murder of people who are related to me. But I will admit that I've detected an arithmetical gleam in Freddie's eye of late."

"Arithmetical?"

"You know. Two into one gives one half, but one into one isn't properly division at all, now is it? No; cynical as it may sound, I do not really trust Freddie."

"All right," David said. "I'm about as fit to move as I ever will be."

"Good." John uncoiled himself from the floor and stood up. "Let me give you a hand. Good God, my dear fellow, it requires two hands, doesn't it? You can't go far in that state. Let me think."

He whistled softly to himself. Then he said cheerfully, "Right, I've got it. We'll stash you away, my lad, in one of the uninhabited rooms in this wing. Freddie won't look for you; he'll assume you've fled with Jess. Who will dash along down the road to town and seek out the police."

Jess, propping David's swaying height on the other side, peered suspiciously at her cousin.

"What about you?"

He beamed at her across David's chest.

"Nice of you to think of me. I do have a little scheme worked out. . . ."

"Oh, gosh," Jess said weakly.

"Your lack of confidence hurts me. The scheme means making Freddie the sole villain, but he won't mind; he'll have departed by the time you get back with the police. I'll simply explain that he held you hostage and threatened to kill you if I interfered. Tonight I managed to free you, and nobly held the killer at bay while you escaped. Now all you need do is back me up, and—er—one other small favor—"

"Like forgetting about the treasure?"

"That's not much to ask, is it, in return for your lives? It's not as if I were robbing anyone; only the Crown, and though I am, of course, a loyal Tory, I do believe that the Crown has plenty already. And think what I'm giving up for you. We'll have to dispose of the treasure through Freddie's disreputable acquaintances abroad, and I shall lose my shirt that way. I must also abandon my pleasant schemes, including my plan for turning the old family mansion into a luxury hotel. I'd have called it The Camelot, probably; right on the spot, ladies and gents, next to King Arthur's veritable tomb! I'm ready to lose all this, for your sake, plus risking my own neck. If Freddie ever found out—"

This time the door did not creak, or, if it did, the creaking was drowned in the greater sound as the whole heavy object crashed, shivering, back against the wall. Jess didn't need to look. She knew who was standing in the doorway.

She had never admired her cousin more. After the first reflexive recoil and guilty gasp, John straightened to his full height and flung out the arm that was not engaged in supporting David.

" 'Lo, where it comes again! I'll cross it, though it blast me . . .' Freddie, I beg you—keep calm!"

"Calm, is it, you so-and-so," said Freddie; the word was one Jess had never heard, and it was followed by several more of unfamiliar etymology, all obviously epithets and obviously uncomplimentary. Cousin John winced. In the light of the dim flashlight she could see that he had gone rather pale, but his eyes had a lively glitter.

"Don't act rashly, Freddie," he said. "I've hidden the loot."

For a moment Freddie did not react. Then his foot lifted and the door crashed again, this time back into its frame.

"Where?" he asked.

"You don't really think I'd be simple enough to tell you? I'll split with you, as I promised. We'll have to make a run for it now."

"There is an alternative," said Freddie.

"There is always an alternative. Almost always . . . Look here, old boy, the game is up, why not accept the fact gracefully? It wouldn't have worked out; you can't simply exterminate people; they have friends and relatives who'll be inquiring after them. For our little scheme we required peace and quiet, time, and an absence of curiosity. You can't—"

"We've discussed this before," said Freddie. The gun remained in position, fixed on the center of Cousin John's pale-blue sweater. "I never cared much for your scheme. The only reason why I let you talk me into it was because we'd have lost such a lot otherwise. Now I'll take the lot."

"You'll have to find it first," said Cousin John valiantly.

"That can be arranged."

Jess decided that the most alarming thing about Freddie was that he was capable of only two emotions—black rage and icy malevolence. The second of the two was in evidence now.

The muzzle of the gun dropped, deliberately, a few inches.

"I've never shot anyone in the kneecap," said Freddie. "But I've heard that it's the most painful of all wounds. I'll start with your right knee. On the count of four. One . . ."

"Oh, God," said Cousin John devoutly.

"Two . . ."

Jess propped David's limp body up against the cot; he had slid silently out of consciousness some time before, and she was glad he was no longer with them; he'd have tried to fight, and gotten himself efficiently killed. Surreptitiously she flexed her hands. She didn't need to have the rest of Freddie's program outlined to her. Once he had extracted the information he wanted from John, he would shoot them all. On the whole, she preferred to be killed in action. Coldly and without malice she waited for the first shot, planning under cover of its effect to do something. She didn't know what. Just something.

"Three . . ."

"Freddie, stop and think . . ."

"F—"

"All right, I'll tell you." Her cousin mopped his brow with his shirt sleeve; he was, apparently, afraid to reach for a handkerchief, and Jess didn't blame him. "You are so damned hotheaded," he complained.

"Where is it?"

"In my room. In a shoebox under the bed."

"Why, you complete fool, I'd have found that at once."

"I know. But *you* didn't know till now, did you?"

Freddie's dark face congealed into something that might have stepped off the towers of Notre Dame, rainspout and all. For a second Jess thought that sheer exasperation would tighten his trigger finger. But greed triumphed over rage.

"I'll have a look," he said. "If it's not there . . ."

He reached backward for the door handle, not taking his eyes or his aim off the huddled trio. Jess was suddenly wet with perspiration, produced by a fear which she had not had time to enjoy when death seemed imminent. She understood now why men sold out their allies and friends for five minutes more of life. Looking up at her cousin's poised, immobile shape, she could not make out from his expression whether he had told the truth. She didn't know whether she hoped he had or not.

Freddie pulled the door open and the loud

screech of rusty hinges reverberated. Then Jess echoed the scream. Her eyes were focused, in a stare that showed the whites, on the thing that stood in the open doorway.

Freddie produced a stretched grimace; he was incapable of a genuine smile.

"The oldest trick of them all," he said. "Want me to look round, do you?"

"Well, no," Jess said truthfully.

There was some excuse for her scream; the figure posed eerily in the doorway might have stepped bodily out of a horror film. Its face showed white, disembodied, between the masses of dark hair and the sombre black garment; its features were hideously shadowed by the flickering light of the candle it held in one pale hand. In the other hand, it held a hammer.

As the pair stared, mesmerized, Freddie's smirk faded; their collective surprise was too genuine to be ignored. He started to turn, but he was too late; the shrouded figure lifted the hammer and brought it neatly down on his head with a distinct *bonk!* Freddie fell down.

"This," said Aunt Guinevere fastidiously, "has gone far enough."

I had to let him escape," said Cousin John. He added placatingly, "Do have more sherry."

It was the afternoon of the following day. Bright sunlight poured through the windows of the parlor and Jess wanted to pass her hands through it as if it were water. She would never, ever again, get too much light.

The party assembled over the decanter and glasses looked more like negotiators of an uneasy truce than friends. To be sure, neither mother nor son showed any signs of strain; Aunt Guinevere was as silent as a sphinx, her lips tightly folded, her hands ladylike in her lap, and Cousin John, in a costume of impeccable sartorial perfection, had not a shadow under his blue eyes.

David was shaved and dressed in his best, but he was so swathed in bandages that he looked like an escapee from an operating room. Not even a black silk sling and a bandaged brow could make him look romantic, for the nose triumphed over all. Jess, in her scarlet sweater and plaid skirt, looked a lot brighter than she felt. She could sense the bags under her eyes hanging down on her cheeks, and was aware of a nervous tendency to scream whenever anyone moved.

"I can't believe it's over," she said grumpily. "It's too easy. Too facile."

"That's Cousin John for you." David was disagreeable. "Facile is his middle name."

"Oh, but look here," John said affably. "It is simple; why make it difficult? If we'd had Freddie arrested, he might have said many nasty things about me. I'd have denied them, naturally, but some suspicion might have lingered. This way we blame all the unpleasantness on Fred and remove any cause for revenge that he might harbor. They wouldn't have put him in prison for long, you know—he didn't actually kill anyone—and guess where he'd have gone first when they let him out!"

He produced a realistic shudder, but Jess saw

an unregenerate twinkle in the eye he turned toward her.

"You've a point," David admitted grudgingly. "But that tale you told about the treasure—"

"That Grandfather kept it hidden from us all these years and Freddie found it in the spare room when he came weekending? Weak, I'll admit; but life generally does produce improbable plots."

"In any case, the story has been accepted," said Aunt Guinevere calmly. "I see no reason to cause further unpleasantness."

David studied her with unconcealed exasperation.

"By rights, that precious son of yours ought to be sent up for a few years."

"It would be a very poor return for rescuing you," said Aunt Guinevere.

"And how embarrassing to have a near kin in the jug," added Cousin John. "'My wife's cousin? Oh, yes, old man, he's the one at Wormwood Scrubs. We send him little parcels now and then, soap, you know, and shaving lotion. . . .'"

His mother gave him a look of fond pride.

"John, darling, you mustn't joke. It was naughty of you."

David having been rendered speechless by this comment, Jess returned to the attack.

"The treasure will have to go back to Mr. Pendennis, you know."

"I gathered you felt that way. Jess, wouldn't you like to have a look at it first?"

She knew his real motive when he spread it out before her. Battered and worn by time as it was, it took the breath away—massive armlets of gold and uncut stones, a necklace of twisted granulated gold-work that had a faintly oriental look; most evocative of all, a flattened gold circlet that was too large to have encircled an arm or neck.

"It's a crown, you know," John said softly. "It may have been *the* crown." He added, "That's how I'd have advertised it, at any rate."

"The crown of King Arthur?" Jess meant to scoff; it wasn't her fault that the words sounded a little breathless.

"He wasn't even a king," David said. "Just a British war lord. A local mercenary."

"Tell that to the tourists," John said. He glanced at Jess, and recognized the painful truth; her fascination was for the objects, not for what they might bring. "Ah, well, it was worth trying. . . . Off they go, to Pendennis and the dear old British Museum. Unless you think a small souvenir apiece . . . No? In that case . . ."

"Yes, it's time we left," David said.

"This time you really are off for Sussex to introduce Jess to your parents?"

"Unless some other group of thugs interferes."

"No one asked you to come back last time," said Cousin John petulantly. "Think of all the fuss we'd have avoided if you hadn't. Not that it wasn't frightfully clever of you, but still . . ."

"Your problem is over-elaboration," David said. "If you hadn't harassed Jess, you'd probably have made out all right."

"I suppose you're right; Grandfather most probably wouldn't have said anything to her. But I couldn't be certain. And if I'd pinched the ring after it got here, it would have looked so suspicious. And she'd have been sure to ask why he had to have it back. And then, you see, it all looked so simple. . . ."

"You almost killed me, that's all," said Jess. "Simple, he says."

"But without me you'd never have met David, and settled down amongst us all. You must be our guests when we open the hotel. On your honeymoon, perhaps."

"Hotel?"

"Certainly. There'll be a sensation when this discovery is made public. Pendennis won't cash in on it, so why shouldn't we? We'll erect a few ruins out in the pasture; Camelot was a largish place, I imagine, so we'll simply claim it lapped over onto our land. The hotel will be very picturesque—blackened beams in the ceiling, stone fireplaces, and all that— the Americans adore it. I'm thinking of calling it 'The Camelot Arms.' Or did I tell you that?"

"How are you going to get the money to renovate the place?" Jess demanded.

Her cousin smiled at her.

"Oh, I'll find it," he said gently. "Don't worry about that."

"Let's go," David said hastily. "Before he tells us."

Aunt Guinevere gave them only a cool nod in farewell, but John escorted them to the door, chattering cheerfully. As they came out into the sunlight he asked, "How are you going to manage driving with that arm?"

"I'm driving," Jess said, pulling out her gloves with an air. "And never mind the raised eyebrows,

John. I can't do any more damage to his precious car than the pair of you have managed to do already."

"That's love," murmured Cousin John. He added thoughtfully, "Perhaps 'The Excalibur Arms' would be more effective."

"That's a little farfetched, surely."

"Not at all. Don't tell me you missed that point?" He turned and touched the doorknocker. "The family crest. The same symbol that's cut onto the ring. That gave me something of a shock the first time I saw it. I think Grandpapa must have scratched it on himself, just to add verisimilitude, et cetera. But . . . it would be odd, wouldn't it, if that crest had been there since the fifth century?"

David stirred restlessly.

"I don't follow you. The family crest is a sword. But why should the sword, any old sword, be Excalibur?"

"Don't be dense. Look at the crest here, above the door; it's carved in stone, isn't it? Just as the emblem on the ring is cut into an agate. Wait, though . . ." John pondered, his eyebrows drawn together. "You're right, it wasn't Excalibur, that came later. By George, that's it! That's the perfect name!"

Jess fought the urge, but she couldn't help herself; she had played straight man to her cousin too many times.

"What?" she asked.

John's smile was seraphic.

" 'The Sword on the Stone,' of course."

Meet the Incomparable Heroines of Elizabeth Peters

Vicky Bliss is beautiful, smart, and courageous . . . and she also happens to be an expert art historian specializing in Medieval Europe. This rare combination makes her the perfect sleuth to track down forgers, art thieves, and cold-blooded killers all around the world, from the midwestern United States to the National Museum of Munich in Germany.

THE VICKY BLISS NOVELS
Borrower of the Night
Street of the Five Moons
Silhouette in Scarlet
Trojan Gold
Night Train to Memphis
The Laughter of Dead Kings

Jacqueline Kirby (a.k.a. Jake) is intelligent, glamorous, and flamboyantly quirky, but it's her love of research and her diligent attention to detail that allow her to excel as a detective. The amber-haired, green-eyed librarian-turned-romance novelist is endlessly entertained by people who take themselves—and their hobbies—just a bit too seriously. She is always more than happy to join them in a quest to sate their curiosity, but it is this research that often gets her into trouble as she uncovers long-hidden secrets and deadly mysteries.

THE JACQUELINE KIRBY NOVELS
The Seventh Sinner
The Murders of Richard III
Die for Love
Naked Once More

Amelia Peabody, a well-groomed, well-mannered heiress and archaeologist/Egyptologist, spends her time enjoying her favorite passions: mysteries, pyramids, and her devilishly handsome husband, Radcliffe Emerson. Known as Sitt Hakim or "Lady Doctor" to her Egyptian friends, Amelia is always prepared with her trusty parasol, tool belt, and a pistol that she never *quite* learns to use, all of which come in handy, given her knack for finding dead bodies and getting into trouble, in Egypt and other places in the early years of the twentieth century.

THE AMELIA PEABODY NOVELS